# JOURNEY
## BY
# MOONLIGHT

ANTAL SZERB

# JOURNEY
# BY
# MOONLIGHT

Translated from the Hungarian by
Len Rix

PUSHKIN PRESS
LONDON

# For Bianca

Translated from the Hungarian
by Len Rix

First published as *Utas és Holdvilág*, Budapest, 1937

This edition first published in 2001 by
Pushkin Press
123 Biddulph Mansions
Elgin Avenue
London W9 1HU

British Library Cataloguing in Publication Data:
A catalogue record for this book is available
from the British Library

ISBN 1 901285 37 5

Set in 10 on 12 Baskerville
and printed in Britain
by Sherlock Printing, Bolney, West Sussex
on Legend Laid paper

PART ONE

# HONEYMOON

*Mutinously I submit to the claims of law and order.*
*What will happen? I wait for my journey's wages*
*In a world that accepts and rejects me.* VILLON

# I

ON THE TRAIN everything seemed fine. The trouble began in Venice, with the back-alleys.

Mihály first noticed the back-alleys when the motor-ferry turned off the Grand Canal for a short cut and they began appearing to right and left. But at the time he paid them no attention, being caught up from the outset with the essential Veniceness of Venice: the water between the houses, the gondolas, the lagoon, and the pink-brick serenity of the city. For it was Mihály's first visit to Italy, at the age of thirty-six, on his honeymoon.

During his protracted years of wandering he had travelled in many lands, and spent long periods in France and England. But Italy he had always avoided, feeling the time had not yet come, that he was not yet ready for it. Italy he associated with grown-up matters, such as the fathering of children, and he secretly feared it, with the same instinctive fear he had of strong sunlight, the scent of flowers, and extremely beautiful women.

The trip to Italy might well have been postponed forever, but for the fact that he was now married and they had decided on the conventional Italian holiday for their start to married life. Mihály had now come, not to Italy as such, but on his honeymoon, a different matter entirely. Indeed, it was his marriage that made the trip possible. Now, he reasoned, there was nothing to fear from the danger Italy represented.

Their first days were spent quietly enough, between the

pleasures of honeymooning and the gentler, less strenuous forms of sightseeing. Like all highly intelligent and
self-critical people, Mihály and Erzsi strove to find the
correct middle way between snobbery and its reverse.
They did not weary themselves to death "doing" everything prescribed by Baedeker; still less did they wish to be
bracketed with those who return home to boast, "The
museums? Never went near them," and gaze triumphantly
at one another.

One evening, returning to their hotel after the theatre,
Mihály felt he somehow needed another drink. Quite
what of, he wasn't yet sure, but he rather hankered after
some sort of sweet wine, and remembering the somewhat
special, classical, taste of Samian, and the many times he
had tried it in Paris, in the little wine merchant's at number 7 rue des Petits Champs, he reasoned that Venice
being effectively Greece, here surely he might find some
Samian, or perhaps Mavrodaphne, since he wasn't yet
quite *au fait* with the wines of Italy. He begged Erzsi to go
up without him. He would follow straightaway. It would
be just a quick drink, "really, just a glass" he solemnly
insisted as she, with the same mock-seriousness, made a
gesture urging moderation, as befits the young bride.

Moving away from the Grand Canal, where their hotel
stood, he arrived in the streets around the Frezzeria.
Here at this time of night the Venetians promenade in
large numbers, with the peculiar ant-like quality typical
of the denizens of that city. They proceed only along certain routes, as ants do when setting out on their journey-
ings across a garden path, the adjacent streets remaining

empty. Mihály too stuck to the ant-route, reckoning that the bars and *fiaschetterie* would surely lie along the trodden ways, rather than in the uncertain darkness of empty side-streets. He found several places where drinks were sold, but somehow none was exactly what he had in mind. There was something wrong with each. In one the clientele were too elegant, in another they were too drab; another he did not really associate with the sort of thing he was after, which would have a somehow more *recherché* taste. Gradually he came to feel that surely only one place in Venice would have it, and that he would have to discover on the basis of pure instinct. Thus he arrived among the back-alleys.

Narrow little streets branched into narrow little alley-ways, and the further he went the darker and narrower they became. By stretching his arms out wide he could have simultaneously touched the opposing rows of houses, with their large silent, windows, behind which, he imagined, mysteriously intense Italian lives lay in slumber. The sense of intimacy made it feel almost an intrusion to have entered these streets at night.

What was the strange attraction, the peculiar ecstasy, that seized him among the back-alleys? Why did it feel like finally coming home? Perhaps a child dreams of such places, the child raised in a gardened homestead who fears wide expanses. Perhaps there is an adolescent longing to live in such a closed world, where every square foot has a private significance, ten paces infringe a boundary, decades are spent around a shabby table, whole lives in an armchair.... But this is speculation.

He was still wandering among the alleys when it occurred to him that day was already breaking and he was on the far side of Venice, on the *Fondamenta Nuova*, within sight of the burial island and, beyond that, the mysterious islands which include San Francesco Deserto, the former leper colony, and, in the far distance, the houses of Murano. This was where the poor of Venice lived, too remote and obscure to profit from the tourist traffic. Here was the hospital, and from here the gondolas of the dead began their journey. Already people were up and on their way to work, and the world had assumed that utter bleakness as after a night without sleep. He found a gondolier, who took him home.

Erzsi had long been sick with worry and exhaustion. Only at one-thirty had it occurred to her that, appearances notwithstanding, even in Venice one could doubtless telephone the police. Which she did, with the help of the night porter, naturally to no avail.

Mihály was still like a man walking in his sleep. He was abominably tired, and quite incapable of providing rational answers to Erzsi's questions.

"The back-alleys," he said. "I had to see them by night, just once . . . it's all part of . . . it's what everyone does."

"But why didn't you tell me? Or rather, why didn't you take me with you ?"

Mihály was unable to reply, but with an offended look climbed into bed and drifted towards sleep, full of bitter resentment.

"So this is marriage," he thought. "What does it amount to, when every attempt to explain is so hopeless? Mind you, I don't fully understand all this myself."

# II

Erzsi however did not sleep. For hours she lay, with knitted brow and hands clasped under her head, thinking. Women are generally better at lying awake and thinking. It was not exactly new or surprising to her that Mihály could say and do things she failed to understand. For a time she had successfully concealed her lack of comprehension, wisely asking no questions and acting as if eternally familiar with everything to do with him. She knew that this wordless assumption of authority, which he thought of as her ancestral, intuitive woman's wisdom, was her strongest means of holding on to him. Mihály was full of fears, and Erzsi's role was to comfort him.

But there is a limit to everything, especially as they were now married and on a proper honeymoon. In those circumstances to stay out all night seemed grotesque. For an instant she entertained the natural feminine suspicion that Mihály had in fact been with another woman. But this possibility she then completely dismissed. Setting aside the utter tastelessness of the idea, she well knew how timid and circumspect he was with all strange women, how terrified of disease, how averse to expense, and above all, how little interest he had in the female sex.

But in point of fact it would have been of some comfort to her to know that he had merely been with a woman. It would put an end to this uncertainty, this total blankness, this inability to imagine where and how he had spent the night. And she thought of her first husband,

Zoltán Pataki, whom she had left for Mihály. Erzsi had always known which of the office typists was his current mistress. Zoltán was so doggedly, blushingly, touchingly discreet, the more he wished to hide something the clearer everything became to her. Mihály was just the reverse. When he felt guilty he always laboured to explain every movement, desperately wanting her to understand him completely, and the more he explained the more confusing it became. She had long known that she did not understand him, because Mihály had secrets even from himself, and he did not understand her since it never occurred to him that people other than himself had an inner life in which he might take an interest. And yet they had married because he had decided that they understood each other perfectly, and that, for both, the marriage rested on purely rational foundations and not fleeting passion. For just how long could that fiction be sustained?

# III

A FEW EVENINGS later they arrived in Ravenna. Mihály rose very early the next morning, dressed and went out. He wanted to visit, alone, Ravenna's most important sight, the famous Byzantine mosaics. He now knew there were many things he could never share with Erzsi, and these he reckoned among them. In the matter of art history she was much better informed, and much more discerning, than he, and she had visited Italy before, so he generally left it to her what they would see, and what they would think when they saw it. Paintings only rarely interested him, and then at random, like a flash of lightning, one in a thousand. But the Ravenna mosaics … these were monuments from his private past.

Once in the Ulpius house he, together with Ervin, Tamás, and Tamás's sister Éva, poring over these mosaics in a large French book, had been seized by a restless and inexplicable dread. It was Christmas Eve. In the vast adjoining room Tamás Ulpius's father walked back and forth alone. Elbows on the table, they studied the plates, whose gold backgrounds glittered up at them like a mysterious fountain of light at the bottom of a mineshaft. Within the Byzantine pictures there was something that stirred a sleeping horror in the depth of their souls. At a quarter to twelve they put on their overcoats, and, with ice in their hearts, set off for midnight mass. Then Éva fainted, the only time her nerves ever troubled her. For a month afterwards it was all Ravenna, and for Mihály

Ravenna had remained to that day an indefinable species of dread.

That profoundly submerged episode now re-surfaced in its entirety, as he stood there in the cathedral of San Vitale before the miraculous pale-green mosaic. His youth beat within him with such intensity that he suddenly grew faint and had to lean against a pillar. But it lasted only a second, and he was a serious man again.

The other mosaics held no further interest for him. He went back to the hotel, waited for Erzsi to make herself ready, then together they systematically visited and discussed all there was to see. Mihály did not of course mention that he had already been to San Vitale. He slipped rather ashamedly into the cathedral, as if something might betray his secret, and pronounced the place of little interest, to atone for the morning's painful disclosure.

The next evening they were sitting in the little piazza outside a café. Erzsi was eating an ice-cream, Mihály trying some bitter beverage previously unknown to him but not very satisfying, and wondering how to get rid of the taste.

"This stench is awful," said Erzsi. "Wherever you go in this town there is always this smell. This is how I imagine a gas attack."

"It shouldn't surprise you," he replied. "The place smells like a corpse. Ravenna's a decadent city. It's been decaying for over a thousand years. Even Baedeker says so. There were three golden ages, the last in the eighth century AD."

"Come off it, you clown," said Erzsi with a smile.

"You're always thinking about corpses and the smell of death. This particular stench comes from life and the living. It's the smell of artificial fertiliser. The whole of Ravenna lives off the factory."

"Ravenna lives off artificial fertiliser? This city, where Theodoric the Great and Dante lie buried? This city, besides which Venice is a parvenu?"

"That's right, my dear."

"That's appalling."

In that instant the roar of a motorbike exploded into the square and its rider, clad in leathers and goggles, leapt down, as from horseback. He looked around, spotted the couple and made straight for their table, leading the bike beside him like a steed. Reaching the table he pushed up his visor-goggles and said, "Hello, Mihály, I was looking for you."

Mihály to his astonishment recognised János Szepetneki. In his amazement all he could say was, "How did you know I was here?"

"They told me at your hotel in Venice that you had moved on to Ravenna. And where might a man be in Ravenna after dinner but in the piazza? It really wasn't difficult. I've come here straight from Venice. But now I'll sit down for a bit."

"Er ... let me introduce you to my wife," said Mihály nervously. "Erzsi, this is János Szepetneki, my old classmate, who ... I don't think ... I ever mentioned." And he blushed scarlet.

János looked Erzsi up and down with undisguised hostility, bowed, shook her hand, and thereafter totally ignored her presence. Indeed, he said nothing at all, except to order lemonade.

Eventually Mihály broke the silence:

"Well, say something. You must have some reason for trying to find me here in Italy."

"I'll tell you. I mainly wanted to see you because I heard you were married."

"I thought you were still angry with me. The last time we met was in London, at the Hungarian legation, and then you walked out of the room. But of course you've no reason to be angry now," he went on when János failed to reply. "One grows up. We all grow up, and you forget why you were offended with someone for ten years."

"You talk as if you know why I was angry with you."

"But of course I know," Mihály blurted out, and blushed again.

"If you know, say it," Szepetneki said aggressively.

"I'd rather not here ... in front of my wife."

"It doesn't bother me. Just have the courage to say it. What do you think was the reason I wouldn't speak to you in London?"

"Because it occurred to me there had been a time when I thought you had stolen my gold watch. Since then I've found out who took it."

"You see what an ass you are. I was the one who stole your watch."

"So it was you who took it?"

"It was."

Erzsi during all this had been fidgeting restlessly in her chair. From experience she had been aware for some time, looking at János's face and hands, that he was just the sort of person to steal a gold watch every now and then. She nervously drew her reticule towards her. In it were the passports and traveller's cheques. She was astonished, and dismayed, that the otherwise so diplomatic Mihály should have brought up this watch business, but what was really unendurable was the silence in which they sat, the silence when one man tells another that he stole his gold watch and then neither says a word. She stood up and announced:

"I'm going back to the hotel. Your topics of conversation, gentlemen, are such that...."

Mihály looked at her in exasperation.

"Just stay here. Now that you're my wife this is your business too." And with that he turned to János Szepetneki and positively shouted: "But then why wouldn't you shake hands with me in London?"

"You know very well why. If you didn't know you wouldn't be in such a temper now. But you know I was in the right."

"Speak plainly, will you?"

"You're just as clever at not understanding people as you are at not finding, and not looking for, people who have gone out of your life. That's why I was angry with you."

Mihály was silent for a while.

"Well, if you wanted to meet me ... we did meet in London."

"Yes, but by chance. That doesn't count. Especially as you know perfectly well we're not talking about me."

"If we're talking about someone else ... it would have been no use looking for them."

"So you didn't try, right? Even though perhaps all you had to do was stretch out your hand. But now you've another chance. Listen to this. I think I've traced Ervin."

Mihály's face changed instantly. Rage and shock gave way to delighted curiosity.

"You don't say! Where is he?"

"Exactly where, I'm not sure. But he is in Italy, in Tuscany or Umbria, in some monastery. I saw him in Rome, with a lot of monks in a procession. I couldn't get to him—couldn't interrupt the ceremony. But there was a priest there I knew who told me the monks were from some Umbrian or Tuscan order. This is what I wanted to tell you. Now that you're in Italy you could help me look for him."

"Yes, well, thanks very much. But I'm not sure I will. I'm not even sure that I should. I mean, I am on my honeymoon. I can't scour the collected monasteries of Umbria and Tuscany. And I don't even know that Ervin would want to see me. If he had wanted to see me he could have let me know his whereabouts long ago. So now you can clear off, János Szepetneki. I hope I don't set eyes on you again for a good few years."

"I'm going. Your wife, by the way, is a thoroughly repulsive woman."

"I didn't ask for your opinion."

János Szepetneki climbed onto his bike.

"Pay for my lemonade," he shouted back, and vanished into the darkness that had meanwhile fallen.

The married couple remained where they were, and for a long time did not speak. Erzsi was furious, and at the same time found the situation rather ridiculous. "When old classmates meet," she thought.... "It seems Mihály was deeply affected by these old schoolboy doings. I suppose for once I'd better ask who this Ervin and this Tamás were, however ghastly they might be." She had little patience with the young and immature.

But in truth something quite different bothered her. Naturally she was upset that she had made so little impression on János Szepetneki. Not that it would have had the slightest significance what such a ... such a dubious creature might think about her. All the same there is nothing more critical, from a woman's point of view, than the opinion held of her by her husband's friends. In the matter of women men are influenced with incredible ease. True, this Szepetneki was not Mihály's friend. That is to say, not his friend in the conventional sense of the word. But there was apparently a powerful bond between them. And of course the most foul-minded of men can be especially influential in these matters.

"Damn him. Why didn't he like me?"

Basically, Erzsi was not used to this sort of situation. She was a rich, pretty, well-dressed, attractive woman. Men found her charming, or at the very least sympathetic. She knew it played a large part in Mihály's continuing devotion that men always spoke appreciatively of her. Indeed she often suspected that he looked at her not with his own eyes but those of others, as if he said to himself, "How I would love this Erzsi, if I were like other men." And now along comes this pimp, and he finds me unattractive. She simply had to say something.

"Tell me, why didn't your friend the pickpocket like me?"

Mihály broke into a smile.

"Come on, it wasn't you he didn't like. What upset him was the fact that you're my wife."

"Why?"

"He thinks it's because of you that I've betrayed my youth, our common youth. That I've forgotten all those who ... and built my life on new relationships. And well ... And now you'll tell me that I've obviously got some fine friends. To which I could reply that Szepetneki isn't my friend, which is of course only avoiding the question. But ... how can I put this? ... people like that do exist. This watch-stealing was just a youthful rehearsal. Szepetneki later became a successful con-man. There was a time when he had a great deal of money and forced various sums onto me which I couldn't pay back because I didn't know where he was hanging out. He's been in prison, and he wrote to me from Baja to send him five *pengos*. And every now and then he turns up and always manages to say something really unpleasant. But as I say, people like him do exist. If you didn't know that, at least now you've seen it. I say, could we buy a bottle of wine somewhere round here, to drink in our room? I'm tired of this public life we're leading here in the piazza."

"You can get one in the hotel. There's a restaurant."

"And won't there be an awful fuss if we drink it in the room? Is it allowed?"

"Mihály, you'll be the death of me. You're so scared of waiters and hotel people."

"I've already explained that. I told you, they're the most grown-up people in the whole world. And, especially when I'm abroad, I do hate stepping out of line."

"Fine. But why do you have to start drinking again?"

"I need a drink. Because I have to tell you who Tamás Ulpius was, and how he died."

# IV

"$\text{I}$HAVE TO TELL YOU about these things from the past, because they are so important. The really important things usually lie in the distant past. And until you know about them, if you'll forgive my saying so, you will always be to some extent a mere newcomer in my life.

"When I was at High School my favourite pastime was walking. Or rather, loitering. If we are talking about my adolescence, it's the more accurate word. Systematically, one by one, I explored all the districts of Pest. I relished the special atmosphere of every quarter and every street. Even now I can still find the same delight in houses that I did then. In this respect I've never grown up. Houses have so much to say to me. For me, they are what Nature used to be to the poets—or rather, what the poets thought of as Nature.

"But best of all I loved the Castle Hill district of Buda. I never tired of its ancient streets. Even in those days old things attracted me more than new ones. For me the deepest truth was found only in things suffused with the lives of many generations, which hold the past as permanently as mason Kelemen's wife buried in the high tower of Deva.

"I'm putting this rather well, don't you think? Perhaps it's this excellent bottle of Sangiovese. . . .

"I often saw Tamás Ulpius on Castle Hill, because he lived up there. This in itself made him a highly romantic figure. But what really charmed me was his pale face, his princely, delicate melancholy, and so much else about him. He was extravagantly polite, dressed soberly, and kept aloof from his classmates. And from me.

"But to get back to me. You've always known me as a thick-set, well-built, mature young man, with a smooth calm face, what they call a 'po-face' in Budapest. And as you know I've always been rather dreamy. Let me tell you, when I was at school I was very different. I've shown you my picture from those days. You saw how thin and hungry, how restless my face was, ablaze with ecstasy. I suppose I must have been really ugly, but I still much prefer the way I looked then. And imagine, with all that, an adolescent body to match—a skinny, angular boy with a back rounded by growing too fast. And a corresponding lean and hungry character.

"So you can imagine I was pretty sick in mind and body. I was anaemic, and subject to fits of terrible depression. When I was sixteen, after a bout of pneumonia, I began to have hallucinations. When reading, I would often sense that someone was standing behind my back peering over my shoulder at the book. I had to turn round to convince myself that there was no one there. Or in the night I would wake with the terrifying sensation that someone was standing beside my bed staring down at me. Of course there was no one there. And I was permanently ashamed of myself. In time my position in the family became unbearable because of this constant sense of shame. During meals I kept blushing, and at one stage the least thing was enough to make me want to burst into tears. On these occasions I would run out of the room.

You know how correct my parents are. You can imagine how disappointed and shocked they were, and how much my brothers and Edit teased me. It got to the point where I was forced to pretend I had a French lesson at school at two-thirty, and so was able to eat on my own, before the others did. Later I had my supper kept aside as well.

"Then on top of this came the worst symptom of all: the whirlpool. Yes, I really mean whirlpool. Every so often I would have the sensation that the ground was opening beside me, and I was standing on the brink of a terrifying vortex. You mustn't take the whirlpool literally. I never actually saw it; it wasn't a vision. I just knew there was a whirlpool there. At the same time I was aware that there wasn't anything there, that I was just imagining it— you know how convoluted these things are. But the fact is, when this whirlpool sensation got hold of me I didn't dare move, I couldn't speak a word, and I really believed it was the end of everything.

"All the same, the feeling didn't last very long, and the attacks weren't frequent. There was a really bad one once, during a natural history lesson. Just as I was called on to answer a question, the ground opened beside me. I couldn't move, I just stayed sitting in my place. The teacher kept on at me for a while, then when he saw that I wasn't going to move, got up and came over to me. 'What's the matter?' he asked. Of course I didn't reply. So he just looked at me for a while, then went back to his chair and asked someone else to answer. He was such a fine, priestly soul: he never said a word about the incident. But my classmates talked about it all the more. They thought I had refused to reply out of cheek, or stubbornness, and that the teacher was afraid of me. At a stroke, I had become a public character and enjoyed unprecedented popularity throughout the school. A week later, the same teacher called out János Szepetneki—the one you met today. Szepetneki put on his tough-guy face and stayed in his seat. The teacher got up, went over to him, and soundly boxed his ears. From that time on Szepetneki was convinced I had some special status.

"But to get onto Tamás Ulpius. One day the first snow fell. I could barely wait for school to finish. I gulped down my solitary lunch and ran straight to Castle Hill. Snow was a particular passion of mine. I loved the way it transformed the city, so that you could get lost even among streets you knew. I wandered for ages, then came to the Fisherman's Bastion, and stood gazing out at the Buda hills. Suddenly the ground beside me opened again. The whirlpool was all the more believable because of the height. As so often before, I found myself not so much terrified by it as waiting with calm certainty for the ground to close again, and the effect vanish. So I waited there for a while, I couldn't say how long, because in that state you lose your sense of time, as you do in a dream or in love-making. But of this I am sure: that whirlpool lasted much longer than the previous ones. Night was already falling and it was still there. 'This one's very stubborn,' I thought to myself. And then to my horror I noticed it was growing in size, that just ten centimetres remained between me and the brink, and that slowly, slowly, it was approaching my foot. A few more minutes and I would be done for: I'd fall in. I clung grimly on to the safety railing.

"And then the whirlpool actually reached me. The ground opened under my feet and I hung there in space, gripping the iron bar. 'If my hand gets tired,' I thought, 'I shall fall.' And quietly, with resignation, I began to pray and prepare for death.

"Then I became aware that Tamás Ulpius was standing beside me.

"'What's the matter?' he asked, and put his hand on my shoulder.

"In that instant the whirlpool vanished, and I would have collapsed with exhaustion if Tamás hadn't caught me up. He helped me to a bench and waited while I rested. When I felt better I told him briefly about the whirlpool thing, the first time I had ever told anyone in my life. I don't know how it was: within seconds he had become my best friend, the sort of friend you dream about, as an adolescent, with no less intensity, but more deeply and seriously than you do about your first love.

"After that we met every day. Tamás did not want to come to my house because, he said, he hated being introduced, but he soon invited me to his place. That's how I got to know the Ulpius ménage.

"Tamás's family lived in the upstairs part of a very old and run-down house. But only the outside was old and run-down: inside it was fine and comfortable, like these old Italian hotels. Although, in many ways, it was a bit creepy, with its large rooms and works of art, rather like a museum. Because Tamás's father was an archaeologist and museum director. The grandfather had been a clock-maker—his shop had been in the house. Now he just tinkered for his own amusement with antique clocks and all sorts of weird clockwork toys of his own invention.

"Tamás's mother was no longer alive. He and his younger sister Éva hated their father. They blamed him for driving their mother to her death with his cold gloominess when she was still a young woman. This was my first, rather shocking, experience of the Ulpius household at the start of my first visit. Éva said of her father that he had eyes like shoe-buttons (which, by the way, was very true), and Tamás added, in the most natural voice you can imagine, 'because, you know, my father is a most thoroughly loathsome fellow,' in which he too was right. As you know, I grew up in a close-knit family circle. I adored my parents and siblings, I worshipped my father and couldn't begin to imagine that parents and children might not love one another, or that the children should criticise their parents' conduct as if they were strangers. This was the first great primordial rebellion I had ever encountered in my life. And this rebellion seemed to me in some strange way endlessly appealing, although in my own mind there was never any question of revolt against my own father.

"Tamás couldn't stand his father, but conversely, he loved his grandfather and sister all the more. He was so fond of his sister that that too seemed a form of rebellion. I too was fond of my brothers and sister. I never fought with them very much. I took the idea of family solidarity very seriously, as far as my withdrawn and abstracted nature would allow. But it wasn't our way, as siblings, to make a show of mutual affection—any tenderness between us would have been considered a joke, or a sign of weakness. I'm sure most families are like that. We never exchanged Christmas presents. If one of us went out or came in, he wouldn't greet the others. If we went away, we would just write a respectful letter to our parents and add as a postscript, 'Greetings to Péter, Laci, Edit and Tivadar'. It was quite different in the Ulpius family. Tamás and Éva would speak to one another with extreme politeness, and when parting, even if only for an hour, would kiss one another lovingly. As I realised later, they were very jealous of each other, and this was the main reason why they had no friends.

"They were together night and day. By night, I tell you, because they shared a room. For me, this was the strangest thing. In our house, from the time Edit was twelve she was kept away from us boys, and thereafter a separate female ambience grew up around her. Girlfriends called on her, boyfriends too, people we didn't know and whose pastimes we thoroughly scorned. My adolescent fantasy was thoroughly exercised by the fact that Éva and Tamás lived together. Because of it, the gender difference became somehow blurred, and each took on a rather androgynous character in my eyes. With Tamás I usually spoke in the gentle and refined way I always did with girls, but with Éva I never experienced the bored restlessness I felt with Éva's girlfriends—with those officially proclaimed females.

"The grandfather I did have difficulty getting used to. He would shuffle into their room at the most unlikely hours, often in the middle of the night, and wearing the most outlandish clothes, cloaks and hats. They always accorded him a ceremonial ovation. At first I was bored by the old fellow's stories, and couldn't follow him very well since he spoke Old German with a trace of Rhineland accent, because he had come to Hungary from Cologne. But later on I acquired a taste for them. The old chap was a walking encyclopaedia of old Budapest. For me, with my passion for houses, he was a real godsend. He could tell the story of every house on the Hill, and its owners. So the Castle District houses, which up till then I had known only by sight, gradually became personal and intimate friends.

"But I, too, hated their father. I don't recall ever once speaking with him. Whenever he saw me he would just mutter something and turn away. The two of them went through agonies when they had to dine with him. They ate in an enormous room. During the meal they spoke not a word to each other. Afterwards, Tamás and Éva would sit while their father walked up and down the enormous room, which was lit only by a standard lamp. When he reached the far end of the room his form would disappear into the gloom. If they spoke to one another he came up and aggressively demanded, 'What's that? What are you talking about?' But luckily he was rarely at home. He got drunk alone in bars, on brandy, like a thoroughly bad sort.

"Just at the time we got to know each other, Tamás was working on a study of religious history. The study was to do with his childhood games. But he approached it with the method of a comparative religious historian. It was a really strange thesis, half parody of religious history, half deadly serious study of Tamás himself.

"Tamás was just as crazy about old things as I was. In his case it was hardly surprising. Partly it was inherited from his father, and partly it was because their house was like a museum. For Tamás what was old was natural, and what was modern was strange and foreign. He constantly yearned for Italy, where everything was old and right for him. And, well, here am I sitting here, and he never made it. My passion for antiquity is more of a passive enjoyment, an intellectual hankering. His was the active involvement of the whole imagination.

"He was forever acting out bits of history.

"You have to understand that life for these two in the Ulpius house was non-stop theatre, a perpetual *commedia dell'arte*. The slightest thing was enough to set them off on some dramatisation, or rather, they acted things out as they talked. The grandfather would tell some story about a local countess who had fallen in love with her coach-man, and instantly Éva was the countess and Tamás the coachman. Or, he would tell how the state judge Majláth was murdered by his Wallachian footman, so Éva became the judge and Tamás the footman. Or they would develop some historical melodrama, much longer and more involved, as an ongoing serial. Naturally these plays sketched the events only in broad strokes, like the *commedia dell'arte*. With one or two items of clothing, usually from the grandfather's inexhaustible and amazing wardrobe, they would suggest costume. Then would ensue some dialogue, not very long, but highly baroque and convoluted, followed by the murder or suicide. Because, as I think back now, these little improvisations always culminated in scenes of violent death. Day after day, Tamás and Éva strangled, poisoned, stabbed or boiled one another in oil.

"They could imagine no future for themselves, if they ever did think about one, outside the theatre. Tamás was preparing to be a playwright, Éva a great actress. But to call it 'preparation' is a bit inaccurate, because he never wrote any plays, and it never occurred to Éva in her dreamworld that she would have to go to drama school. But they were all the more passionate in their theatre-going. But only to the National: Tamás despised the popular stage in exactly the same way he despised modern architecture. He preferred the classical repertoire, with its wealth of murder and suicide.

"But going to the theatre requires cash, and their father, I am sure, never gave them pocket money. One small source of income was their cook, the slovenly old family housekeeper, who set aside a few pennies for the two youngsters from her housekeeping money. And the grandfather, who from a secret cornucopia donated a few crowns now and again. I think he must have earned them on the side. But of course none of this was enough to satisfy their passion for the theatre.

"It was Éva's job to think about money. The word was not to be uttered in front of Tamás. Éva took charge. In such matters she was highly inventive. She could find a good price for anything they possessed which might sell. From time to time she would sell off some priceless museum-piece from the house, but this was very risky because of their father, and also Tamás took it badly if some familiar antique went missing. Sometimes she made really surprising loans—from the greengrocer, in the confectionery, in the pharmacy, even from the man collecting the electricity money. And if none of this worked, then she stole. She stole from the cook, she stole with death-defying courage from her father, taking advantage of his drunkenness. This was the surest and in some respects the least reprehensible source of income. But on one occasion she managed to lift ten crowns from the confectioner's till. She was very proud of that. And no doubt there were other episodes she didn't mention. She even stole from me. Then, when I found out, and bitterly remonstrated with her, instead of stealing she imposed a regular levy on me. I had to pay a certain sum into the family kitty every week. Tamás was of course never allowed to know of this."

Erzsi butted in: "Moral insanity."

"Yes, of course," continued Mihály. "It's very comforting to use expressions like that. And to a certain extent it absolves one. 'Not a thief, but mentally ill'. But Éva was not mentally ill, and not a thief. Only, she lacked moral awareness when it came to money. The pair of them were so cut off from the real world, from the economic and social order, they simply had no idea what were the permitted and what the forbidden ways to raise money. Money for them did not exist. All they knew was the certainty that without those pretty bits of paper and bronze crowns they couldn't go to the theatre. Money has its own great abstract mythology, the basis of modern man's religious and moral sensibility. The religious rites of the

34

money-god, honest toil, thrift, profitability and suchlike, were quite unknown to them. Ideas like these everyone is born with but they weren't; or we learn them at home, as I did. But all they ever learned at home was what their grandfather taught them about the history of the neighbourhood houses.

"You can't begin to imagine how out of touch they were, how they shrank from every practical reality. They never held a newspaper in their hands, they had no idea what was happening in the world. There was a world war going on at the time—it didn't interest them. At school it became obvious once during questions that Tamás had never heard of István Tisza. When Przemysl fell, he thought it was something to do with a Russian general, and politely expressed his pleasure. They nearly thrashed him. Later, when the more intelligent boys discovered Ady and Babits, he thought they were talking about generals, and he actually believed for ages that Ady was a general. The clever boys thought Tamás was stupid, as did his teachers. His real genius, his knowledge of history, went totally unnoticed in the school, which he for his part didn't mind in the least.

"In every other sense too, they stood outside the common order of life. It would occur to Éva at two in the morning that the week before she had left her French exercise book on Sváb Hill, so they would both get up, get dressed, go to Sváb Hill and wander there till morning. The next day Tamás, with lordly indifference, would absent himself from school. Éva would forge an absence note for him over the signature of the older Ulpius. Éva

35

cut school regularly, and had absolutely nothing to do, but she was as happy as a cat on her own.

"One could call on them at any time. Visitors never bothered them. They just carried on with their own lives as if no one else was present. Even at night you were made welcome. But while I was still at school I couldn't visit them at night because of family rules: at the very most, after the theatre and then very briefly, and I dreamed constantly about how wonderful it would be to sleep at their house. Once I'd left school, I often spent the night there.

"Later I read in a famous English essay that the chief characteristic of the Celts was rebellion against the tyranny of facts. Well, in this respect the two of them were true Celts. In fact, as I recall, both Tamás and I were crazy about the Celts, the world of Parsifal and the Holy Grail. Probably the reason why I felt so at home with them was that they were so much like Celts. With them I found my real self. I remember why I always felt so ashamed of myself, so much an outsider, in my parents' house. Because there, facts were supreme. At the Ulpius house, I was at home. I went there every day, and spent all my free time with them.

"The moment I came into the atmosphere of the Ulpius house my chronic sense of shame vanished, as did my nervous symptoms. When Tamás pulled me from the whirlpool, that was the last time it afflicted me. Nobody peered over my shoulder again, or stared at me in the darkness of night. I slept peacefully, and life granted what I expected of it. Physically I knitted together, and my face became unlined. This was the happiest time of my life, and if some smell or effect of the light stirs up the memory of it, I still experience the same rapturous, deceptive, elusive happiness, the first happiness I ever knew.

"This happiness was not of course without a price. In order to belong to the Ulpius house I had to renounce the objective world. Or rather, it became impossible to lead a double life. I gave up reading newspapers, broke off with my more intelligent friends. Gradually they came to think I was as stupid as Tamás. This really hurt, because I was proud, and I knew I was clever. But it couldn't be helped. I severed all links with the family at home. To my parents and siblings I spoke with the measured formality I had learned from Tamás. The rift that this brought between us I have never been able to repair, however hard I try, and ever since I've felt guilty towards my family. Later on I laboured to remove this sense of estrangement by being extremely compliant, but that's another story.

"My parents were deeply dismayed by my transformation. The family sat in anxious council, with all my uncles, and they decided that I needed a girl. My uncle put this to me, much embarrassed, and with many symbolic expressions. I listened with polite interest, but showed little inclination to agree, the less so because at that time Tamás, Ervin, János Szepetneki and I had undertaken never to touch any woman since we were the new Knights of the Grail. However with time the girl idea faded, and my parents came to accept that I was as I was. My mother, I am sure, to this day carefully warns our domestics and new acquaintances when they come to the house, to be on their guard, because I am not a normal sort of person. And yet, for how many years now, there hasn't been the slightest thing about me to suggest that I am other than perfectly normal.

"I really couldn't say what caused this change which my parents noted with such alarm. It's true that Tamás and Éva demanded absolutely that one should fit in with them, and I heartily, even happily, went along with this. I ceased to be a good student. I revised my opinions and came to despise a whole lot of things which up till then I had liked—soldiers and military glory, my classmates, native Hungarian cooking—everything that would have been described in school terms as 'cool' and 'good fun'. I gave up football, which until then I had followed passionately. Fencing was the only permissible sport, and the three of us trained for it with all the more intensity. I read voraciously to keep up with Tamás, although this wasn't difficult for me. My interest in religious history dates from this time. Later, I gave it up, like so many other things, when I became more serious.

"Despite all this, I still felt guilty towards Tamás and Éva. I felt like a fraud. Because what for them was natural freedom was for me a difficult, dogged sort of rebellion. I was just too petty-bourgeois. At home they had brought me up too much that way, as you know. I had to take a deep breath and reach a major decision before dropping my cigarette ash on the floor. Tamás and Éva couldn't imagine doing anything else. When I summoned up the courage every so often to cut school with Tamás,

I'd have stomach cramps for a whole day. My nature was such that I would wake early in the morning and be sleepy at night, I'd be hungriest at midday and dinner-time, I'd prefer to eat from a dish and not begin with the sweet. I like order, and am mortally afraid of policemen. These sides to my nature, my whole order-loving, dutiful bourgeois soul, I had to conceal when I was with them. But they knew. They took exactly the same view, and they were very good about it. They said nothing. If my love of order or thrift somehow betrayed itself, they magnanimously looked the other way.

"The hardest thing was that I had to take part in their plays. I don't have the slightest instinct for acting. I am incurably self-conscious, and at first I thought I would die when they gave me their grandfather's red waistcoat so that I could become Pope Alexander the Sixth in a long-running Borgia serial. In time I did get the hang of it. But I never managed to improvise the rich baroque tapestries they did. On the other hand, I made an excellent sacrificial victim. I was perhaps best at being poisoned and boiled in oil. Often I was just the mob butchered in the atrocities of Ivan the Terrible, and had to rattle my throat and expire twenty-five times in a row, in varying styles. My throat-rattling technique was particularly admired.

"And this I have to tell you, though it's difficult for me to talk about it, even after so much wine, but my wife must know everything: I really enjoyed being the sacrificial victim. It was the first thing I thought of when I woke up, and I looked forward to it the whole day long, yes. . . ."

"Why did you enjoy being the victim?" asked Erzsi.

"Hmmm ... well, for erotic reasons, if you follow me. I think ... yes. After a while, I would dig up these stories myself, so I could be the victim according to my taste. For example: Éva would be an Apache girl (the cinema had already begun to channel her fantasy—there were films about them at the time) and would lure me into her camp. She would get me drunk, then they would rob me and murder me. Or, the same thing done historically, say, Judith and Holofernes. That story I really adored. Or I would be a Russian general, Éva a spy. She puts me to sleep and steals the plan of campaign. Tamás is the heroic assistant. He chases after Éva, recovers the secret plans. But Éva frequently neutralises him, and the Russians suffer horrific losses. That sort of story would take shape as the game developed. It's interesting that Tamás and Éva really enjoyed these games. It's only me that's still embarrassed by them, and even now I speak of them with some shame. They never did. Éva loved to be the woman who cheats, betrays and murders men, Tamás and I loved to be the man she cheats, betrays, murders, or utterly humiliates...."

Mihály stopped talking and sipped his wine. After a while Erzsi asked:

"Tell me, were you in love with Éva Ulpius?"

"No, I don't think so. If you really must know if I was in love with anyone, then it was more like Tamás. Tamás was my ideal. Éva was just a bonus, and the erotic catalyst in these games. But I wouldn't really agree that I was in love with him, because the phrase is misleading, and you would continue to think there was some unhealthy homoerotic bond between us, which simply wasn't the case. He was my best friend, using the word in a very adolescent sense, and what was unhealthy in the affair was, as I said before, something quite different and of a deeper nature."

"But tell me, Mihály ... this is rather difficult to believe ... you were with her for years on end, and there was never any question of an innocent flirtation between you and Éva Ulpius?"

"No, none."

"How was that?"

"How? ... in fact ... probably, that we were so intimate that it wasn't possible to flirt or fall in love with one another. For love, there has to be a distance across which the lovers can approach one another. The approach is of course just an illusion, because love in fact separates people. Love is a polarity. Two lovers are the two oppositely charged poles of the universe."

"This is all very deep, for so late at night. I don't get the full picture. Perhaps the girl was ugly?"

"Ugly? She was the most beautiful girl I've ever seen. No, that isn't quite right. She was the one beautiful woman against whom I have since measured all others. All my later loves were like her in some particular. With one, it would be the legs, with another, the way she lifted her head, with a third, her voice on the telephone."

"Myself included?"

"You included ... yes."

"In what way am I like her?"

41

Mihály blushed and fell silent.

"Tell me. I insist."

"How can I put it? ... Stand up, would you, and come over here beside me."

Erzsi stood beside his chair. He put his arm around her waist and looked up at her. She smiled.

"Now ... that's it," said Mihály. "When you smile down at me like that. That's how Éva smiled when I was the victim."

Erzsi disengaged herself and sat down again.

"Very interesting," she said, somewhat crestfallen. "You're certainly holding something back. Never mind. I don't consider it necessary that you should tell me everything. I don't feel any pangs of conscience about the fact that I've not told you about my adolescence. I don't think it very important. But tell me—you were in love with this girl. It's just a matter of words. Where I come from it was what you would call love."

"No. I tell you I wasn't in love with her. Just the others."

"What others?"

"I'm about to explain. For years there was no other visitor at the Ulpius house but me. When we were eighteen the situation changed. Then we were joined by Ervin and János Szepetneki. They came to see Éva, not Tamás, as I did. What happened was that around that time the school put on a drama festival, as it did every year, and as we were the final year group we did the main item of the whole event. Any chance to do a play was good news. The only trouble was that there was a large female role in it.

To fill it, the boys brought along their fantasy-heroines from the skating rink and the dancing school, but the teacher producing the play, an extremely clever young priest who hated women, didn't find any of them suitable. I somehow mentioned the fact in Éva's hearing. From that moment she would not rest. She felt that this was her chance to begin her career as an actress. Tamás of course wouldn't hear of it. He thought it grotesque and degrading that she should begin in the context of school, such an intimate, almost family setting. But Éva positively terrorised me until I took the matter up with the teacher in question. He was very fond of me, and told me to bring her along. This I did. She had barely opened her mouth before he declared, 'You must have the part, you and no one else.' Éva plucked up the nerve to raise the subject with her puritanical, theatre-hating father and pleaded with him for half an hour until at last he consented.

"Of course I don't want to talk about the performance itself just now. I'll just observe in passing that Éva, generally speaking, was not a success. The assembled parents, my mother included, found her too forward, insufficiently feminine, a little common—in a word, somehow not quite the thing. Or rather, they sensed the rebellion latent in her, and even though there was nothing objectionable in her acting, her costume, or her general behaviour, they took exception to her morals. But this didn't make her a success with the boys either, despite the fact that she was so much more beautiful than the heroines of the skating-rink and the dancing school. They conceded she was very attractive, 'but somehow … ' they said, and shrugged their shoulders. These young bourgeois types already carried the germ of their parents' attitude to the unconventional. Only Ervin and János recognised the enchanted princess in her. Because they too were rebels by this time.

"János Szepetneki you saw today. He's always been like that. He was the best verse-reader in the class. In particular he was a great hit in the literary and debating society as Cyrano. He carried a revolver about with him and every week shot burglars dead in the middle of the night, trying to steal secret documents from his widowed mother. While the other lads were still laboriously treading on their dancing partners' toes, he was having wild adventures. Every summer he went off to the battlefront and took up the rank of second lieutenant. His new clothes would be torn within minutes—he always seemed to fall off something. His greatest ambition was to prove to me that he was my superior. I think it all started when we were thirteen. One of our teachers took up phrenology and decided from the bumps on my head that I was gifted, whereas János's skull showed he wasn't very bright. He never got over this. Years after we'd left school he was still going on about it. He had to be better than me at everything—football, study, intellectual things. When later on I gave up all three he was really at a loss and didn't know where to turn. So then he fell in love with Éva, because he thought that Éva was in love with me. Yes, that was János Szepetneki."

"And who is this Ervin?"

"Ervin was a Jewish boy who'd converted to Catholicism,

perhaps under the influence of the priests who taught us, but more probably I think following his own inner promptings. Earlier, at sixteen, he'd been the brightest of all the clever and conceited boys: Jewish boys tend to mature early. Tamás really hated him for his cleverness, and became thoroughly anti-Semitic whenever he was mentioned.

"It was from Ervin that we first heard about Freud, Socialism, the March Circle. He was the first of us to be influenced by the strange world of what later became the Károlyi revolution. He wrote wonderful poetry. In the style of Ady.

"Then, practically from one day to the next, he changed completely. He shut himself off from his class-mates. I was the only one he communicated with. But as for his poetry, to my mind, I just didn't understand it, and I didn't like the fact that he started writing long lines without any rhyme. He became a recluse, read books, played the piano—we knew very little about him. Then one day in Chapel we noticed him going up to the altar, with the other boys, for the sacrament. That was how we knew he had converted.

"Why did he become a Catholic? Ostensibly, because he was drawn to the strange beauty of the religion. He was also attracted by the dogma and the harshness of its moral code. I do believe there was something in him that craved austerity the way other people crave pleasure. In a word, all the usual reasons why outsiders convert.... And he became a model Catholic. But there was another side to it too, which I didn't see so clearly at the time.

Ervin, like everyone else in the Ulpius house except me, was a role-player by nature. When I think back now, even as a younger pupil he was always playing at being something. He played the intellectual and the revolutionary. He was never relaxed and natural, the way a boy should be, not by a long way. Every word and gesture was studied. He used archaic words, he was always aloof, always wanting the biggest role for himself. But his acting wasn't like Tamás's and Éva's. They would just walk away from their part the moment it was over and look for something new. He wanted a role to fill with his whole being, and in the Catholic religion he finally found the hugely demanding role he could respect. After that he never altered his posture again. The part just grew deeper and deeper.

"He was a really devout Catholic, as Jewish converts often are. Their centuries of tradition haven't been eroded the way they have for us. He wasn't like his pious and impoverished schoolmates who worshipped every day, went to mass, and trained for a career in the church. Their Catholicism was a matter of conformity, his a form of rebellion, a challenge to the whole unbelieving and uncaring world. He took the Catholic line on everything—books, the war, his classmates, the mid-morning buttered roll. He was much more inflexible and dogmatic than even the most severe of our religious teachers. 'No man, having put his hand to the plough, should look behind him'. That text was his motto. He cut out of his life everything that was not purely Catholic. He guarded his soul's salvation with a revolver.

"The only vice he retained from his former life was smoking. I cannot recall ever seeing him without a cigarette.

"But he still had his share of life's temptations. Ervin had adored women. With his comical single-mindedness he'd been the great lover of the class, the way János Szepetneki had been its great liar. The whole form knew about his loves, because he would walk his sweetheart for the whole afternoon on Gellért Hill, and write verses to her. The boys respected Ervin's attachments because they felt the intensity and the poetic quality. But when he became a Catholic he naturally renounced love. At that time the lads were beginning to visit brothels. Ervin turned away from them in horror. They, I am quite sure, went to those women for a lark, or out of bravado. Ervin was the only one who really knew the meaning of physical desire.

"Then he met Éva. Of course Éva set her cap at him. Because Ervin was beautiful, with his ivory face, his high forehead, his blazing eyes. And he radiated differentness, stubbornness, rebellion. And with it he was gentle and refined. I only came to appreciate him after he and János turned up at the Ulpius house.

"That first afternoon was horrible. Tamás was aloof and aristocratic, contributing only the occasional totally irrelevant remark, *pour épater les bourgeois*. But Ervin and János were not *épatés* because they weren't bourgeois. János talked the entire afternoon about his whale-hunting experiences and the plans of some big company to harvest coconuts. Ervin listened, smoked, and gazed at Éva.

Éva was quite unlike her usual self. She simpered, she put on airs, she was womanish. I was utterly miserable. I felt like a dog discovering that two other dogs have come to share his privileged place under the family table. I growled, but really I wanted to howl with misery.

"I began to visit less often. I arranged to call when Ervin and János weren't there. Besides, we were approaching our school-leaving exams. I had to take them seriously. What's more, I made a huge effort to drill the essential information into Tamás. Somehow we got by, Tamás on the strength of my cramming him—mostly he didn't even want to get out of bed. And after that there began a whole new phase of life at the Ulpius house.

"Now everything changed for the better. Tamás and Éva emerged as the stronger personalities. They completely assimilated Ervin and János into their way of life. Ervin relaxed his morbid severity. He adopted a terribly kind, if somewhat affected, manner, speaking always as if in quotation marks to dissociate himself in some way from what he was saying or doing. János was more quiet and sentimental.

"In time we got back to the play-acting, but the plays were now much more crafted, enriched by János's escapades and Ervin's poetical fantasy. János naturally proved a great actor. His declamation and sobbing were always over the top (because what he really wanted to play was unrequited passion). We had to stop in mid-scene for him to calm down. Ervin's favourite role was a wild animal. He did a wonderful bison, slain by Ursus (me), and an extremely accomplished unicorn. With his single mighty

48

horn he shredded every obstacle—curtains, sheets, and the rest of us put together.

"During that period our horizons gradually opened out. We began to go for long walks among the Buda hills. We even went bathing. And then we took up drinking. The idea came from János. For years he'd told us stories about his exploits in bars. Apart from him, the best drinker among us was Éva—it was so hard to tell whether she was drunk or just her normal self. Ervin took to drinking with the same passion as with his smoking. I don't like to confirm a prejudice, but you know how strange it is when a Jew hits the bottle. Ervin's drinking was every bit as odd as his Catholicism. A sort of embittered plunging headlong into it, as if he wasn't simply getting drunk on Hungarian wine but on some vicious substance like hashish or cocaine. And with it, it was always as if he was saying goodbye, as if he was about to drink for the very last time, and generally doing everything as if for the last time in this world. I soon got used to the wine. I came to depend on the feeling of dissolution and the shedding of inhibition it produced in me. But at home the next day I would feel horribly ashamed of my hangovers, and always swore I'd never drink again. And then when I did drink again, the knowledge of my own weakness grew, as did the sense of death, which was my overwhelming feeling during these years of the second phase at the Ulpius house. I felt I was 'rushing headlong towards ruin', especially at those times when I was drinking. I felt I was irretrievably falling outside the regular life of respectable people, and everything my father expected of me. This feeling, despite the horrible agonies of remorse, I really enjoyed. By this stage I was virtually in hiding from my father.

"Tamás drank very little, and grew steadily more taciturn.

"Then Ervin's religiosity began to affect us. We had by now started to look at the world, at the reality we'd always shied away from, and it terrified us. We believed that man was degraded by his material needs, and we listened reverently to Ervin who told us we must never follow that path. We too began to pass judgement on the whole modern world with the same severity and dogmatism as Ervin himself, and for a while he became the dominant influence in the group. We deferred to him in everything. János and I strove to outdo each other in pious deeds. Every day we searched out new poor unfortunates in need of assistance, and even newer immortally great Catholic authors requiring to be rescued by us from undeserved obscurity. St Thomas and Jacques Maritain, Chesterton and St Anselm of Canterbury buzzed in our conversation like flies. We went to mass, and János of course had visions. Once St Dominic appeared at the window before dawn, with the gesture of the raised finger, and pronounced: 'We watch over you individually and completely.' I guess János and I in this pose must have been irresistibly comic. Tamás and Éva took little part in this Catholicism of ours.

"This period lasted for perhaps a year. Then things began to disintegrate. I couldn't say exactly what began the process, but somehow common reality began to flow back. And with it, it brought decay. The Ulpius grandfather died.

He suffered for weeks. He struggled for air, his throat rat-
tled. Éva nursed him with surprising patience, staying up
whole nights at his bedside. I remarked to her later how
good it was of her. She smiled absent-mindedly and said
how interesting it was to watch someone die.

"At that point their father decided that things really
couldn't carry on as they were. Something would have to
be done about his children. He wanted to marry Éva off
as a matter of urgency. He bundled her off to a rich old
aunt in the country, who took a large house where she
could go to county balls and Lord knows what else. Éva
of course returned after a week, with some marvellous
stories, and submitted phlegmatically to her father's chas-
tisement. Tamás did not share his sister's easy nature. His
father put him in an office. It's horrible to think ... even
now it brings tears to my eyes when I think how he suffered in that office. He worked in the city hall, with conventional petty-bourgeois types who regarded him as
mentally unsound. They gave him the most stupid, most
dully routine work possible, because they reckoned he
wouldn't be able to cope with anything requiring a little
thought or initiative. And perhaps they were right. The
worst of the many humiliations he received at their hands
amounted to this: not that they insulted him, but that
they pitied and cosseted him. Tamás never complained
to us, just occasionally to Éva. That's how I know. He just
went pale and became very withdrawn whenever the
office was mentioned.

"Then came his second suicide attempt."

"The second?"

"The second. I should have mentioned the first one earlier. That was actually much more serious and horrific. It happened when we were sixteen, just at the start of our friendship. I called there one day as usual and found Éva alone, doing some drawing with rather unusual concentration. She said Tamás had gone up to the attic, and I should wait, he would soon be down. Around that time he often went up to the attic to explore. He turned up countless treasures in the old trunks, which fed his antiquarian fantasies and were used in our plays. In an old house like that the attic is a specially romantic sort of place, so I wasn't really surprised, and I waited patiently. Éva, as I said, was unusually quiet.

"Suddenly she turned pale, leapt to her feet, and screamed at me that we should go up to the attic to see what was wrong with Tamás. I had no idea what this was all about, but her fear ran through me. In the attic it was as black as could be. I tell you, it was a vast ancient place, full of nooks and crannies, with the doors of mysterious bureaux open everywhere, and trunks and desks blocking the main passage at intervals. I bumped my head on low-hanging beams. There were unexpected steps to go up and down. But Éva ran through the darkness without hesitation, as if she already knew where he might be. At the far end of the corridor there was a low and very long niche, and at the end of that the light of a small round window could be seen. Éva came to a sudden stop, and with a scream grabbed hold of me. My teeth were also chattering, but even at that age I was the sort of person who finds unexpected courage in moments of greatest fear. I went into the darkness of the niche, dragging Éva along, still clinging to me.

"Tamás was dangling beside the little round window, about a metre off the floor. He had hanged himself. Éva shrieked, 'He's still alive, he's still alive,' and pressed a knife into my hand. It seems she had known perfectly well what he intended. There was a trunk next to him. He'd obviously stood on it to attach the noose to the strength of the joist. I jumped up on the trunk, cut the cord, supported Tamás with the other hand and slowly lowered him down to Éva, who untied the noose from his neck.

"Tamás quickly regained consciousness. He must have been hanging only a minute or two, and no damage was done.

"'Why did you give me away?' he asked Éva. She was covered in shame and didn't reply.

"In due course I asked, rather guardedly, why he had done it.

"'I just wanted to see...' he replied, with indifference.

"'And what was it like?' asked Éva, wide-eyed with curiosity.

"'It was wonderful.'

"'Are you sorry I cut you down?' I asked. Now I too felt a little guilty.

"'Not really. I've plenty of time. Some other time will do.'

"Tamás wasn't able at the time to explain what it was really all about. But he didn't have to. I knew all the same. I knew from our games. In the tragedies we played we were always killing and dying. That's all they were ever about. Tamás was always preoccupied with dying. But try to understand, if it's at all possible: not death, annihilation, oblivion, but the act of dying. There are people who commit murder again and again from an 'irresistible urge', to savour the heady excitement of killing. The same irresistible urge drew Tamás towards the supreme ecstasy of his own final passing away. Probably I can't ever explain this to you, Erzsi. Things like this just can't be explained, just as you can't describe music to someone who is tone-deaf. I understood him completely. For years we never said another word about what happened. We just knew that each understood the other.

"The second attempt came when we were twenty. I actually took part in it. Don't worry, you can see I'm still alive.

"At that time I was in utter despair, mainly because of my father. When I matriculated I enrolled as a philosophy student at the university. My father asked me several times what I wanted to be, and I told him a religious historian. 'And how do you propose to earn your living?' he would ask. I couldn't answer that, and I didn't want to think about it. I knew he wanted me to work in the firm. He had no real objection to my university studies because he thought it would simply give status to the firm if one of the partners had a doctorate. For my part, I looked on university, in the last analysis, as a few years' delay. To gain a bit of time, before becoming an adult.

"*Joie de vivre* wasn't my strong point during that time. The feeling of mortality, of transience, grew stronger in me, and by then my Catholicism was no longer a consolation. In fact it increased my sense of weakness. I wasn't a role-player by nature, and by that stage I could clearly see that my life and being fell hopelessly short of the Catholic ideal.

"I was the first of us to abandon our shared Catholicism. One of my many acts of betrayal.

"But to be brief. One afternoon I called at the Ulpius house and invited Tamás to come for a walk. It was a fine afternoon in spring. We went as far as Old Buda and sat in an empty little bar under the statue of St Flórián. I had a lot to drink, and moaned about my father, my prospects, the whole horrible misery of youth.

"'Why do you drink so much?' he asked.

"'Well, it's fun.'

"'You like the dizzy feeling?'

"'Of course.'

"'And the loss of consciousness ?'

"'Of course. It's the one thing I really do like.'

"'Well then, I really don't understand you. Imagine how much better it would be to die properly.'

I conceded this. We think much more logically when we are drunk. The only problem was, I have a horror of any form of pain or violence. I had no wish to hang or stab myself or jump into the freezing Danube.

"'No need,' said Tamás. 'I've got thirty centigrams of morphine here. I reckon it would do for the two of us, though it's really just enough for one. The fact is, the time has come. I'm going to do it in the next few days. If you come with me then so much the better. Naturally I don't want to influence you. It's just as I say: only if you feel like it.'

"'How did you get the morphine?'

"'From Éva. She got it from the doctor—said she couldn't sleep.'

"For both of us it was fatally significant that the poison came from Éva. This was all part of the world of our dramatics, those sick little plays which we had had to change so much after Ervin and János arrived. The thrill was always in the fact that we died for Éva, or because of her. The fact that she had provided the poison finally convinced me that I should take it. And that's what happened.

"I can't begin to describe how simple and natural it was just then to commit suicide. I was drunk, and at that age drink always produced the feeling in me that nothing mattered. And that afternoon it freed in me the chained demon that lures a man towards death, the demon that sleeps, I believe, in the depths of everyone's consciousness. Just think, dying is so much more easy and natural than staying alive...."

"Do get on with the story," said Erzsi impatiently.

"We paid for our wine and went for a walk, in a blaze of happy emotion. We declared how much we loved each other, and how our friendship was the finest thing in the world. We sat for a while beside the Danube, somewhere in Old Buda, beside the tramlines. Dusk was falling on the river. And we waited for it to take effect. At first I felt absolutely nothing.

"Suddenly I experienced an overwhelming sense of grief that I was leaving Éva. Tamás at first didn't want to hear about it, but then he too succumbed to his feelings for her. We took a tram, then ran up the little stairway to Castle Hill.

"I realise now that the moment I wanted to see Éva I had already betrayed Tamás and his suicide attempt. I had unconsciously calculated that if we went back among people they would somehow rescue us. Subconsciously I had no real wish to die. I was weary to death, as weary as only a twenty-year-old can be, and indeed I yearned for the secret of death, longed for the dark delirium. But when the feeling of mortality inspired by the wine began to wear off, I didn't actually want to die.

"In the Ulpius house we found Ervin and János in their usual chairs. I gaily announced the fact that we had each taken fifteen centigrams of morphine and would soon be dead, but first we wanted to say goodbye. Tamás was already white as a sheet and staggering. I just looked as if I had had a glass too many, and I had the thick speech of a drunk. János instantly rushed out and phoned Casualty to tell them there were two youths who had each taken fifteen centigrams of morphine.

"'Are they still alive?' he was asked.

"When he said we were they told him to take us there immediately. He and Ervin shoved us into a taxi and took us to Markó Street. I still couldn't feel anything.

"I felt a lot more when the doctor brutally pumped out my stomach, and removed any desire I had for suicide. Otherwise, I can't help the suspicion that what we had taken wasn't morphine. Either Éva had deceived Tamás, or the doctor had deceived her. His illness could have been auto-suggestion.

"Éva and the boys had to stay up with us the whole night to watch that we didn't fall asleep, because the Casualty people had said that if we did it would be impossible to wake us again. That was a strange night. We were somewhat embarrassed in each other's company. I was thrilled because I had committed suicide—what a great feeling!—and happy to be still alive. I felt a delicious fatigue. We all loved one another deeply. The staying awake was a great self-sacrificing gesture of friendship, and wonderfully in keeping with our current mood of intense friendship and religious fervour. We were all in a state of shock. We engaged in long Dostoyevskian conversations, and drank one black coffee after another. It was the sort of night typical of youth, the sort you can only look back on with shame and embarrassment once you've grown up. But God knows, it seems I must have grown up already by then, because I don't feel the slightest embarrassment when I think back to it, just a terrible nostalgia.

"Only Tamás said nothing. He just let them pour icy water over him and pinch him to keep him awake. He really was ill, and besides, he was tortured by the knowledge that once again he had failed. If I spoke to him he would turn away and not answer. He regarded me as a traitor. From then on we were never really friends. He never spoke about it again. He was just as kind and courteous as before, but I know he never forgave me. When he did die, he made sure I had nothing to do with it."

Here Mihály fell silent and buried his head in his hands. After a while he got up and stared out of the window into the darkness. Then he came back, and, with an absent smile, stroked Erzsi's hand.

"Does it still hurt so much?" she asked softly.

"I never had a friend again," he said.

Again they were silent. Erzsi wondered whether he was simply feeling sorry for himself because of the maudlin effect of the wine, or whether the events in the Ulpius house had really damaged something in him, which might explain why he was so remote and alienated from people.

"And what became of Éva?" she finally asked.

"Éva by then was in love with Ervin."

"And the rest of you weren't jealous?"

"No, we thought it natural. Ervin was the leader. We thought him the most remarkable person among us, so it seemed right and proper that Éva should love him. I certainly wasn't in love with Éva, though you couldn't be so sure about János. By that stage the group was beginning to drift apart. Ervin and Éva were increasingly sufficient for one another and kept looking for opportunities to be alone together. I was becoming genuinely interested in the university and my study of religious history. I was filled with ambition to be an academic. My first encounter with real scholarship was as heady as falling in love.

"But to get back to Ervin and Éva. Éva now became much quieter. She went to church and to the English Ladies' College, where she'd once been a pupil. I've already mentioned that Ervin had an exceptionally loving nature: being in love was as essential to him as wild adventures were to Szepetneki. I could well understand that even Éva couldn't remain cold in his presence.

59

"It was a touching affair, very poetic, a passion permeated with the ambience of Buda Castle and being twenty years old—you know how it is—so that when they went along the street I almost expected the crowd to part reverentially in front of them, as if before the Sacrament. At least, that was the sort of respect, the boundless respect, we had for their love. Somehow it seemed the fulfilment of the whole meaning of the group. And what a short time it lasted! I never knew exactly what happened between them. It seems Ervin asked for her hand in marriage and old Ulpius threw him out. János believed he actually struck him. But Éva simply loved Ervin all the more. She would willingly have become his mistress, I have no doubt. But for Ervin the sixth commandment was absolute. He became even paler and quieter than before, and never went to the Ulpius house. I saw him less and less. And in Éva the big change must have finally happened around this time, the one I personally found so hard to understand later. Then one fine day Ervin simply vanished. I learned from Tamás that he had become a monk. Tamás destroyed the letter in which Ervin told him of his decision. Whether he knew Ervin's religious name, or where he was, and in which Order, was a secret that went with Tamás to the grave. Perhaps he revealed it only to Éva.

"Ervin certainly did not become a monk just because he couldn't marry Éva. We had in the past talked a great deal about the monastic life, and I know that Ervin's religion went too deep—he would never have become a monk merely out of despair and romantic sensibility, without any definite sign of an inner calling. Certainly he saw it as a sign from above that he couldn't marry Éva. But the fact that he left so hastily, virtually fled, could have been largely to do with the fact that he wanted to escape from Éva and the temptation she represented for him. So although he ran away, perhaps a bit like Joseph, he nonetheless accomplished what we had dreamed about so much at that time. He offered up his youth as a willing sacrifice to God."

"But I don't understand," said Erzsi. "If, as you say, he was so loving by nature, why offer that up as a sacrifice?"

"Because, my dear, in the spiritual life opposites meet. It's not the cold passionless ones who become great ascetics, but the most hot-blooded, people with something worth renouncing. That's why the Church won't allow eunuchs to become priests."

"And what did Éva have to say to all this?"

"Éva remained unattached, and from this point on she was impossible to put up with. By this time Budapest was in the hands of the currency sharks and the officers of the Entente. Éva somehow or other got herself into the officers' set. She knew various languages and her manner was somehow not typically Hungarian but more cosmopolitan. I know she was very much in demand. She went, from one day to the next, from a little adolescent girl to a stunning woman. This was when, in place of the earlier friendly and open expression, her eye took on that other quality: that look, as if she were listening to some far off, murmuring sound.

"Earlier on, Tamás and Ervin had dominated the

group. Now it was János's turn. Éva needed money so that she could make her exquisite appearance among the exquisite people. She was very clever at sewing herself elegant things out of nothing, but even that nothing costs a little something. That was where János came in. He'd always been able to get hold of money for Éva. Where from, he alone knew. Often he swindled the very same Entente officers she danced with. 'I've been realising the group assets,' he would say cynically. But by then we all talked cynically, because we always adapted ourselves to the leadership style.

"I didn't like János's methods very much. They were pretty unscrupulous. I didn't like it, for example, when he called one day on Mr Reich, an old bookkeeper in my father's firm and, with a horribly convoluted story about my gambling debts and proposed suicide, lifted a fairly serious sum of money from him. Of course I then had to agree that I had incurred a debt at cards, though I never had a card in my hand in all my life.

"And what I particularly didn't like was his stealing my gold watch. It happened on the occasion of a grand 'do' out of doors somewhere, in a then fashionable summer inn, I no longer remember the name. There were several of us present—Éva's friends, two or three foreign officers, some young inflation-millionaires, some strange women, remarkably daring for those times in their dress and general behaviour. My usual sense of impermanence was made worse by the fact that Tamás and I were mixing with people not our own, people we had nothing in common with, and by the same old feeling that nothing mattered. But then I wasn't the only one with this sense of impermanence. The whole city had it, it was in the air. People had a lot of money and they knew that it made no difference: it might vanish from one day to the next. The sense of impending disaster hung over the garden like a chandelier.

"They were apocalyptic times. I don't know if we were still sober when we sat down to drink. As I recall, it's as if I became drunk in the first few moments. Tamás drank little, but the universal feeling that the world was going to end was so much in accord with his state of mind that he moved with unaccustomed ease among all those people, even the gypsies. I talked with him a lot that night. Not perhaps so much in words, but the words we did speak had a profoundly sinister resonance. And once again, marvellously, we understood each other—understood each other in our impermanence. And we shared this sympathy with the strange women: at least, I felt that my modest religious-historical thesis about the Celts and the Islands of the Dead found an echo in the drama student sitting near me. Then I got into a *tête-à-tête* with Éva. I courted her as if I hadn't known her since her skinny, big-eyed adolescence and she received my courtship with a complete womanly seriousness, talking in half-finished sentences and staring into the distance, in the full glitter of her pose of that time.

"By the time it started to become light I felt really ill. Then, when I'd sobered up a bit, I realised my gold watch had disappeared. I was really shocked. My despair verged on hysteria. You have to understand: the mere loss of a gold watch is not in itself such a misfortune, not even when you are twenty and have nothing else of value in the world, nothing but your gold watch. But when you are twenty, and you sober up in the light of dawn to find your gold watch has actually been stolen, then you begin to see a symbolic importance in the loss. I had it from my father, who is not by nature a great giver of gifts. I tell you, it was my only object of value, the only one worth mentioning—admittedly a bulky, commonplace thing, whose pretentious, petty-bourgeois quality stood for everything I disliked. But its loss, now that it appeared to me in its full symbolic significance, filled me with panic. It was the feeling that I was now irrevocably damned: that they had stolen the very possibility that I might one day sober up and get back to the bourgeois world.

"I staggered over to Tamás, told him that my watch had been stolen, said that I would telephone the police and tell the innkeeper to lock the gate. They would have to search every guest. Tamás calmed me down in his own special way:

"'It's not worth it. Let it go. Of course it was stolen. They'll steal everything you've got. You'll always be the victim. It's what you really want.'

"I stared at him in amazement. But in fact I never said a word to anyone about the disappearance of the watch. As I gazed at Tamás I suddenly understood that only János Szepetneki could have stolen it. In the course of the evening there had been a game of exchanging clothes. Szepetneki and I had swapped coats and ties. Probably when I got my coat back the watch had already gone. I started to look for János to confront him, but he'd already left. I didn't see him the next day, or the day after that.

"And on the fourth day I still hadn't been able to challenge him about it. I was sure that only he could have taken it, and that he had done so because Éva needed money. In all probability he had taken it with her full knowledge. She had set up the whole clothes-swapping game—and that was the point of the scene when I sat alone with her. Perhaps its whole purpose was so that I wouldn't immediately notice that it had gone. When I stumbled on this possibility I was able to accept what had happened. If it happened because of Éva, it was all right. It was all part of the game, the old games in the Ulpius house.

"From that moment I was in love with Éva."

"But then why have you so strenuously denied all along that you were ever in love with her?" Erzsi interjected.

"Of course. I was quite right to. It's only for want of a better word that I call what I felt for her, love. That feeling wasn't in the least like the feeling I have for you, and had, if you'll forgive me, for one or two of your predecessors. In a way it was quite the reverse. I love you because you're part of me. I loved Éva because she wasn't. That's to say, loving you gives me confidence and strength, but when I loved her, it humiliated and annihilated me.... Of course these expressions are merely antithetical. When it happened, I felt that the truth of the old plays was supreme, and I was being slowly destroyed in the great climax. I was being destroyed because of Éva, through Éva, just as we had played it in our adolescence."

Mihály got up and walked restlessly round the room. It had at last begun to worry him that he had so given himself away. To Erzsi, a stranger....

Erzsi remarked:

"Before that, you said something about ... that you couldn't possibly be in love with her, because you knew each other too well, there wasn't the necessary distance between you for you to fall in love."

("Good—she hasn't understood," he thought. "She's taking in only as much as her basic jealousy can grasp.")

"It's good that you mention that," he continued, calmly. "Until that memorable night there was no distance. Then I discovered, as the two of us sat there, like a lady with her gentleman, that she had become a totally different woman, a strange, splendid, stunning woman, whereas the old Éva would have carried within her, ineradicably, the old dark, sick sweetness of my youth.

"But generally Éva didn't give a damn for me. I rarely managed to see her and when I did she showed no interest in me. Her restlessness was somehow pathological. Especially after the serious suitor appeared—a wealthy, famous, not-exactly-young collector of antiques, who had turned up once or twice at the Ulpius house with the old man, caught the odd glimpse of her, and had long busied himself with plans to make her his wife. The old Ulpius informed Éva he would hear not a word of protest: she had lived off him quite long enough. She would marry, or go to hell. Éva asked for two months' delay. The old man consented, at the fiancé's request.

"The more she neglected me, the stronger was my

feeling of what I called, for want of a better word, love. It seems I had a real bent at that time for hopeless gestures: standing around by her gate at night to spy on her as she came home with her laughing and noisy crowd of admirers; neglecting my studies; spending all my money on stupid presents which she didn't even acknowledge; being cravenly sentimental and creating unmanly scenes if I met her. That was my style. Then I was truly alive. No joy I ever experienced afterwards ever ran as deep as the pain, the exulting humiliation, of knowing I was lost for love of her and that she didn't care for me. Is that what you call love?"

("Why am I saying all this? Why?... Once again I've drunk too much. But I had to tell her at some stage, and she isn't really taking it in....")

"Meanwhile the delay Éva had been granted was coming to its end. Old Ulpius would occasionally burst into her room and make terrible scenes. In those days he was never sober. The fiancé himself appeared, with his greying hair and apologetic smile. Éva asked for one more week. So that she could go away with Tamás, in a calm atmosphere, so they could take their leave of one another. Somehow money was found for the journey.

"Off they went, to Hallstatt. It was late autumn. There wasn't a soul there besides them. There's nothing more funereal than an old historical watering place like that. A castle or cathedral might be ancient, past its time, crumbling away here and there. It's natural, that's its function. But when that sort of place, a coffee-house or a promenade, designed for the pleasures of the moment, when that shows its impermanence—there's nothing more ghastly."

"Yes, yes," said Erzsi, "just get on with it. What happened to Tamás and Éva?"

"My dear, if I beat about the bush and philosophise, it's because from that point on I don't know what happened to them. I never saw them again. In Hallstatt Tamás Ulpius poisoned himself. This time he made no mistake."

"And Éva?"

"You mean, what part did she have in Tamás's death? Perhaps none. I've no way of knowing. She never returned. It was said that after he died some high-ranking foreign officer came and took her away.

"Perhaps I might have been able to meet her. Once or twice in the following years there might have been a chance. From time to time János would pitch up out of the blue, make obscure reference to the fact that he could possibly arrange for me to see her, and would be happy to do so I if I would reward his services. But by then I had no desire to meet Éva. That's why János said earlier tonight that it was my fault, because I walked out on the friends of my youth, when all I had to do was hold out my hand. . . . He was right. When Tamás died I believe I went out of my mind. And then I decided I would change, I would tear myself away from the spell. I didn't want to go the way he went. I would become a respectable person. I left the university, trained for my father's profession, went abroad to get a better grasp of things, then went home and worked hard to become just like everyone else.

"As regards the Ulpius house, my sense of impermanence

was not misplaced. Everything was destroyed. Nothing was left. Old Ulpius didn't live long after. He was beaten to death while making his way home drunk from a bar on the outskirts of town. The house had earlier been bought by a rich fellow called Munk, a business friend of my father's. I visited there once. It was awful. They'd fitted it out wonderfully, as if it were much older than it really was. There's now a genuine Florentine well in the courtyard. The grandfather's room became an Altdeutsch dining-room with oak panelling. And our rooms! My God, they turned them into some sort of old Hungarian guest house or God knows what, with painted chests, jugs and knick-knacks. Tamás's room! Talk about impermanence.... Holy God, it's so late! Sorry, love, but I had to tell you all this at some time, no matter how stupid it might sound from the outside.... Now, I'm off to bed."

"Mihály ... you promised to tell me how Tamás Ulpius died. And you haven't told me why he died."

"I haven't told you how he died because I don't know. And why he died? Hmmm. Perhaps he was bored to death. Life can be really boring, no?"

"No. But let's get some sleep. It's very late."

# V

IN FLORENCE their luck ran out. It rained the whole time they were there. As they stood outside the Cathedral in their raincoats Mihály suddenly burst into laughter. He had just understood the complete tragedy of the building. There it rose in its unparalleled beauty, and no one took it seriously. For tourists and art-historians it had become a landmark, and no one gave it a second thought. No one believed in it, or that its purpose there was to proclaim the glory of God and the city.

They went up to Fiesole, and watched a storm hurrying with busy speed over the hills to overtake them. They retreated inside the monastery and viewed the copious oriental bric-a-brac which the pious brothers had brought back from their missions over the centuries. Mihály stood in wonder for some time over a series of pictures from China. It took him several minutes to work out what they represented. In the upper part of each an alarmingly ferocious Chinaman sat enthroned, with a large book before him. What gave the face its special ferocity was the hair flaring upwards from the temples on either side. In the lower half, all sorts of gruesome events were taking place: people being tossed with pitchforks into some ghastly liquid; some having their legs sawn off; someone whose intestines were being drawn out, very carefully, like a rope; and in one a contraption like an automobile, driven by a monster with flying hair, attacking a crowd of people and chopping them up with blades attached to its snout.

It suddenly struck him that this was the Last Judgement, as seen by a Chinese Christian. What craftsmanship, and what objectivity!

He began to feel faint and went out into the square. The landscape, so magical when viewed from the train between Bologna and Florence, was now damp and hostile, like the face of a weeping woman with the make-up peeling off.

When they arrived back in Florence Mihály went to the main Post Office. Since Venice, their mail had been directed there. On one of the envelopes addressed to him he recognised the hand of Zoltán Pataki, Erzsi's previous husband. Thinking it might contain something better not seen by her, he sat down with it outside a café. "There's male solidarity for you," he thought, with a smile.

The letter ran as follows:

*Dear Mihály,*

*I know it's a bit much, my writing you a long and friendly letter after you 'seduced and ran off with' my wife, but you never were a conventional sort of chap, and so perhaps you won't be shocked if I too disregard convention just this once, even though you've always branded me an old conformist. I'm writing to you because I won't be at rest until I do. I'm writing to you because, quite honestly, I don't see why I shouldn't, since we are both perfectly aware that I'm not angry with you. We only keep up the appearance because it's better for Erzsi's self-esteem to have the romantic situation where we are locked into deadly enmity over her. But between ourselves, my dear Mihály, you are well aware that I always thought highly of you, and this hasn't changed simply because you 'seduced and ran*

71

off with' my wife. Not as if this 'crime' of yours hasn't left me absolutely distraught. I needn't deny—this of course is strictly between us—how much I still adore her. But I realise you aren't responsible for that. As a general fact—don't take this amiss—I don't believe you're responsible for anything I can think of in the whole world.

It's precisely for this reason that I am writing to you. To be honest, I'm rather anxious about Erzsi. You see, after all these years I've got used to looking after her, always making a careful note of things so that I could provide her with everything she needed (and often with things she didn't), making sure she was dressed warmly enough when she went out in the evening, and I can't just give up all that concern, from one day to the next. This concern is what binds me so strongly to her. I must tell you, a few nights ago I had a silly dream. I dreamed that Erzsi was leaning far out of a window, and that if I hadn't caught her she would have fallen. Then it occurred to me that you wouldn't have noticed if she was leaning too far out the window, you're such an absent-minded and introverted fellow. And so, I thought, I'll make a few requests, so you can take special care of her, and I wrote them down in note form, as they came to me. Don't be offended, but we can't get away from the fact that I've known her so much longer than you have, and that does give me certain rights.

1. Make sure she eats enough. Erzsi (perhaps you've already noticed) is terrified of putting on weight. This fear sometimes gets her in a panic, when she will starve for days, and then she has attacks of hyperacidity, which in turn are bad for her nerves. It occurred to me that perhaps the fact that you (touch wood!) have such a good appetite might encourage her to eat. I myself, sorry to say, am just an old man with a weak stomach, and could never set her a good example.

*2. Take special care over her manicurists. If she requires their services while you are travelling, make it your personal business and use only the best establishments. Ask the hotel porter for details. Erzsi is extremely sensitive, and it has happened more than once that her fingers have gone septic because of an unskilled practitioner. Which you certainly wouldn't want.*

*3. Don't let her get up too early. I know that on one's travels there is strong temptation to do that sort of thing. When we were last in Italy I made this mistake myself, because in Italy the inter-city coaches leave at the crack of dawn. To hell with the coaches. Erzsi goes to bed late and gets up late. Early rising does her no good—she takes days to get over it.*

*4. Don't let her eat* scampi, frutti di mare, *or any other disgusting sea creature—they give her a rash.*

*5. A rather delicate matter. I don't know how to put this. Perhaps I should just assume you're aware of it, but I really don't know if such an absent-minded, philosophical sort of person is aware of such things as the incredible frailty of women, and how much they are at the mercy of certain physical functions. But I beg you to take careful note of Erzsi's times of the month. A week before the onset you must be patient and tolerant in the extreme. At such times she is not fully responsible. She will pick quarrels. The wisest course is to stand your ground. It gives her an outlet for her irritation. But you mustn't quarrel in earnest. Remember, it's just a physiological function you're dealing with. Don't get carried away, and don't say anything you might later regret. Above all, don't let Erzsi say anything that she might later regret, as that's no good for her nerves.*

*Now, don't be offended. There are a thousand things I should write about—a thousand little details for you to attend to—these are just the most important—but I can't at this moment think of them.*

*I really lack imagination. All the same, still in confidence, I am extremely worried, not only because I know Erzsi, but, more to the point, because I know you. Now please don't get me wrong. If I were a woman, and had to choose between the two of us, I too would have chosen you without hesitation, and Erzsi surely loves you for being just the sort of person you are—so utterly withdrawn and abstracted that you have no real relationship with anybody or anything, like someone from another planet, a Martian on Earth, someone who never really notices anything, who cannot feel real anger about anything, who never pays proper attention when others speak, who often seems to act out of vague goodwill and politeness as if just playing at being human. Now, this is all very well, and I too would appreciate it if I were a woman. The only problem is, you are now Erzsi's husband. And Erzsi is used to a husband who looks after her in every detail, shielding her from the very wind, leaving her nothing to think of but her mind, her inner life, and, by no means least, care of her person. Erzsi is by nature a lady of leisure. That's how they brought her up at home, and I respected it—and I don't know if, being with you, she will now have to face up to the realities her father and I carefully protected her from.*

*There is another delicate matter I have to touch upon. I realise that you (or rather your father whose firm you work for) are well off, and your wife will lack for nothing. But I do sometimes worry, because I know how pampered Erzsi has been, and I fear that someone as absent-minded as you might not take proper account of her needs. Your own nature is that of an amiable bohemian, undemanding, always bound up in your own solid existence, on a rather different level to what Erzsi is accustomed to. Now one of you is going to have to adapt to the other's standard. If she adapts to yours, that will sooner or later create trouble, because she is going to feel herself* déclassée *the moment she comes into contact with the old set. For example, in Italy you might meet one of her girlfriends, who pulls a face when she hears you're staying at a hotel that isn't exactly top notch. The alternative is that you move up to Erzsi's level, and this, sooner or later, will have material consequences because—if you will forgive me—I probably know the strength of the firm better than you do, you being such an abstracted sort of fellow—not to mention that you are four brothers, and your respected father a somewhat conservative, rather puritanical old gentleman who believes in saving rather than using his income ... in a word, to be brief, you are hardly in a position to maintain Erzsi's standard of living on your own account. And since it is a matter close to my heart that she should never want for anything, I beg you not to take it amiss when I tell you that should the need ever arise I am absolutely at your disposal, should you ever ask for help in the form of a long-term loan. Quite frankly, I would much prefer to pay you a regular monthly sum, but I know that would be an impertinence. But in any event this much I have to tell you: if ever you are in need, just turn to me.*

*Now please don't be angry with me. I'm a simple businessman with nothing better to do than to make money, and that, thank God, I do pretty well. I think it's only fair that I should be able to give it away to whoever I choose, if I want to, no?*

*Well, once again,* nichts für ungut. *Keep well and happy.*

*With affectionate greetings and true respect,*

*Zoltán.*

The letter left Mihály very angry. He felt nauseated by Pataki's effete "decency", which, properly speaking, was not "decency" but unmanliness, or, if it was genuine, then hardly more acceptable because he had rather a low opinion of that quality. And such obsequiousness! It was no good. Pataki, for all his acquired wealth, still had the soul of a shop-assistant.

If Zoltán Pataki was still in love with Erzsi after she had treated him so truly shamefully, then that was his affair, and his problem. But it wasn't that that made Mihály angry. It was those parts of the letter that bore on himself and Erzsi.

First of all, the financial considerations. Mihály had an extreme respect for "economic necessity." Perhaps precisely because he had so little talent for it. If someone said to him, "material considerations compel you to this or that course of action," he would immediately fall silent, and see the justification for every form of baseness. For just that reason, this aspect of the matter made him particularly uneasy. It had arisen as an issue long before the present, but Erzsi had always treated it as a joke. From a materialistic point of view she had made a very poor choice in him. Previously married to a man of substance, now the wife of a modest bourgeois—this sooner or later was bound to make itself felt, as the cool-headed and worldly Zoltán Pataki had already seen so clearly.

There rushed into his mind a host of details which, even on their honeymoon, had sharply exposed the difference in their living standards. One needed to look no further than the hotel where they were staying. Having discovered in Venice and Ravenna that Erzsi's Italian was so much better than his own, and that she dealt so much more competently with hotel staff, of whom he had a particular horror, Mihály had in Florence delegated the hotel and all other practical considerations to her. Whereupon Erzsi, without further ado, had taken a room overlooking the river, in an old but extremely expensive little hotel, on the grounds that if one is in Florence one simply must lodge on the banks of the Arno. The cost of the room, Mihály felt vaguely, because he was too lazy to work it out, was generally out of scale with the amount they had set aside for their Italian accommodation. It was much more expensive than their room in Venice, and that for a moment had shocked his habitual thriftiness. But then he had driven the mean thought from him in disgust, telling himself, "after all, we're on our honeymoon," and thinking no more about it. Now, having read Pataki's letter, it rose before him as a sign.

But the greatest problem was not financial but moral. When after six months of agonised deliberation he had finally decided to detach Erzsi, with whom he had been having an affair for a full year, from her husband, and take her as his wife, he had taken that momentous step in order to "atone for everything", and indeed, through a serious marriage, to enter at last into man's estate and become a serious person on the same level as, for example, Zoltán Pataki. So he had pledged to try with all his might to be a good husband. He wanted to make Erzsi forget what a fine spouse she had left on his account, and in particular he wanted to "make amends" retrospectively for his adolescence. Pataki's letter had now shown him the hopelessness of this undertaking. He could never become as good a husband as this man, who could look after a wife, so unfaithful and now so distant, with more care and skill than he, who was actually with her, but so unused to the role of protector that he had already had to load her with the responsibility of their hotel and other practical arrangements on that most transparent of pretexts, that she spoke better Italian.

"Perhaps it's true what Pataki says," he thought. "I am so abstracted and introverted by nature. Of course that's a simplification—no one can ever be so neatly categorised—but this much is certain, that I am singularly useless and incompetent in all practical matters, and generally not the man in whose calm superiority a woman can trust. And Erzsi is precisely the sort of woman who loves to entrust herself to someone, who likes to know that she belongs completely to someone. She isn't one of those motherly types (perhaps that's why she has no children) but one of those who really want to be their lover's child. My God, how deceived she is going to be in me, sooner or later. I could more easily become a Major-General than play the role of father. That's one human quality I completely lack, amongst others. I can't bear it when people depend on me, not even servants. That's why I did everything on my own, as a boy. I hate responsibility and I always come to despise people who expect things from me.

"The whole thing's crazy: crazy from Erzsi's point of view. She would have been better off with ninety-nine men out of a hundred than she is with me. Any average, normal fellow would have made a better husband than me. Now I can see it not from my own point of view, but

78

purely from hers. Why didn't I think of all this before I got married? Or rather: why didn't Erzsi, who is so wise, think it through more carefully?"

But of course Erzsi couldn't have thought it through, because she was in love with Mihály, and, when it came to him, was not wise, had not recognised his shortcomings, and still, it seems, did not recognise them. It was just a game of feelings. Erzsi with raw, uninhibited appetite was seeking the happiness in love she had never found with Pataki. But perhaps once she had had her fill, because such passionate feeling does not usually last very long....

By the time he got back to the hotel, after a long rambling walk, it seemed inevitable to him that she would, one day, leave him, and do so after horrible crises and sufferings, after squalid affairs with other men, her name "dragged through the mud", as the saying goes. To a certain extent he took comfort in the inevitable, and when they sat down to dinner he could already, a little, look upon her as a lovely fragment of his past, and he was filled with solemn emotion. Past and present always played special games inside Mihály, lending each other colour and flavour. He loved to relocate himself in his past, at one precise point, and from that perspective re-assemble his present life: for example, "What would I have made of Florence if I had come here at sixteen?" and this re-ordering would always give the present moment a richer charge of feeling. But it could also be done the other way round, converting the present into a past: "What fine memories will I have, ten years from now, of once having been in Florence with Erzsi ... what will such memories hold, what associations of feeling, which I cannot guess at at this moment?"

This sense of occasion he expressed by ordering a huge festive meal and calling for the most expensive wine. Erzsi knew Mihály. She knew that the fine meal signified a special mood, and she did her best to rise to the occasion. She skilfully directed the conversation, putting one or two questions bearing on the history of Florence, prodding him to think about such matters, because she knew that historical associations, together with wine, drew him out of his solemnity, and were in fact the only thing that could overcome his apathy. Mihály poured out enthusiastic, colourful, factually unreliable explanations, then with shining eyes tried to analyse the meaning for him, the wonder, the ecstasy of the mere word: Tuscany. "Because there is no part of this land that hasn't been trodden by the armies of history. The Caesars, the gorgeously apparelled troops of the French kings, all passed this way. Here every pathway leads to some important site and one street in Florence holds more history than seven counties back home."

Erzsi listened with delight. The actual history of Tuscany did not for one minute interest her, but she adored him when he came alive like this. She loved the way that at these moments, in his historical day-dreams, precisely when he reached the furthest point from actual living people and the present world, his remoteness left him and he became a normal person. Her sympathy soon merged with more powerful feelings, and she thought with pleasure of the expected sequel later that night, all the more because the night before he had been in a bad mood, and fell asleep, or pretended to, the moment he lay down.

She knew that Mihály's exalted mood could easily be diverted from history towards herself. It was enough to put her hand in his and gaze deep into his eyes. He forgot Tuscany, and his face, flushed as it was with wine, grew pale with sudden desire. Then he began to woo and flatter her, as if trying to win her love for the very first time.

"How strange," Erzsi thought. "After a year of intimacy he still woos me with that voice, with that diffidence, as if totally unsure of success. In fact the more he wants me, the more distant and fastidious his manner becomes, as if to embellish his desire, to give it the proper respect—and the greatest intimacy, physical intimacy, doesn't bring him any closer. He can only feel passion when he senses a distance between us."

So it was. Mihály's desire spoke to her across a distance, in the knowledge that she would leave him. Already she had become for him a sort of beautiful memory. He drank heavily to sustain this mood, to make himself believe that he wasn't with Erzsi but with the memory of Erzsi. With Erzsi as history.

But meanwhile Erzsi drank too, and on her wine always had a strong effect. She became loud, jolly and extremely impatient. This Erzsi was rather new to him. Before their marriage she had had little opportunity for unguarded behaviour when with him in public. He found this new Erzsi extremely attractive, and they went up to the bedroom with equal haste.

That night, when she was at once the new Erzsi and the Erzsi of history, Erzsi-as-memory, when Zoltán Pataki's letter, with its implicit reminder of the Ulpius days, had so deeply shaken him, Mihály forgot his long-standing resolution and admitted elements into his married life which he had always wanted to keep away from Erzsi. There is a kind of lovemaking fashionable among certain adolescent boys and still-virgin girls, which lets them seek pleasure in a roundabout way, avoiding all responsibility. And there are people, like Mihály, who actually prefer this irresponsible form of pleasure to the serious, adult, and, as it were, officially approved variety. But Mihály, in his heart, would have been thoroughly ashamed to acknowledge this inclination, being fully aware of its adolescent nature, of its adolescent limitations. Once he had arrived at a truly serious adult relationship with Erzsi he had determined it would express itself only along the "officially approved lines", as befitting two serious-minded adult lovers.

That night in Florence was the first and only derogation. Erzsi was filled with wonder, but she accepted him willingly and reciprocated his unaccustomed gentleness. She did not understand what was happening, nor did she understand afterwards his terrible depression and shame.

"Why?" she asked. "It was so good that way, and anyhow I love you."

And she fell asleep. Now he was the one who lay awake for hours. He felt that finally, definitively, he was facing the bankruptcy and collapse of his marriage. He had to acknowledge that here too he had failed as an adult, and, what was even worse, he had to concede that Erzsi had never before given him so much pleasure as now, when he made love to her not as a partner in adult passion but as an immature girl, a flirtation on a springtime outing.

He climbed out of bed. As soon as he was sure she was still asleep he went to the dressing table where her reticule lay. He rummaged in it for the cheques (Erzsi was their cashier). He found the two National Bank *lira* cheques, each for the same amount, one in his name, the other in hers. He withdrew his own, and in its place smuggled in a sheet of paper of similar size. Then, very carefully, he put it in his wallet, and went back to bed.

# VI

THE NEXT MORNING they continued on their way to Rome. The train pulled out of Florence into the Tuscan landscape, between hillsides green with spring. It made slow progress, stopping for ten minutes at every station, where the passengers disembarked until it was ready to leave, then drifted back, chattering and laughing, at the comfortable pace of the South.

"Just look," observed Mihály. "You see so much more from the window of a train, here in Italy, than you can in any other country. I don't know how they do it. The horizon is wider here, or the objects smaller, but I bet you can see five times as much in the way of villages, towns, forests, rivers, clouds and sky here, than you would from a train window in, say, Austria."

"Indeed," said Erzsi. She felt sleepy, and his worship of all things Italian was beginning to irritate. "All the same, Austria's more beautiful. We should have gone there."

"To Austria?!" cried Mihály. He was so offended he couldn't continue.

"Put your passport away," said Erzsi. "Once again you've left it out on the table."

The train stopped at Cortona. When he saw the little hilltop town Mihály had the feeling that once, long ago, he had known many such places and was now savouring the pleasure of renewing old acquaintance.

"Tell me, why do I feel as if I spent part of my youth among these hilltop towns?"

But Erzsi had nothing to say on the subject.

"I'm bored with all this travelling," she remarked. "I wish I was already in Capri. I'll have a good rest when we get there."

"What, Capri! It would be so much more interesting to get off here in Cortona. Or anywhere. Somewhere unplanned. For example, the next stop, Arezzo. Arezzo! It's just incredible that there really is a place called Arezzo, that Dante didn't make it up when he compared their gymnasts to devils because they used their backsides as trumpets. Come on, let's get off at Arezzo."

"I see. We're getting off at Arezzo because Dante wrote that sort of rubbish. Arezzo will be just another dusty little birdsnest, doubtless with a thirteenth century cathedral, a Palazzo Communale, a bust of the Duce on every street-corner, with the usual patriotic inscriptions, several cafés, and a hotel called the Stella d'Italia. I really am not very interested. I'm bored. I just wish I was already in Capri."

"That's interesting. Perhaps you no longer swoon at the sight of a Fra Angelico or a Bel Paese because you've been to Italy so often. But I still feel I am committing a mortal sin at every station where we don't get off. There's nothing more frivolous than travelling by train. One should go on foot, or rather in a mailcoach, like Goethe. Take me, for example. I've been to Tuscany, but I haven't really been there. Oh yes, I travelled past Arezzo, and Siena was somewhere nearby, and I never went there. Who knows if I will ever get to Siena if I don't go there now?"

"Tell me: when you were at home you never showed what a snob you are. What does it matter if you don't get to see the Siena Primitives?"

"Who wants to see the Siena Primitives?"

"What else would you want to do there?"

"What do I know? If I knew, perhaps it wouldn't be so exciting. But just to say the name Siena gives me the feeling that I might stumble across something there that would make everything all right."

"You're daft. That's the problem."

"Perhaps. And I'm hungry. Have you got anything to eat?"

"Mihály, it's appalling how much you've been eating since we came to Italy. And you've only just had breakfast."

The train pulled in to a station called Terontola.

"I'll get out here and have a coffee."

"Don't get off. You're not an Italian. The train might start at any moment."

"Of course it won't. It always stands for a quarter of an hour at every station. Cheers. God bless."

"Bye, silly monkey. Do write to me."

Mihály left the train, ordered a coffee, and, while the espresso machine coaxed the marvellous steaming liquid out of itself, drop by drop, he began to chat with a local about the sights of Perugia. Finally he drank the coffee.

"Come, quickly," said the Italian, "the train's going."

By the time they got there the train was half way out of the station. Mihály just managed to clamber onto the last coach. This was an old-fashioned third-class carriage, with no corridor. Every compartment was a separate world.

"Never mind," he thought. "I'll move up to the front at the next station."

"Will this be your first visit to Perugia?" asked the friendly native.

"To Perugia? I'm not going to Perugia, unfortunately."

"Then you must be going on to Ancona. That's not a good idea. Stop off at Perugia. It is a very old city."

"But I'm heading for Rome."

"For Rome? You are joking."

"I'm what?" asked Mihály, thinking he must have mis-heard the word in Italian.

"Joking," shouted the Italian. "This train doesn't go to Rome. My, what a witty fellow" (using the appropriate idiom).

"And why shouldn't this train go to Rome? I got on at Florence with my wife. It said Rome on it."

"But that wasn't this train," the Italian replied with glee, as if this was the greatest joke of his life. "The train to Rome went earlier. This is the Perugia-Ancona train. The line forks at Terontola. Wonderful! And the *signora* is happily on her way to Rome."

"Terrific," replied Mihály, and stared helplessly out of the window at Lake Trasimene, as if an answer might come paddling across it towards him.

When he had taken his cheque and passport the night before he had thought—of course, not really seriously— that they might perhaps find themselves separated during the journey. When he got off at Terontola it had again flitted across his mind that he might leave Erzsi to continue on the train. But now that it had really happened he was amazed and disturbed. But at all events—it had happened!

"And what will you do now?" urged the Italian.

"I shall get off at the next station."

"But this is an express. It doesn't stop before Perugia."

"Then I'll get off at Perugia."

"Didn't I just say you were going to Perugia? You'll get there, no problem. A very old city. And you must visit the surrounding countryside."

"Great," thought Mihály. "I'm on my way to Perugia. But what will Erzsi do? Probably go on to Rome and wait there for the following train. But she might also get off at the next station. Perhaps she'll go back to Terontola. And she won't find me there. It won't be easy for her to work out that I left on the Perugia train.

"Yes, that'll fox her. So if I now get off at Perugia, it'll certainly be a day or two before anybody finds me. It will take even longer if she doesn't stop in Perugia but carries on from there on God knows what line.

"Lucky that I've got my passport with me. Luggage? I'll buy myself a shirt and whatnot—underwear is good and cheap in Italy. I was going to buy some anyway. And money . . . how are we off for money?"

He took out his wallet and in it discovered his National Bank *lira* cheque.

"Of course, last night! . . . I'll change it in Perugia, there must be a bank there that will take it."

He snuggled into his corner and fell deeply asleep. The friendly Italian woke him when they reached Perugia.

PART TWO

# IN HIDING

*Tiger, Tiger, burning bright*
*In the forests of the night....*
WILLIAM BLAKE

# VII

THE SCENE is the great Umbrian plain. In one corner, on its high table of rock, stands Perugia. In the other, propped against the vast hill of Subasio, Assisi gleams white, or, for a few days every year, is ablaze with flowers. Everywhere teeming fruit-trees filled the air with their annual jubilation: the strange, twisting-branched mulberries, the pale Italian-green olives, and those great lilac-coloured trees whose name Mihály could learn from no one. By day one could go about in shirt-sleeves. The evenings were still rather cool, but not unpleasantly so.

Mihály went on foot from Spello to Assisi, and thence up to the town's highest point, the Rocca. There he listened while a wise and beautiful Italian boy explained its history, sat on a wall of the old fortress, gazed for long hours across the Umbrian landscape, and was happy.

"Umbria is totally different from Tuscany," he thought: "more rustic, more ancient, more holy, and perhaps a shade bleaker.

"The land of the Franciscans, and the true hilltop town. Back home, they always built down in the valleys, under the hills. But here they build up on the hills, above the plain. Did those early founders harbour some obscure race memory of enemy attack? What was the terror that drove them ever upwards to the protection of steep rocks? Wherever a hill rose up out of the plain they immediately built a town on it.

"And here every town is in fact a city. Spello, for

example. Back home it would be a mean little village. Here it's a real city, with a cathedral and a coffee-house, much more so than, say, Szolnok or Hatvan. And no doubt some great painter was born here, or some great battle took place nearby.

"The Italian landscape isn't as simply friendly and merely pretty as I had imagined it. Certainly not here in Umbria. Here there is something desolate, something dark and rugged, like the bay-tree: that exactly epitomises the harsh attractiveness of Italy. Perhaps it's the great barren hills that do it. I would never have thought there were so many barren and really high mountains. There are still patches of snow on Subasio."

He broke off a branch of the tree whose name he did not know and, bedecked with flowers, cheerfully made his way down to the town. In the *piazza*, opposite the ancient temple of Minerva—the first ancient temple Goethe saw on his Italian travels—he sat down outside a little café, ordered vermouth, and asked the waitress the name of the tree.

"Salsify," she lisped, after a slight hesitation. "Salsify," she repeated, without conviction. "At least that's what they call it back home, up in Milan. But here everything has a different name," she added, with contempt.

"Like hell it's salsify," thought Mihály. "Salsify would be the houseleek. This must be the Judas tree."

But this detail aside, he felt very content. The Umbrian landscape diffused a general happiness, an unassuming Franciscan happiness. He felt, as so often in his dreams, that the important things happened not here but elsewhere, up there in Milan perhaps, where the sad exile, the little lisping girl, came from, or where Erzsi was ... but now he was filled with the happy feeling that he did not have to be where the important things happened, that he was somewhere entirely other, behind God's back.

During his walk to Assisi the hope had occurred to him that he might perhaps meet Ervin. In their youth, when Ervin was dominant in the group, they had read everything they could about the great saint of Assisi. Ervin must surely have joined the Franciscan order. But Mihály did not meet him, nor could the Franciscan churches revive the religious fervour of his youth, not even Santa Maria degli Angeli, built around the Portiuncula where the saint died. He decided not to wait around there until nightfall, fearing that anyone looking for him might well find him in such an obvious venue for tourists. He moved on, and by evening reached Spoleto.

Here he dined, but did not enjoy the wine at all. These Italian reds sometimes end up smelling of methylated spirits, or onions, God knows why, when at other times they can be so unaccountably fine. He became even more depressed when he realised at the counter that, despite every economy, the money he had cashed in Perugia would soon run out, and he had no idea what he would then do. The outside world, which he had been so happy to forget in Perugia and its plain, began here to breathe once more down his neck.

He took a cheap room in a cheap *albergo*—there really wasn't much choice in this tiny place—and then set off for one more little stroll before dinner round the back streets of Spoleto. Clouds veiled the moon. It was dark and the narrow lightless alleys of the sombre town closed around him, but not in the welcoming way the little pink streets had in Venice. Somehow he ended up in the sort of district where, with every step, the lanes grew darker and more menacing, the stairways led to ever more mysterious doors. He could see absolutely no one about—he had quite lost his way—and then he suddenly felt sure that someone was following him.

He turned. Just at that moment the person loomed round the corner: a huge, dark-clad form. An unnameable fear seized him, and he stepped hurriedly into an alleyway that proved darker and narrower than any so far.

But the alley was blind. He could only turn back to where the stranger was already waiting at the narrow exit. Mihály began a few hesitant steps towards him, but, catching a better view of the man, he stopped in horror. The stranger wore a short, black, circular cape, of the sort common in the last century, and over it, a white silk scarf. On his ancient, soft, oddly crumpled face was a sort of indescribable smile. He spread his arms in a little gesture towards Mihály, and screeched in a thin, neutered voice, "Zacomo!", or some such name.

"Not me," said Mihály. The stranger considered this, and a hasty apology passed between them. Mihály could now see that the indefinable smile on the old man's face was quite witless.

The fact that his escapade had arisen out of a purely irrational fear and had ended on this somewhat comic note, did nothing to reassure him. Rather, given his readiness to find symbolic significance, he concluded from this foolish episode that he was indeed being pursued, and that someone was indeed close on his tracks. In growing panic, he sought out the way back to his lodging, hurried up to his room, shut the door and blocked it with a chest. Even so, the room remained an alarming place. First of all, it was far too big for one person. Second, Mihály couldn't bear that fact that in Italy the smaller hotels have tiled floors. He felt like a child who had been banished into the kitchen, a harsh enough punishment in itself (though one that in practice could never have happened to him). Third, the room was on the very edge of the hill town. Below the window the cliff fell sheer some two hundred metres, and, defying comprehension, a glass door had been cut beside it into the wall. Perhaps it had at one time opened onto a balcony, but the balcony had either been removed centuries before, or had collapsed from neglect. Only the door remained, opening into the sky two hundred metres up in the air. For any potential suicide this room would have been certain death. The door would have been irresistible. In addition to this, the vast wall was hung with a single picture, an illustration from some picture-book, of a hideously ugly woman dressed in the fashion of the last century, holding a revolver.

Mihály decided that he had slept in more reassuring places. What worried him even more was that his passport was downstairs with the grim-faced, but no less sly-looking, proprietor, who had resisted his cunning suggestion that he fill in the registration form himself on the pretext that his passport was written in an incomprehensible foreign tongue. The innkeeper insisted that the passport should remain in his keeping as long as Mihály continued on the premises. It seemed he had had some bad experiences. The inn was indeed just the sort to guarantee its owner his fair share of those. During the day, Mihály reckoned, probably only down-at-heel revellers frequented the place, while in the evening horse-thieving types guffawed over cards in the so-called *sala da pranzo*, an eating area pervaded with kitchen smells.

But in whoever's hands, for whatever reason, the passport was a potential threat to him, betraying his name to his pursuers. Just to make off, leaving the passport behind, would have been as distressing as going out without his trousers on, as we do in our dreams. He lay on the questionably clean bed, feeling very tense. He slept little. A mixture of sleep, dozing and anxious wakefulness blended themselves together into the all-pervasive night-time feeling of being closely followed.

He rose at the crack of dawn, sneaked downstairs, roused the innkeeper after a long struggle, paid his bill, reclaimed his passport, and hurried off to the station. A half-awake woman made coffee for him at the bar counter. After a while, some sleepy labourers came in. Mihály's anxiety would not leave him. He was in constant terror that someone would arrest him. The appearance of every soldier or policeman fuelled his suspicion, until, at last, the train pulled in. He began to breathe more freely and prepared to abandon his cigarette and climb on board.

Just then a very young and startlingly handsome little

*fascista* stepped up to him and asked for a light before he threw down his cigarette.

"*Ecco*," said Mihály, and offered him the cigarette. He was entirely off his guard. Especially now that the train had come.

"You're a foreigner," said the fascista. "I can tell from the way you said '*ecco*'. I've a sharp ear."

"*Bravo*," said Mihály.

"You're Hungarian," the little man beamed up at him.

"*Si, si,*" said Mihály, smiling.

In that instant the *fascista* seized him by the arm, with a strength he would never have thought possible in such a small person.

"Ah! You're the man the whole of Italy is searching for! *Ecco*! This is your picture!" he added, producing a piece of paper. "Your wife is looking for you."

Mihály jerked his arm away, pulled out a calling card, and quickly scribbled on it, "I am well. Don't try to find me," and gave it, with a ten *lira* note, to the little fascista.

"*Ecco*! Send this telegram to my wife. *Arrivederci!*"

Once again he tore himself away from the man, who had renewed his grip, jumped onto the moving train, and slammed the door behind him.

The little train went up to Norcia, in the hills. When he disembarked the Sibilline mountains stretched out before him with their two-thousand-metre peaks. To the right lay the Gran Sasso, Italy's highest range.

It was fear that had driven him to the mountains, as it once had the builders of those towns. Up there, in the wilderness of ice and snow, they would not find him. He wasn't thinking now of Erzsi. Indeed he felt that Erzsi, as an individual, had been disarmed by his telegram. But Erzsi was only one of many. It wasn't so much people that were following him as whole institutions, and the whole dreaded terrorist army of the past.

For indeed, what had been his life during the past fifteen years? At home and abroad he had been schooled in mastery. Not self-mastery, but the mastery of his family, his father, the profession which did not interest him. Then he taken his place in the firm. He had really tried to learn the pleasures befitting a partner in the firm. He had learned to play bridge, to ski, to drive a car. He had dutifully entangled himself in the sort of love affairs appropriate to a partner in the firm. And finally he had met Erzsi, who was sufficiently talked about in high society for the level of gossip to satisfy what was due to the young partner in a fashionable firm. And he had ended by marrying her, a beautiful, sensible, wealthy woman, notorious for her previous affairs, as a partner should. Who knows, perhaps it needed only another year and he would become a real partner: the attitudes were already hardening inside him like calluses. You start off as Mr X, who happens to be an engineer, and sooner or later you're just an engineer who happens to be called Mr X.

He made his way on foot up into the hills and meandered around the villages. The natives remained peaceful, did not pursue him. They accepted him as just another crazy tourist. But a middle-class person meeting him on the third or fourth day of his wanderings would have taken him not for a tourist but a madman. He was unshaven, unwashed, and sleeping in his clothes: he was simply a man on the run. And inside, he was utterly in turmoil, up there among the harsh outline of pitiless mountains, the inhuman solitude, the utter abandonment. The faintest shadow of purpose never flickered across his consciousness. All he knew was that there was no going back. The whole horde of people and things pursuing him, the lost years and the entire middle-class establishment, fused in his visionary consciousness into a concrete, nightmarish shape. The very thought of his father's firm was like a great steel bar raised to strike him. At the same time he could see that he was slowly ageing, his body was somehow caught up in slow but visible processes of change, as if his skin was shrivelling at the speed of a minute hand ticking round a clock. These were the first signs of a delirious fever of the nerves.

His doctors later agreed that the nervous fever was the result of exhaustion. It was little wonder. For fifteen years Mihály had systematically driven himself too hard. He had forced himself to become something other than what he was, to live never after his own inclination but as he was expected to. The latest and not least heroic of these exertions had been his marriage. Then the excitement of travel, and the wonderful series of unwindings and unfoldings which the Italian landscape had induced in him, together with the fact that throughout his honeymoon he had drunk practically non-stop and never taken enough sleep, all had contributed to the collapse. Essentially, it was a case of a man not realising how tired he is until he sits down. The accumulated exhaustion of fifteen years had begun to overwhelm him from that time in Terontola when he involuntarily, but not unintentionally, took the other train, the train that carried him ever further from Erzsi, towards solitude and himself.

One evening he arrived in one of the larger hill towns. By then he was in such a surreal state of mind that he never inquired after the name, being all the more reluctant to do so since he had realised, around midday, that he could not remember a single word of Italian—so we need not record the name of the town. In the main square stood a friendly-looking *albergo*, where he called in, and dined with a perfectly good, normal appetite on *gnocchi* in tomato sauce, the local goat's cheese, oranges and white wine. But when the time came to pay he noticed the waitress looking at him suspiciously and whispering with two other people sitting in the room. He instantly rushed out, then roamed restlessly up and down on the scrubby *macchia*-covered hill above the town until, forced to leave by a howling wind, he let himself down a steep hillside.

He ended up in a deep, well-like valley where the wind was less fierce. But the place was so closed-in, so dark and desolate it would have seemed to him quite natural to come upon a few skeletons, with a royal crown amongst them, or some other bloody symbol of ancient dignity and tragedy. Even in his normal mind he was highly susceptible to the mood of place: now he was ten times so. He ran headlong out of the deep recess, then became exhausted. A pathway led him up a gentle hill. Arriving at the top he stopped at the base of a low wall. It was a friendly, inviting place. He jumped up on to the wall. So far as he could see, by the weak light of the stars, he was in a garden, in which fine cypress trees grew. A small mound beside his foot offered itself as a natural pillow. He lay down and immediately fell into a deep sleep.

Later the starlight grew much stronger. The stars became so bright it was as if some strange disturbance filled the sky with energy, and he awoke. He sat up, looked hesitantly around in the eerie luminosity. From behind a cypress tree, pale and melancholy, stepped Tamás.

"I must go back now," Tamás said, "because I can't sleep under this terrible starlight." Then he moved away, and Mihály wanted to rush after him, but could not get onto his feet, however much he struggled.

He awoke at dawn, with cold and the first light, and looked sleepily around the garden. At the foot of the cypress trees, extending in all directions, stood crosses marking graves. He had slept in the town's garden of rest, the cemetery. Nothing could have been more horrible. By day, and perhaps also by moonlight, the Italian cities of the dead were indeed perhaps more friendly and inviting than those of the living, but for Mihály the episode had a horrific symbolic meaning. Again he fled in terror, and from that moment one might properly date the onset of his illness. What happened to him afterwards he was unable to recall.

On the fourth, fifth or perhaps sixth day, on a narrow mountain path, he became aware of the sunset. The pink and gold hues of the setting sun were, to his fevered condition, quite overwhelming, even more so perhaps than when he was rational. In his saner moments he would have been ashamed to respond so strongly to the familiar, banal and utterly meaningless colours of the sky. But as the sun went down behind a mountain he suddenly clambered impulsively onto a rock, seized with the feverish notion that from its top he would be able to watch for a little longer. In his clumsiness he took a wrong hold and slithered down into the ditch beside the road, where he no longer had the strength to get up. There he remained prostrate.

Luckily, towards dawn some peddlers came by on mules, saw him lying in the moonlight, recognised the genteel foreigner and with respectful concern took him down to the village. From there the authorities sent him on, with many changes of transport, to the hospital at Foligno. But of this he knew nothing.

# VIII

WHEN HE RECOVERED consciousness he was still unable to speak a word of Italian. In a weary, timorous voice, using Hungarian, he asked the nurse the usual questions: where was he, and how had he got there? The nurse being unable to reply, he worked out for himself—it was not very difficult—that he was in hospital. He even remembered the strange feeling he had experienced in the mountains, and grew calmer. All he wanted to know was, what was wrong with him? He felt no pain, just very weak and tired.

Luckily there was in the hospital a doctor who was half English, and who was called to his bed. Mihály had lived in England for many years and the language flowed in his veins, so much so that it did not desert him now, and they could communicate fully.

"There's nothing wrong with you," said the doctor, "just horrendous exhaustion. What were you doing, to get yourself so tired?"

"Me?" he asked, meditatively. "Nothing. Just living." And he fell asleep again.

When he woke again he felt a great deal better. The English doctor visited him again, examined him, and informed him there was nothing wrong and he would be able to get up in a few days.

The doctor was interested in Mihály and talked with him a great deal. He was keen to establish the cause of his extreme exhaustion. He gradually became aware how much comfort Mihály took in the thought that he would be well in a few days and would have to leave the hospital.

"Do you have business in Foligno or the area?"

"Not at all. I had no idea there was such a place as Foligno."

"Where will you go? Back to Hungary?"

"No, no. I'd like to stay in Italy."

"And what would you want to do here?"

"I haven't the faintest idea."

"Do you have any relations?"

"No, no one," said Mihály, and, in his state of nervous debilitation, burst into tears. The tender-hearted doctor felt extremely sorry for this poor abandoned soul and began to treat him with even greater kindness. But Mihály had not wept because he had no relations, just the opposite—because he had so many—and he feared he would not long be able to preserve the solitude he so much enjoyed in the hospital.

He told the doctor that all his life he had longed to be in bed in a hospital. Of course not seriously ill or suffering, but as at present, just lying there in passive and involuntary exhaustion, being nursed, without purpose or desire, far from the normal business of men.

"It's no use. Italy has everything I ever longed for," he said.

It became apparent that the doctor shared his love of historical connections. By degrees he came to spend all his free time at Mihály's bedside, in historical discussions that flitted about lethargically. Mihály learned a great deal about Angela da Foligno, saint and mystic, the most famous daughter of the town, who was virtually unheard of in Foligno itself. And he came to know a lot about the doctor, since, as with all Englishmen, his family history proved rather colourful. His father had been a naval officer who had caught yellow fever in Singapore, was tormented in his delirium with terrible visions, and on his recovery turned Catholic, thinking that would be the only way he could escape the torments of the devil. His family, a religious one consisting for the most part of Anglican clergymen, rejected him, whereupon he became fiercely anti-British, left the Navy, joined the Italian merchant service, and later married an Italian woman. Richard Ellesley—that was the doctor's name—had spent his childhood in Italy. From his Italian grandfather they inherited a considerable fortune, and his father had educated the young Ellesley at Harrow and Cambridge. During the war the old man went back into the British Navy, fell at the battle of Skagerrak, the fortune evaporated, and Ellesley had to earn his living as a doctor.

"The only thing I inherited from my father," he said with a smile, "was the fear of damnation."

Here the roles were reversed. Mihály lived in terror of a great number of things, but hell was certainly not among them. He had little feeling for the afterlife. So he undertook to cure the doctor. A cure was urgently needed. About every third day the little English doctor would be seized by terrible fear.

The terror was not induced by bad conscience. He was a virtuous and kindly soul, with no obvious cause for self-reproach.

"Then why should you think you'll be damned?"

"My God, I've no idea why I should be damned. It won't be because of what I am. They'll just take me."

"But devils have power only over the wicked."

"That we can never know. Even the prayer says it. You know: 'Saint Michael Archangel, defend us in our struggles; be our shield against the wickedness of Satan and his snares. As God commands you, so we humbly beseech you; and you who command the Heavenly Armies, with the strength of the Lord deliver unto eternal damnation Satan and all the evil spirits who lead us into danger'."

The prayer reminded Mihály of his school chapel, and the horror its words had always conjured up inside him as an adolescent. But it was not Satan and damnation that disturbed him. It was the prayer with its bleak reminder of bygone days. He generally thought of Catholicism as a modern phenomenon, which indeed it is, but that one prayer seemed like a relic of buried ages.

Whenever the terror of Satan seized him, Ellesley would hurry off to priests and monks for absolution of his sins. But this was of little use. For one thing, because he did not feel himself to be in sin, the act of forgiveness did not help. Another problem was that his confessors, for the most part, were simple country priests who persisted in carefully and repeatedly drawing his attention to the horrific nature of Satan, which merely made his condition worse. But at least the amulets and other magic charms were a help. On one occasion a saintly old woman blessed him with a sacred incense, and that kept him calm for two whole months.

"But what about you?" he asked Mihály. "Aren't you afraid? What do you think happens to the soul after death?"

"Absolutely nothing."

"And you have no hope of survival after death, and eternal life?"

"The names of great men live forever. I am not great."

"And you can endure life on those terms?"

"That's another question."

"I don't understand how anyone can believe that when a man dies he vanishes completely. There are a thousand proofs to the contrary. Every Italian can tell you that. And every Englishman. In all these two nations there isn't a single person who hasn't met with the dead, and these, after all, are the two most honest races. I had no idea Hungarians were so cynical."

"Have you met with the dead?"

"Of course. More than once."

"How?"

"I won't describe it, it might just upset you. Although, one occasion was so straightforward it shouldn't disturb you. I was a pupil at Harrow before the war. One day I was lying in my bed—with the 'flu—and staring out through the window. Suddenly I saw my father standing on the window sill in his naval uniform, saluting me. The only strange thing was that his officer's cap had two wings, as in pictures of Mercury. I jumped up from the bed and opened the window. But he had gone. This was in the afternoon. That same morning my father was killed. That was the time it took for the spirit to get from Skagerrak to Harrow."

"And the other occasion?"

"That was much more mysterious. It happened in Gubbio, not long ago. But that I really shouldn't tell you about."

"Gubbio? Why does that name seem so familiar?"

"Presumably from the legend of Saint Francis in *The Little Flowers*."

"Of course, yes, the wolf of Gubbio ... the one Saint Francis made a pact with, that he wouldn't trouble the townspeople, and they in return provided him with food?..."

"And every evening the wolf could be seen, with two baskets round his neck, going about the houses of Gubbio one after the other, collecting love-gifts."

"Is this Gubbio still in existence?"

"Of course. It's quite near here. You must visit it when you are better. It's very interesting, not only for the wolf legend...."

They talked a lot about England, Doctor Ellesley's other home, which he greatly missed. Mihály too was very fond of England. He had spent two very serious, dreamy years there, before going on to Paris and home. In London he had wallowed in an orgy of solitude. Sometimes he went for weeks without speaking to anyone, just a few working men in suburban pubs, and then only a few words. He loved the appalling London weather, its foggy, watery softness, in which one can sink as low as the temperature in solitude and spleen.

"In London November isn't a month," he said, "it's a state of mind."

Ellesley readily agreed.

"You see," Mihály continued, "now it comes back to me: in London one November I also experienced something which, with people like yourself, would no doubt have strengthened their belief that the dead somehow survive. In me it only strengthens the conviction that there is something wrong with my nervous system. Listen to this. One morning I was working down in the factory (as I said, this was in November) when I was called to the telephone. An unknown woman asked me to go without fail that afternoon, on important business, to such and such a place, and gave me an unfamiliar name and address. I protested that there must be some error. 'Oh no,' said this unknown female voice, 'I'm trying to contact a Hungarian gentleman who works in the Boothroyd factory as a volunteer. Is there another one of that description?' 'No one,' I replied, 'and you have my name correctly. But tell me, what is it about?' She couldn't say. We talked about it for some time and eventually I agreed to go.

"I went because I was curious. Is there any man who wouldn't respond to the dulcet tones of an unknown woman on the telephone? If women really knew men they would ask us for everything over the telephone—in unfamiliar voices. The street, Roland Street, was in that rather forbidding bit of London behind Tottenham Court Road, just north of Soho, where the painters and prostitutes live who can't afford Soho proper or Bloomsbury. I don't know for certain, but I think it very likely that this is the part of London where you find the founders of new religions, Gnostics and the seedier kinds of spiritualist. The whole area gives off an aura of religious dereliction. Well, anyway, that's where I had to go. You have to understand I am incredibly sensitive to the atmosphere of streets and places. As I made my way through the dark streets looking for Roland Street in the fog—it was mist rather than fog, a white, transparent, milky mist, typical of November—I was so overcome by this sense of spiritual abandonment I was almost seasick.

"I finally found the house, and a plate beside the door with the name given me by the strange voice on the telephone. I rang. After some time I could hear shuffling, and a sleepy slattern of a maid opened the door.

"'What do you want?' she asked.

"'Well, I've no idea,' I said, and felt rather embarrassed.

"Then someone shouted down, as from a long way off. The maid pondered this and for some time said nothing. Then she led me to a grubby little stairway and said, in the usual English way, 'Just go straight up.' She herself remained below.

"At the top of the stairs I found an open door and a room in semi-darkness. There was no one in it. Just then the door opposite closed, as if someone had just that instant left the room. Remembering the maid's instructions, I crossed the room and opened the door that had just closed. I found myself in another semi-dark, old-fashioned, dusty and tasteless room, with no one in it, and again the door across the way closed, as if someone had just that instant gone out. Again I crossed the room and entered a third room, then a fourth. Always a door quietly closing before me, as if someone was walking ahead of me. Finally, in the fifth room ... well, it's an overstatement to say finally, because although there was no one in that fifth room, there at least was no door closing before me. In this room there was only one door, the one I had come through. But whoever had been walking ahead of me was not in the room.

"There was a lamp burning in the room, but no furniture apart from two armchairs. On the walls pictures, rugs hanging everywhere, every sort of worthless old-fashioned lumber. I sat down rather hesitantly in one of the armchairs and prepared to wait. Meanwhile I kept glancing restlessly about me, because I was quite sure something very strange was happening.

"I don't know how long I had been sitting like that, when suddenly my heart began to knock horribly, because I had realised what I had unconsciously been looking for. From the moment I entered this room I had had the feeling that I was being watched. Now I had found who it was. On one of the walls hung a Japanese rug, depicting various sorts of dragon and other fantastic animals, and the eyes of these animals were made of large coloured-glass buttons. I now saw that one of the animals had an eye that wasn't glass, but a real eye, and was staring at me. Presumably someone was standing behind the rug looking at me.

"In any other circumstances it would have seemed to me like something out of a detective novel. You read so much about foreigners vanishing in London without trace, and this seemed just the sort of start you would imagine for such a story. I tell you, the natural thing would have been for me to panic, suspect criminal intent, and put myself in a defensive posture. But I didn't. I just sat there, stock-still, frozen with terror. Because, you see, I recognised the eye."

"What do you mean?"

"That eye was the eye of a friend of my youth, a certain Tamás Ulpius who died young in tragic, although rather unclear, circumstances. For a few moments my fear was suspended, and a sort of pallid ghostly happiness filled me, a sort of ghost of happiness. I called out, 'Tamás,' and wanted to rush over to him. But in that instant the eye vanished."

"And then?"

"Properly speaking, that's all there was. But what happened next is quite inexplicable. An old lady came into the room, a strange, old-fashioned, repulsive, large-eyed woman, and with a fairly expressionless face asked me something. I didn't understand, because she wasn't speaking English. I tried her in French, German, even Hungarian, but she just shook her head sadly. Then she said something in a strange tongue, with much greater expression, besieging me with more and more questions. I listened hard, if only to try and catch what language she was speaking. I have a good ear for languages, especially those I don't speak. I decided that what she was talking was not Latinate, Germanic, or Slav. It was not even Finno-Ugric, because I had studied Finnish at one stage at university. And then suddenly I just knew that she was the only person in the whole world speaking that language.

Where that idea came from, I really don't know. But I was so horrified I jumped up, rushed out of the room and back home."

"And how do you explain it all?" asked Ellesley.

"I can think of no other than that it was November. I had got into that house through some strange random mistake. Our lives are full of inexplicable coincidences...."

"And the eye?"

"The eye was surely in my imagination, an effect of the situation I was in and the London November. Because I am unshaken in my belief that the dead are dead."

# IX

His time was up. Mihály was well again and due to leave the hospital. No thief released after twenty years' prison could have felt more cut off from everything, or more devoid of purpose, than Mihály did when, with his little suitcase (his only possessions were the few frugal purchases he had put together on the day of his escape) he made his solitary way between the low-roofed houses of Foligno.

He was in no mood to go home. It would have been impossible to appear among his family after his desertion, which he would be unable and unwilling to explain. And he could not bear the thought of returning to Pest, going in to the office, involving himself in the firm's business, and relaxing over bridge and small talk.

He still had so many Italian cities to see. They would surely have so much for him to discover. He decided to write home and ask for money.

But he put off the business of writing the letter from one day to the next. He had so far remained in Foligno, to be near Dr. Ellesley, the only person with whom he had any connection, however slight. He took a room, where he lived quietly, read the English novels the doctor lent him, and enjoyed his lunches and dinners. Food was the only thing that tied him to reality in those blank days. He loved the undisguised sentimentality of Italian cooking. Conventional French-European cuisine approves only subtle, subdued, qualified flavours, like the colours of

114

men's suits. The Italian loves intense sweetness, extreme tartness, strongly distinctive aromas. Even the huge servings of pasta could be seen as an expression of this sentimentality.

One evening he was sitting with Ellesley outside the main coffee-house of the town. As usual they were speaking English. Suddenly a young girl approached, addressed them in an American accent and joined them at the table.

"Please excuse my troubling you," she said, "but I've spent the whole day wandering around this godforsaken town and found no one I could communicate with. Can you please explain something? It's the reason I came here. It's very important."

"We are at your disposal."

"You see, I'm studying art history at Cambridge."

"Ah, Cambridge?" cried Ellesley with delight.

"Oh yes, Cambridge, Massachusetts. Why? Did you graduate there?"

"No. I was at Cambridge, England. But how can we be of service?"

"Well, I'm studying art history and I came to Italy because, as you probably know, there are lots of great pictures here they don't have anywhere else. And I've seen everything."

She took out a little notebook, and continued:

"I've been to Florence, Rome, Naples, Venice, and a whole lot of other places whose names I can't read just now, the light's so bad here. The last place was Per ... Perugia. Did I say that right?"

"Yes."

"In the museum there I met a French gentleman. He was French, that's why he was so kind. He explained everything beautifully, and then told me that I absolutely must go to Foligno, because there is a very famous picture there, painted by Leonardo da Vinci, you know, the guy who did the *Last Supper*. So I came here. And I looked for this picture the whole day and didn't find it. And nobody in this revolting little birdsnest can direct me to it. Would you please tell me where they hide this painting?"

Mihály and the doctor looked at one another.

"A Leonardo? There's never been one in Foligno," replied the doctor.

"That's impossible," said the girl, somewhat offended. "The French gentleman said there was. He said there's a wonderful cow in it, with a goose and a duck."

Mihály burst out laughing.

"My dear lady, it's very simple. The French gentleman was having you on. There is no Leonardo in Foligno. And although I'm no expert, I have the feeling that there is no such picture by Leonardo, with a cow, a goose and a duck."

"But why did he say there was?"

"Probably because cynical Europeans tend to liken women to these animals. Only European women, of course."

"I don't get it. You're not telling me the French gentleman was playing a trick on me?" she asked, red-faced.

"You could see it that way, I'm sorry to say."

The girl thought deeply. Then she asked Mihály:

"You aren't French?"

"No, no. Hungarian."

Her hand made a gesture of indifference. Then she turned to Ellesley:

"But you're English."

"Yes. Partly."

"And do you agree with your friend?"

"Yes," said Ellesley, nodding sadly.

The girl again thought for a while, then clenched her fist.

"But he was so kind to me! I just wish I knew the bastard's name."

Her eyes filled with tears. Ellesley consoled her:

"But there's no great harm done. Now you can write in your notebook that you've been to Foligno."

"I already did," she said with a sniffle.

"Well, there you are," said Mihály. "Tomorrow you'll go happily back to Perugia and continue your studies. I'll take you to the train. I've already had the experience of getting on the wrong one."

"That's not the point. The shame of it, the shame of it! To treat a poor defenceless girl like that! Everyone told me not to trust Europeans. But I'm such a straightforward person myself. Can you get whisky here?"

And they sat together until midnight.

The girl's presence had a lively effect on Mihály. He too drank whisky, and became talkative, although mostly it was the girl who spoke. The little doctor became very quiet, being naturally shy, and finding her rather attractive.

The girl, whose name was Millicent Ingram, was quite wonderful. Especially as an art historian. She knew of Luca della Robbia that it was a city on the Arno, and claimed that she had been with Watteau in his Paris studio. "A very kind old man," she insisted, "but his hands were dirty, and I didn't like the way he kissed my neck in the hallway." That aside, she talked about art history, passionately and pompously, without stopping.

It gradually emerged that she was the daughter of wealthy Philadelphia parents who enjoyed considerable influence in high society, at least as she saw it, but that some Rousseauistic tendency in her drove her towards solitude and nature, which from her point of view meant Europe. She had attended study semesters in Paris, Vienna and other fine places, but none of it had had any effect. Her soul had preserved its American innocence.

And yet, as Mihály walked home and prepared for bed, he hummed cheerfully to himself, and his apathy slipped away. "Millicent," he said. "There's someone in the world actually called Millicent! Millicent."

Millicent Ingram was not the mind-boggling, soppily-named, beautiful American girl to be seen in Paris in the years after the war, when everything else in the world was so drab. It was only in the second of those contexts that Millicent could be classed as an American beauty. The basis of this beauty, though the word is perhaps an over-statement, was that her face was quite devoid of expression. But in any event she was very good-looking, with a little nose, a wholesome mouth that was large (and painted larger), a fine athletic figure: her muscles seemed as elastic as rubber.

And she was American. Indisputably of that class of

wonderful creatures exported to Paris in Mihály's youth. The "foreign woman" is an element of young manhood, of footloose youth. What remains in later years is the undying nostalgia, for in the footloose years we are still gauche and timid, and let slip the better opportunities. Mihály had now lived for so long in Budapest that his lovers had all been from that city. The "foreign woman" now rather denoted his youth. And liberation: after Erzsi, after the serious marriage, after so many serious years. An adventure, at last: something coming unexpectedly and moving towards an unforeseen conclusion.

Even Millicent's stupidity was attractive. In the deepest stupidity there is a kind of dizzying, whirlpool attraction, like death: the pull of the vacuum.

It so happened that the next day, when he had escorted her to the station, and they were about to buy the ticket, he said:

"Why are you going back to Perugia? Foligno is a city too. Why not stay here?"

Millicent looked at him with her stupidly serious eyes, and said:

"You're right."

And she stayed. That day was rather hot. They spent the whole of it eating ice-cream and talking. Mihály had the skill that makes English diplomats so feared in their profession: he knew how to be extremely dim when the need arose. Millicent noticed nothing of the intellectual distance between them. Indeed, she felt herself at an advantage because of her art history studies, and this rather flattered her.

"You are the first European I've met who really understood me intellectually," she said. "The others were so dull, and took no interest in art."

He had won her complete confidence. By evening he had gleaned everything there was to know about her, not that there was anything worth knowing.

That evening they met Ellesley at the café. The doctor was quite surprised that the girl was still in Foligno.

"You know, I decided I can't always be thinking about problems of art," she told him. "A doctor friend of mine said that prolonged intensive study is bad for the skin. Isn't that so? Anyway I decided to switch myself off for a bit. I'm giving myself an intellectual holiday. Your friend has such a calming influence on me. Such a kindly, simple, harmonious soul, don't you think?"

Ellesley noted with resignation that his patient was courting the American girl, and grew even quieter. For he was still very attracted to Millicent. She was so different from Italian women. Only the Anglo-Saxon type can be so clean, so innocent. Millicent—innocent: what a splendid rhyme that would have been, if he had been a poet. But no matter. The main thing was that this heaven-sent delight was doing visible good to his dear Hungarian patient.

The next day Mihály and the girl went for a long walk. They ate their fill of pasta in a modest village tavern, then lay down in a classical-looking wood and slept. When they awoke, Millicent observed:

"There's an Italian painter who painted trees just like these. What was his name?"

"Botticelli," replied Mihály, and kissed her.

"Ooooh," she said, with horror on her face. Then she kissed him back.

Now that he held the girl between his arms, Mihály decided happily that she did not disappoint. Her body was as elastic as rubber. Oh the "foreign woman" made flesh—how much she means to the man whose passion pursues fantasy and not physiological fact! The pleasure of the preliminary and quite innocent kiss suggested that every detail of Millicent's body would prove foreign, other, wonderful. Her healthy mouth was entirely American (Oh, the prairies!), the little hairs on her neck were foreign, the caresses of her large strong hands, the transcendent cleanliness of her well-scrubbed body (Oh Missouri-Mississippi, North against South, and the blue Pacific Ocean!)....

"Geography is my most potent aphrodisiac," he thought to himself.

But in the evening a letter was waiting for Millicent at the post-office, forwarded from Perugia. It was from a Miss Rebecca Dwarf, Professor of Medieval Art History at the University of Cambridge (Mass.), Millicent's tutor and chief spiritual adviser. Over dinner Millicent tearfully explained that Miss Dwarf was very satisfied with her previous letter in which she had spoken about the progress of her studies, but deemed it absolutely essential that she should now travel forthwith to Siena, to see the famous Primitives.

"But it was so good to be with you, Mike," she sniffled, and put her hand in his.

"So you must go without fail to Siena?"

"Of course. If Miss Dwarf says in her letter...."

"To hell with the old cow," Mihály broke in. "Look, Millicent, listen to me. Don't go and see the Siena Primitives. The Siena Primitives are probably almost identical to the Umbrian Primitives you saw in Perugia. And anyway, does it really matter whether you see ten pictures more or less?"

Millicent looked at him in astonishment and withdrew her hand. "But Mike, how can you talk like that? I really thought you felt so strongly about painting, for a European." And she turned away.

Mihály saw that he had struck the wrong note. He was obliged to go back to the stupid type of voice. But he could not think of stupid arguments with which to reason with her. He tried sentimentality.

"But I shall miss you terribly if you go now. Perhaps we'll never meet again in this life."

"Sure," said Millicent. "I'll miss you horribly too. And I've already written to Philadelphia, to Doris and Ann Mary, telling them how wonderfully well you understand me. And now we have to part."

"But stay here."

"That isn't possible. But you come with me to Siena. You're not really doing anything here."

"That's true. I could leave what I'm doing here."

"Then why not come?"

After some hesitation, he confessed:

"Because I haven't any money."

Which was true. By now his money was almost entirely spent. It had gone on the few decent items of clothing he had bought the day before, out of respect for Millicent, and on buying her meals, which were very substantial and extremely well-chosen. True, it would be gone in a day or two even if he stayed in Foligno ... but if you stay in one place you don't feel the lack of money as much as when you are travelling.

"You've no money?" she asked. "How's that?"

"It's run out," he said with a smile.

"And your parents don't send you any?"

"Oh yes. They'll send some. When I write to them."

"Now look. Until then I'll make you a loan." And she took out her cheque book. "How much do you need? Will five hundred dollars be enough?"

The amount shocked Mihály, as did the offer itself. Every bourgeois scruple in him, and indeed every quiver of romantic sensibility, protested against borrowing from the object of an *amour*, from the heaven-sent stranger, whom he had kissed for the very first time that day. But Millicent, with charming innocence, insisted on the offer. She was always lending money to her boyfriends and girl-friends, she said. In America it was quite natural. And besides, Mihály would pay her back soon. They finally left it that Mihály would think about it overnight.

Mihály very much wanted to go to Siena, even without considering Millicent. Foligno by now bored him to death, and he really longed to go to Siena because, now that his apathy had lifted, the Italian cities once again began to press their sweet, terrible claim, that he should see every one of them and experience their secrets before it was too late. As at the start of his honeymoon, he again carried inside him the mystery Italy stood for, like a great delicate treasure he might at any moment let slip from his hands. Moreover, ever since he had kissed her, Millicent had become much more desirable, and it is in the nature of such adventures that a man likes to see them through.

But could a serious adult, a partner in a well-known Budapest firm, actually borrow money from a young girl? No, a grown-up, serious partner could not. Of that there could be no doubt. But was that what he still was? Or had he, with his desertion, his exile, returned to that earlier level, that way of life in which money was just paper and bits of silver? To put it plainly, had he reverted to the ethics of the Ulpius household?

Mihály was appalled at the thought. No, he couldn't. It would mean that the paradise of youth had succumbed to the reality it had always denied, the reality whose chief manifestation was money.

But the conscience is easily placated when we really want something. Of course it was just a matter of a very short-term loan, a small sum. He wouldn't take five hundred dollars: one hundred would be enough. Or, let's say, two. Perhaps after all we should say three hundred.... He would write home straightaway, and pay the money back very shortly.

He sat down and finally penned the letter. He wrote not to his father, but to his youngest brother, Tivadar. Tivadar was the *bon viveur* and prodigal of the family, a friend of the turf, reputed to have had an liaison with an actress. He perhaps would understand and take a tolerant view of the case.

He told Tivadar that, as he no doubt already knew, he and Erzsi had separated, but quite amicably, and that as a gentleman he would soon put everything to rights. Just why they had separated, he should say straight out, was too complicated to put in a letter. The reason he had not written earlier was that he had been lying in hospital, very ill, in Foligno. Now he was well again, but the doctors absolutely advised rest, and he would like to spend the period of convalescence here in Italy. So he really had to ask Tivadar to send him some money. In fact, as soon as possible, and as much as possible. His money had run out, and he had had to borrow three hundred dollars from a local friend, which he would like to repay as soon as possible. The money should be sent direct to his friend, at Dr Richard Ellesley's address. He hoped everyone was well at home, and that they would see each other again soon. Any letters should be sent to the Ellesley address in Foligno, because he was moving on but did not yet know where he would be spending any length of time.

The next morning he sent the letter by airmail, and hurried off to Millicent's room.

"So you thought it through and you're coming, Mike?" she asked, radiantly.

Mihály nodded and with furious blushes accepted the cheque. Then he went to the bank, and to buy himself a good suitcase. The two of them bade farewell to Ellesley and set off.

They were alone in the first-class compartment and exchanged uninhibited kisses, the way the French do. For both, this was a legacy of their student years in Paris. A little later on a somewhat patrician old gentleman joined them, but by then they were past caring, and exercised the privilege of barbaric foreigners.

By evening they had reached Siena.

"Will the *signore* and *signora* require a room?" was the obliging inquiry of the porter of the hotel outside which their hansom-cab had stopped. Mihály nodded in affirmation. Millicent, unaware of the significance of the exchange, simply went up, but registered no protest on arrival.

It may perhaps seem from a distance that Millicent was not quite as innocent as Doctor Ellesley had imagined. But for just that reason she was, in her amorous mode, every bit as fresh-tasting and quietly awe-struck as at other times. Mihály found that his journey to Siena had been most worthwhile.

# X

S IENA was the most beautiful Italian city Mihály had
ever seen. It was more beautiful than Venice, finer
than aristocratic Florence, lovelier even than dear Bologna
with its arcades. Perhaps an element in this was that he
was there not with Erzsi, officially, but with Millicent,
and on the loose.

The whole city with its steep, pink streets undulated
over several hills in the shape of a happy-go-lucky star.
On the faces of its people you could see that they were
very poor, but very happy—happy in their inimitable
Latin way. The city had the quality of a fairytale, a happy
fairytale, lent it by the fact that from everywhere you
could see, at its highest point, the cathedral hovering over
it like a towered Zeppelin, in the livery of a pantomime
zebra.

One of the walls of the cathedral stood away from the
main mass of the building, a good two hundred metres
distant, as a grotesque and wonderful spatial symbol of
the failure of the most grandiose human plans. Mihály
loved the feckless way the old Italians set about building
their cathedrals. "If Florence has one, then we must have
one, and as large as possible," they said, and then built
the longest wall in existence in order to fill the Florentines
with panic about the intended size of their project. Then
the money ran out, the builders naturally downed tools
and lost all interest in the cathedral. "Yes, yes," thought
Mihály, "that's the way to go about a church. If the

127

Ulpius set were ever to go about building a church, that is exactly how they would do it."

They went down to the Campo, the main square, the scallop shape of which was like the city's smile. He could not tear himself away, but Millicent overruled him:

"Miss Dwarf said nothing about it," she argued, "and it isn't Primitive."

In the afternoon they worked their way round the sequence of city gates. They stopped before each one, and Mihály inhaled the view, the sparse sweetness of the Tuscan landscape.

"This is the landscape of humanity," he told Millicent. "Here a hill is exactly the size a hill should be. Here everything is to scale, tailored to the human form."

Millicent thought about this.

"How would you know exactly what size a hill should be?" she asked.

Over one gate was an inscription which read: *Cor magis tibi Sena pandit*—Siena opens its heart to you. "Here," Mihály thought, "the gates still utter wisdom ánd truth: 'Siena opens its heart' so that life can be filled with the simple delirium of yearning, in harmony with the veiled beauty of the season."

The following day he woke at dawn, rose and stared out of the window. The window looked out from the city towards the hills. Slight, lilac-coloured clouds were sailing over the Tuscan landscape, and a tinge of gold slowly and timidly prepared for dawn. And nothing existed but lilac and the gold of first light over distant hills.

"If this landscape is reality," he thought, "if this beauty

really exists, then everything I have done in my life has been a lie. But this landscape is reality."

And he loudly declaimed Rilke's verses:

*Denn da is keine Stelle,*
*Die dich nicht sieht. Du musst dein Leben andern.*

Then he turned in alarm towards Millicent, who was still sleeping peacefully. And it occurred to him that there was no reality in Millicent. Millicent was no more than a simile, a random phenomenon of the mind. And she was nothing. Nothing.

*Cor magis tibi Sena pandit.* Suddenly he was seized by a mortal yearning, the kind of yearning he had felt only as a young child. But this was both more specific and more urgent. He now yearned for that same childhood emotion, with such intensity that he had had to shout his feelings aloud.

Now he saw that his little adventure, his return to the vagabond years, was merely a transition, a step leading him downwards, and backwards, into the past, into his private history. The "foreign woman" remained a foreigner, just as his years of wandering had been a time merely of pointless locomotion, before he had had to turn home, back to those who were not strangers. But then they ... were already long dead, and the stray winds blowing round the four corners of the world had swept them away.

Millicent was awakened by the sensation of Mihály sinking his head on her shoulder and sobbing. She sat up in the bed, and asked in horror: "What's the matter? Mike, for God's sake, what's the matter?"

"Nothing," he replied. "I dreamed that I was a little boy, and a huge dog came and ate my bread and butter."

He embraced her and drew her towards him.

That day they could find nothing to say to each other. He left the girl to study the Siena Primitives on her own, and, at noon, listened with only half an ear to her charming stupidities on the subject of her experiences.

He did not leave the room all afternoon, but simply lay on the bed, fully-dressed.

"... My God, what is the whole civilisation coming to if they have forgotten what even the modern Negroes know: *summon up the dead*."

This was how Millicent found him.

"Have you a fever?" she asked, and put her large lovely hand on his brow. At her touch, Mihály turned slightly towards her.

"Come for a walk, Mike. It's such a beautiful evening. And everyone's out in the streets, and they've all got children with such marvellous names, like Emerita and Assunta. Such a tiny little girl and she's called Annunziata."

With the greatest difficulty he struggled to his feet and went out. He walked heavily and uncertainly. It was as if he was seeing everything through a veil, and listening to the sounds of the Italian evening through ears filled with wax. His feet were heavy as lead. "When have I felt this way before?" he wondered.

They went down to the Campo, and he stared at the Torre del Mangia, the huge tower of the city hall that rose over a hundred metres, like a needle piercing the evening sky. His gaze slowly followed the tower upwards to its dizzy height. And the tower itself seemed to go on and on, soaring into the reverberating dark-blue sky.

Then it happened. The ground opened up around a deep well, and again he stood before the whirlpool. It must have lasted only a moment, then vanished. Everything was back in its place. The Torre del Mangia was again merely an extremely tall tower. Millicent had noticed nothing.

But that evening, when their sated bodies finally turned away from each other, and he was alone in that profound solitude that a man feels after he has embraced a woman with whom he has nothing in common, the whirlpool opened again (or was he just remembering it?) and this time it remained. He knew he had only to stretch out his hand to feel the presence of the other person, the comforting reality of the friendly body. But he could not bring himself to reach out, and he lay in solitary distress, by choice, for endless hours.

The next morning his head ached and his eyes were horribly red from sleeplessness.

"I'm ill, Millicent," he told her. "The problem has come back, the one that kept me in bed in Foligno."

"What sort of illness is it?" she asked suspiciously.

"I can't exactly say. Some sort of sporadic cataleptic apodictitis," he declared nonsensically.

"I see."

"I must get back to Foligno, to the good Doctor Ellesley. Perhaps he can do something. At least I know him. What will you do, Millicent?"

"Well naturally I'll go with you, if you're sick. I won't

just leave you on your own. In any case I've seen all the Siena Primitives."

He kissed her hand with emotion. They reached Foligno late that afternoon.

They took separate rooms, at his suggestion. "On the whole, it's better that Ellesley shouldn't know," he explained.

Ellesley called on Mihály towards evening. He listened thoughtfully to his complaints, and made humming noises over the whirlpool sensation.

"It's a kind of agoraphobia. For the time being, simply rest. Then we'll see."

He spent several days in bed. The whirlpool did not recur, but he had no desire to get up. He felt that if he did it would return. He slept as much as possible. He took every tranquilliser and mild sedative Ellesley brought him. If he slept, he might manage to dream of Tamás and Éva.

"I know what's wrong with me," he told the doctor. "Acute nostalgia. I want to be young again. Is there a cure for that?"

"Hmmm," said Ellesley. "Certainly, but not one I can tell you about. Think of Faust. Don't hanker after youth. God gave you manhood and old age too."

Millicent visited him regularly and dutifully, though she seemed rather bored. She would call in on Ellesley towards evening, and they would also leave together after the visit.

"Tell me honestly," the doctor asked one day, in her absence, as he sat on Mihály's bed. "Tell me honestly, is there some dead person who is very dear to you?"

"Of course."

"Do you think about them nowadays?"

"I do."

From that point onwards his methods became less medically orthodox. On one occasion he brought a Bible with him, on another a garland of roses, then a Virgin Mary from Lourdes. Once Mihály became aware as he was talking with Millicent that Ellesley was drawing crosses on his door. And one fine day he produced a string of garlic.

"Tie this round your neck when you go to sleep. The smell of garlic is very good for the your nerves."

Mihály burst out laughing.

"Doctor, even I have read Dracula. I know what garlic is supposed to do: keep the vampire at bay, who sucks human blood in the night."

"That's right. I'm glad you understand. Because there's no point in your insisting that the dead don't exist in some form or other. They are what is making you ill. They visit you and suck your life out. Medical science can't help you with that."

"Then take your garlic back home. My dead can't be kept away by that sort of thing. They're inside me."

"Naturally. Nowadays they work with psychological instruments. But their nature hasn't changed in the least. It's just that you have to be on your guard against them."

"Leave me in peace," said Mihály, with mild exasperation. "Tell me that I have cerebral anaemia and prescribe iron tonic and bromide for my nerves. That's what you're supposed to do."

"Of course it is. I can't do anything more for you. Medicine can't help against the dead. But there are stronger, supernatural weapons...."

"You know I'm not superstitious. Superstition only works if you believe in it...."

"That's a very outmoded point of view. At any rate, why not try it? You've nothing to lose."

"Of course not. Just my self-respect, my pride, my integrity as a rational being."

"Those are long meaningless words. You really should try. You should go to Gubbio. There is a monk up there, in the Sant' Ubaldo monastery, who works miracles."

"Gubbio? You spoke to me about it once before. If I remember rightly, you said that you had some supernatural experience there."

"Yes. And now I will tell you about it, because the story might persuade you. It's about that very monk."

"Let's hear it."

"You know how I was a city doctor in Gubbio before I came to the hospital here. One day I was called out to a patient who seemed to be suffering from some deep-seated nervous condition. She lived in the Via dei Consoli, one of those completely medieval streets, in a dark old house. She was a young woman, not from Gubbio, not even Italian, I don't know in fact what her nationality could have been, but she spoke excellent English. A very good-looking woman. The people of the house, where she lived as a paying guest, explained after a while that she was suffering from hallucinations. She had the fixed idea that at night the door of the dead was open."

"The what?"

"The door of the dead. You see, these old houses in Gubbio had two doorways, the usual one for the living, and next to it a second one, rather narrower, for the dead. This door is opened only when a corpse is taken out of the house. Then they wall it up again, so that the dead won't return. Because they know that the dead can only come back in the way they went out. The door isn't on the same level as the paving, but about a metre higher, so you can pass a coffin out to people standing in the street. The woman I mentioned lived in one of these houses. One night she was woken by the realisation that the door of the dead was open, and someone was coming in, someone she greatly loved, who had been dead a long time. And from then on the dead person came every night."

"But it would be easy to cure that. She would simply have to move house."

"That's what we said, but she didn't want to move. She was very happy to be visited by the dead person. She just slept all day, as you do, and waited for the night. Meanwhile she was rapidly losing weight, and the people of the house were very worried about her. And they weren't exactly pleased about a dead man calling at the house every night. It was a rather patrician family with strict moral views. The truth was, they had sent for me so that I would use my authority as a doctor to make her leave."

"And what did you do?"

"I tried to explain to her that she was having hallucinations, and that she should seek a cure. But she laughed at me. "How could I be having hallucinations," she asked, "when he's here every night, truly, beyond all doubt, just as you are now? If you don't believe me, stay here tonight."

"This was not exactly what I would have wanted, because I am perhaps a little too impressionable in these matters, but I really had no alternative than to stay, out of my duty as a doctor. The waiting was not otherwise unpleasant. The woman was neither terrified or crazed. She was remarkably calm, indeed rather cheerful. In fact, though I don't wish to seem boastful, her behaviour was frankly quite flirtatious towards me.... I almost forgot why I was there, and that midnight was approaching. Just before midnight she suddenly seized my hand, took a night-light in the other, and led me down to the ground floor room, the one into which the door of the dead opened.

"I have to admit I did not see the dead man. But that was my fault. I was too scared to wait. I just felt that it was getting horribly cold, and the flame from the wick was guttering in the draught. And I felt—somehow I felt this with my whole body—that there was someone else in the room. And I tell you sincerely, this was more than I could bear. I rushed out of the room, all the way home, shut the door, and buried my head in the eiderdown. Of course you will tell me that I had succumbed to her powers of suggestion. It could be...."

"And what happened to her?"

"Ah, I was just coming to that. When they realised that a doctor, or rather my sort of doctor, was no use, they called in Father Severinus, from the Sant' Ubaldo monastery.

This Father Severinus was a very special and holy person. He had turned up in Gubbio from some faraway country, no one could discover which. He was rarely seen in the town. Apart from major festivals or funerals he never left the mountain, where he lived his life of strict self-denial. However he was now somehow prevailed upon to come down and visit the disturbed woman. The meeting between them, they say, was harrowing and dramatic. When she caught sight of him she screamed and collapsed. Father Severinus himself turned pale and staggered on his feet. It seems he realised what a difficult case it would be. But he did succeed in the end."

"How?"

"That I don't know. It seems he exorcised the ghost. After he'd talked with her for a full hour in some strange tongue, he went back up the mountain. She calmed down and left Gubbio. And after that nobody ever saw her again, or the ghost."

"Very interesting. But tell me," asked Mihály, giving way to a sudden suspicion, "this Father Severinus, did he really come from some foreign country? Do you honestly not know where he was from?"

"I'm sorry, I don't. Nobody does."

"What sort of person, I mean, in outward appearance?"

"Quite tall, rather gaunt. As monks usually are."

"And he is still up there, in the monastery?"

"Yes. You should go and see him. Only he can help someone in your condition."

Mihály thought profoundly. Life was full of inexplicable

coincidences. This Father Severinus could be Ervin, and the woman Éva, haunted by the memory of Tamás....

"You know what, doctor? Tomorrow I'll go to Gubbio. For your sake, because you are such a kind person. And because, as an amateur of religious history, I am curious about these doors of the dead."

Ellesley was delighted with this outcome.

The next day Mihály packed his things. When Millicent arrived to visit him he told her: "I have to travel to Gubbio. The doctor says that only there will I get better."

"Truly? Then I'm afraid it means we shall have to part. I'm staying on here for a time in Foligno. I really love this place. And at first I was so angry with that Frenchman, who tricked me into coming here, do you remember? But now I don't mind. And the doctor is such a nice man."

"Millicent, I am sorry, I still owe you money. I feel really bad about it, but you know, back home it has to be channelled abroad through the National Bank, and the banking machinery is very complicated. Do please bear with me. Truly, it should come in the next few days."

"Don't mention it. And if you see any good pictures, do write to me."

# XI

G<small>UBBIO</small> is reached by the narrow-gauge motor-train that runs between Fossato di Vico and Arezzo. Despite the shortness of the distance, it is a tedious journey. It was also hot, and Mihály was exhausted by the time he arrived. But the city, as it came into view a little way up the road from the station, filled him, from the very first glance, with delight.

It cowered on the side of a huge, barren, typically Italian hill, as if it had collapsed while fleeing upwards in terror. As you looked at it, not a single house seemed less than hundreds of years old.

At the centre of a topsy-turvy tangle of streets, there towered an incredibly high building. Quite why it had been erected in the centre of this godforsaken place, and by whom, he could not imagine: a vast, gloomy medieval skyscraper. It was the Palazzo dei Consoli, from which the consuls ruled the little community of Gubbio until the fifteenth century, when it came under the sway of the Montefeltri, princes of Urbino. And above the town, almost at the peak of the Monte Ingino, stood a long, vast white block of a building, the monastery of Sant' Ubaldo.

Meanwhile down below, on the road leading up from the station, Mihály found an inn that appeared to be of the better sort. He took a room, had lunch, rested a little, then set out to explore Gubbio. He inspected the interior of the cavernous Palazzo dei Consoli, which reminded him somewhat of a vast studio, with its extremely ancient *tavole eugubine*—bronze tablets dating from pre-Roman times and preserving the sacred texts of the Umbrian people. He also looked round the old cathedral. There was not much else to see. The main sight here was the city itself.

In most of the towns in this part of Italy (as in so many ancient cities elsewhere) the houses give an impression of dilapidation, of being within a few short years of total ruin. This is because where the Italians built with local stone it was not the practice to plaster the outer walls. Consequently an observer from Middle Europe concludes that the plaster has fallen off and the house, and indeed the entire city, been left to desolation and ruin. Gubbio was even more unplastered, even more tumbledown, than other towns in Italy. It was absolutely desolate. It was off the beaten tourist track. There was scarcely any industry or commerce. It was a mystery how the few thousand people hemmed within its walls could make a living.

Mihály came out of the cathedral and turned into the Via dei Consoli. "This is the street Ellesley talked about," he thought. It was a street to make the imagination riot: medieval houses, blackened by age, with a bleak, penniless dignity, and, one suspected, inhabitants to match, people living off bread and water in the shadow of a glorious past that had vanished centuries before.

And straightaway, in the third house along, there actually was a door of the dead: next to the usual door, about a metre above the ground, a narrow gothic door-opening, bricked up. There was one in almost every house along the Via dei Consoli, but almost nowhere else in the town; and, strangely, there was no one about.

He went down a narrow back-alley to the street running parallel behind. This was no less ancient, only a little more gloomily patrician, but it did seem that living beings might reside there. And also, it seemed, dead ones. For outside one particular house a group of people met his astonished eye. Had he not immediately realised what was happening he would have thought it was a vision. People were standing outside the house holding candles, their faces covered with hoods. A funeral was taking place, and here, still following the ancient Italian ritual, members of the family, a hooded fraternity, were taking out the dead.

Mihály removed his hat and edged closer for a better view of the ceremony. The door of the dead stood open. Through it he could see into the house, into a dark room containing the bier. Priests and their assistants stood around the coffin, chanting and swinging censers. After a few minutes they lifted it up and passed it through the door of the dead into the street, where the hooded relatives hoisted it on to their shoulders.

Then in the gothic doorway a priest appeared in flowing robes. His pale ivory face, with its sombre, all-unseeing eyes, glanced at the heavens. Then with bowed head he placed his hands together in an ancient gesture of inexpressible gentleness.

Mihály did not rush up to him. For he was now a priest, a pale, serious monk performing a religious duty.... No, one couldn't just run up to him, like a schoolboy, like a little boy....

The pallbearers set off with the coffin, followed closely by the priest and the procession of mourners. Mihály joined it at the rear, and trod slowly with hat in hand towards the *camposanto*, up on the hill side. His heart was beating so hard he had to keep pausing for rest. Would they have anything to say to each other, after so many years, journeying along such widely divergent paths?

He asked one of the people in the procession what the priest was called.

"That's Father Severinus," said the Italian. "A very holy man."

They reached the burial ground. The coffin was lowered into the grave, the funeral came to an end, and people began to move away. Father Severinus set off for the town with a companion.

Mihály still could not make up his mind whether to approach him. He felt that Ervin, now that he had become such a holy person, would surely be ashamed of his worldly youth, and, like St Augustine, would look back upon it with lofty disdain. Surely he would see it all quite differently, and had doubtless dismissed him, not wanting even to think about him. Perhaps it would be better to leave straightaway, and be content with the miracle of simply having seen him.

Just then Father Severinus left his companions and turned back. He was coming straight towards him. Every adult response deserted Mihály, and he ran towards him.

"Mishy!" shouted Ervin, and embraced him. Then he offered the right and the left sides of his face to Mihály's cheeks, with the kindliness of a priest.

"I saw you at the graveside," he said quietly. "How did you get here, where no bird flies?"

But this was mere cordiality. It was clear from his tone that he was not in the least surprised. Rather, it was as if he had long anticipated this meeting.

Mihály was unable to say a word. He simply gazed at Ervin's face, now so long and so thin, and his eyes, in which the youthful fire still blazed. Beneath the happiness of the moment he could see in that face the same profound sombreness he had found in the old Gubbio houses. He could think of only one word, "monk". It was borne in upon him that Ervin really was a monk, and his eyes filled with tears. He turned his face away.

"Don't cry," said Ervin. "You have changed too, since those days. Oh Mishy, Mishy, I've thought about you so much!"

Mihály was filled with a sudden impatience. He must tell Ervin everything, everything, things he couldn't tell Erzsi.... Ervin would know a balm for everything, now that he was bathed in the glory and the radiance of another world....

"I knew you would have to come into Gubbio, so I came here. Tell me when I can talk with you, and where. Can you come with me right now, to the hotel? Can we have dinner together?"

Ervin smiled at his naïveté.

"That really isn't possible. I'm sorry, even at this moment I'm not free, my Mihály. I'm busy all evening. I have to be off straight away."

"Have you so much to do?"

"Terrible. You lay people can't imagine how much. I've still got a pile of prayers to get through."

"But then, when will you have time? And where can we meet?"

"There's only one way, Mishy, but I'm afraid it'll be rather uncomfortable for you."

"Ervin! Do you think comfort matters to me, if it's a question of talking with you?"

"Because you'll have to come up to the monastery. We are never allowed out, except on pastoral duty, like the funeral today, for example. And up in the monastery every hour of the day has its tasks. There's only one way we could speak together without interruption. You know we go to church at midnight to say psalms. At nine we usually go to bed and sleep till midnight. But this sleep isn't obligatory. The period isn't governed by regulation, and silence is not prescribed. That's when we could talk together. The wisest thing would be for you to come up to the monastery after dinner. Come as a pilgrim. We're always receiving pilgrims. Bring a small gift for Sant' Ubaldo, to please the brothers. A few candles perhaps, that's the usual thing. And ask the brother at the gate to put you into the pilgrims' room for the night. You realise it'll be pretty uncomfortable compared with what you're used to—but I won't say anything more. Because, if you left at midnight to go back to the town, I'd be very worried. For that you would have to know your way about the hill. If you aren't familiar with it, it can be a very unfriendly place. Hire a boy to bring you up. Will that be good?"

"It will be good, Ervin, very good."

"So, until then, God be with you. I must hurry, I'm already late. See you tonight. God be with you."

And he set off with rapid strides.

Mihály wandered back to the town. Beside the cathedral he found a shop and bought some rather fine candles for Sant' Ubaldo. Then went back to his hotel, dined, and tried to think what sort of accessories to take with him in his guise of pilgrim. He eventually made a neat little package of the candles, his pyjamas and toothbrush, to all appearances the bundle of a genuine pilgrim. Then he commissioned the waiter to find him a guide. The waiter soon returned with a young lad, and they took to the road.

On the way he inquired after the local sights. He asked what had happened to the wolf Saint Francis had befriended, and the bargain it had made with the town.

"That must have been a long time ago," the boy replied thoughtfully, "even before Mussolini. There certainly haven't been any wolves since he became Duce." But he did seem to recall, as something he had heard, that the wolf's head was buried in some faraway church.

"Is it usual for pilgrims to go up to the monastery?"

"Of course, often. Sant' Ubaldo is said to be very good for knee and back pains. Perhaps you have a bad back yourself, sir?"

"Not so much my back...."

"But he's very good for anaemia and bad nerves. The numbers are specially large on May the Sixteenth. That's the Saint's day. On that day they carry up the *Ceri*—

figures made of wax—in a procession from the cathedral up to the monastery. But that's not such a big procession as Corpus Christi or Resurrection Sunday. When they parade the *Ceri* they have to run."

"What do the *Ceri* represent?"

"That nobody knows. They're very old."

The religious historian in Mihály was aroused. He would have to see these later. It was most interesting that they ran with them up to the monastery ... like the Bacchantes running up the hill at the festival of Dionysos, in Thrace. This Gubbio was really remarkably old: the Umbrian tablets, the doors of the dead. Perhaps even the wolf tamed by St Francis was some old Italian deity, related to the she-wolf that mothered Romulus and Remus, living on in the legend. How very strange that Ervin should have come to just this place....

After an hour of strenuous climbing they reached the monastery. A mighty stone wall led them round the building to a little door cut into it, which was shut. They rang. After a long wait a tiny window in the door was pushed open, and a bearded monk peered out. The helpful lad explained that the gentleman was a pilgrim and wished to pay his respects to Sant'Ubaldo. The door opened. Mihály paid the guide and stepped into the courtyard.

The gate-brother was gazing up and down in amazement at his clothes.

"The *signore* is from abroad?"

"Yes."

"No matter. There is a father here who is also from

abroad and who understands foreign languages. I shall tell him you've come."

He led Mihály into one of the buildings where lights were still burning. A few minutes later Ervin arrived, no longer in his flowing robes but his brown Franciscan cowl. It now struck Mihály how thoroughly Franciscan Ervin had become. The tonsure gave quite a different look to the face, as if its owner had expunged from his nature every worldliness, every conceivable worldliness, and elevated himself into the air of the Giottos and Fra Angelicos. And yet, Mihály felt, this was Ervin's true face. From the very first he had been growing towards this face. The tonsure had always been there on his crown. It had simply been hidden by his bushy black hair.... There could be no doubt that, however alarming the result, Ervin had found himself. And before he realised what he was doing he had greeted him the way they had greeted the religious teachers in school:

"*Laudetur Jesus Christus.*"

"*In aeternum,*" was the reply. "But how did you find me here, where no bird flies? Come, I'll take you to the reception room. We're not allowed visitors in our cells. That's a rule we enforce very strictly."

He lit a taper and led Mihály through vast, totally empty whitewashed halls, corridors and smaller rooms, with no sign of a living soul: nothing but their echoing footsteps.

"Tell me, how many people live in the monastery?" Mihály asked.

"Six. Plenty of room for us, as you can see."

147

It was most eerie. Six people in a building where two hundred would not have been a crowd. And where once there certainly had been that many.

"Don't you get scared here?"

Ervin smiled and ignored the childish question.

And so they reached the reception room, a huge, arched, empty hall, in one corner of which stood a table and a few rickety wooden chairs. On the table was a pitcher of red wine and a glass.

"Thanks to the goodness of Pater Prior we are in the happy situation of being able to offer a little wine," said Ervin. Mihály was struck by the peculiar way he spoke. No doubt he hadn't spoken Hungarian for so many years. . . . "Now for a drink. I'll pour you some straight away. It'll do you good to take something after the long walk."

"And you?"

"Oh, I never drink. Since I joined the order. . . ."

"Ervin . . . perhaps you no longer smoke?"

"No."

Mihály's eyes again filled with tears. No, this was beyond imagining. He could have believed anything of Ervin—that he wore a spiked hairshirt under his clothing, that he would receive the stigmata before his death—but his not smoking!

"We've rather more important things to talk about," said Ervin, to divert attention from this sacrifice. "But have a drink, and do smoke if you want to."

Mihály downed a glass of the red wine. There are great myths about the wines stored by monks in cobwebbed bottles for the entertainment of their rare guests. This was not one of those but an ordinary, if very clean-tasting, country wine, its bouquet wonderfully suited to the simplicity of the empty whitewashed hall.

"I don't know if it's any good," said Ervin. "We don't have a cellar of our own. We are a begging order, and you have to take that rather literally. Now, tell me your story."

"Look, Ervin, of our two lives yours is the more remarkable. My curiosity is by rights stronger than yours. You must tell me your story first...."

"What is there to tell, my dear Mishy? We have no personal story. The life of any one monk is the same as any other, and you can read the sum of those lives in the history of the church."

"But tell me, at any rate, how you came here to Gubbio."

"At first I remained back home, in Hungary. I was a novice in Gyöngyös, then for a long time at the monastery in Eger. Then the Hungarian branch of the Order had to send a father to Rome on some business, and I was chosen because I had been learning Italian. Then, some time after I had dealt with that, I was called to Rome again, because they had taken a great liking to me, though I certainly didn't deserve it, and they wanted to keep me there to work with the Pater Prior. But I was concerned that this might lead, in due course, to my making a career, purely in the Franciscan context, naturally—becoming the head of a house somewhere, or filling some rank at Head Office. And that I didn't want. So I asked Pater Prior to place me here in Gubbio."

"Why here, exactly?"

"I really couldn't say. Perhaps because of the old legend, the one about the wolf of Gubbio we were so fond of at school, you remember. Because of the legend I came here once on a visit from Assisi and fell in love with the monastery. This is the place, you know, where no bird flies...."

"And you're happy here?"

"Very. As the years go by I feel a greater sense of peace ... but I mustn't patter on" (a strange little smile put quotation marks around the phrase) "because I know that you didn't come here to see Pater Severinus, but the person who used to be Ervin, not so?"

"I really don't know ... tell me ... these are difficult questions to ask ... isn't it rather monotonous here?"

"Not in the least. Our lives have the same pleasures and pains as those outside, only the terms are different, and the emphasis is on other things."

"Why don't you want a career in the Order? Is that from humility?"

"Not because of that. The kind of office I could attain would be consistent with the ideal of humility, or rather, would give the opportunity to overcome pride. No, I refused a career for quite other reasons. Really, because any advancement would not have been due to my being a good monk but for the sort of qualities I brought with me from the outside world, and in fact from my ancestors —my ability with languages and the fact that I can sometimes deal with matters more quickly and effectively than some of my fellow monks. In a word, my Jewish qualities. And I didn't want that."

"Tell me, Ervin, how do your fellow monks look on the fact that you were Jewish? Hasn't that been a disadvantage?"

"Not at all. It worked only to my benefit. I did run into individual fellow-monks who made it clear how much they disliked my race, but that just presented opportunities to practise meekness and self-control. And then in Hungary, when I was a country pastor, the fact always somehow got about, and the good village faithful saw me as some sort of oddity and paid much greater attention to what I said. Here in Italy nobody bothers about it. I hardly ever think about it myself."

"Tell me, Ervin ... what do you actually do all day? What work is there for you?"

"A great deal. Chiefly prayers and spiritual exercises."

"You don't write any more?..."

Again Ervin smiled.

"No, not for a long time now. You see, it is true that when I first joined the Order I imagined that I would serve the Church with my pen, I would be a Catholic poet.... But later...."

"What? Your inspiration left you?"

"Not at all. I left it. I realised it was all really beside the point."

Mihály thought deeply. He was beginning to understand what sort of worlds separated him from Father Severinus, who had been Ervin.... "How long have you been in Gubbio?" he asked eventually.

"Wait a moment ... it must be ... six years. But it could be seven."

"Tell me, Ervin, I used to think about this a lot, if you remember. Do you monks also have the feeling that time goes forward, and that every little bit of it has a special truth? Do you have a sense of history? If you recall some event, can you say if it happened in 1932 or in 1933?"

"No. It is one of the blessings of our lot that God lifts us out of time."

Ervin began to cough violently. Mihály realised only then that he had been coughing for some time, a dry, ugly cough.

"Tell me, Ervin, isn't there something wrong with your lungs?"

"Well, they're certainly not in perfect order ... in fact you could say they're in a pretty bad way. You know, we Hungarians are really pampered. Houses in Hungary are so well-heated. These Italian buildings really wear you down, always in unheated cells and cold churches ... and in sandals on the stone floor ... and this cowl doesn't warm you very much."

"Ervin, you're ill ... aren't they treating you?"

"You're very good, Mihály, but you mustn't grieve about it," he said, coughing. "You see, it's simply a blessing for me, being ill. Because of it they agreed that I could leave Rome to come here to Gubbio, where the air is so healthy. Perhaps I really will get better. Then again, physical suffering is part of our monastic system. Others have to mortify the body—in my case the body takes care of this itself.... But let's leave all this. You came here to talk about yourself. We shouldn't be wasting precious time on things neither you nor I can do anything about."

"But Ervin, it's not as if ... you shouldn't live like that, and you should go somewhere where they looked after you, and made you drink your milk, and lie in the sun."

"Don't worry about it, Mihály. Perhaps the time for that will come. Even monks have to guard against death, because if we simply allow the illness to take us over it would be a form of suicide. If the problem gets serious, I really will see a doctor ... but we're still a long way from that, believe me. And now you must talk. Tell me everything that's happened to you since I last saw you. And first of all, tell me how you found me."

"János Szepetneki said you were somewhere in Umbria, he didn't know where precisely. And some unusual chance happenings, some really strong indications, made me suspect that you were in Gubbio, and indeed the famous Father Severinus."

"Well, I am Father Severinus. And now tell me about yourself. I'm all attention."

He rested his head in his hand in the classical pose of the father-confessor, and Mihály began to speak, haltingly at first, and with difficulty, though Ervin's questions were a wonderful help. "But that long experience of the confessional is quite wasted on me," Mihály thought to himself, for he could never have withheld the outpouring that was just waiting to burst from him. As he spoke it all came to the surface—everything that since his escape had lived inside him like a repressed instinct: how deeply he felt a failure in his adult, or quasi-adult life, his marriage, his desperation to know where he might start again, what he could expect from the future, how he could get back to his true self. And above all, how he was tortured by nostalgia for his youth and the friends of his youth.

When he reached this point the strength of his emotion overwhelmed him and his voice broke. He was filled with self-pity, and at the same time ashamed of his own sentimentality before Ervin, before Ervin's mountain-peak serenity. Then he suddenly burst out in shocked amazement:

"And you? How can you bear it? Doesn't it upset you too? Don't you miss them? How do you manage it?"

The faint smile again passed over Ervin's face, then he bent his head, and made no answer.

"Answer me, Ervin, answer, I beg of you. Don't you miss them?"

"No," he said in a toneless voice, with a wild look on his face. "I miss nothing."

There was a long silence between them. Mihály was trying to understand Ervin. It couldn't be otherwise. He must have purged everything from himself. Since he had had to tear himself away from everyone, he had dug up from his soul the very roots of anything that might flower into those feelings that bind people together. Now there was no pain, but he lived on in this fallow, this barren, land, on the bare mountain ... Mihály shuddered to think of it.

Then a sudden thought struck him:

"I heard a story about you ... how you exorcised a woman who was visited by the dead, here, in some mansion in the Via dei Consoli. Tell me, Ervin: that was Éva, wasn't it?"

Ervin nodded.

Mihály jumped up in excitement, and gulped down the remaining wine.

"Oh, Ervin, tell me … how was … what was she like, Éva?"

What was Éva like? Ervin considered this. "Well, how should she be? She was very beautiful. She was, as always.…"

"How? She hadn't changed?"

"No. Or rather, I didn't notice any change in her."

"And what is she doing?"

"I'm not very sure. She spoke a lot about how lucky she'd been, and how much she'd moved about in the West."

Had anything flared up in Ervin when they met? He dared not ask.

"You don't know what she's doing now?"

"How should I know. It's a few years, I believe, since she was here in Gubbio. But I have to say, my sense of time is pretty unreliable."

"And tell me … if you can … how did it happen that … how did you get the dead Tamás to leave?"

Mihály's voice sounded with the fear that filled him whenever he thought of it. Ervin again smiled that little smile.

"It wasn't difficult. The old house made her see ghosts. Those doors of the dead have affected others in the same way. I merely had to persuade her to move out. Then again, I believe she played the whole thing up a little. Well, you know Éva … I'm afraid she never actually saw Tamás.

She wasn't having visions. Although it is possible that she was. I can't say. You know, I've had to deal with so many apparitions and ghosts over the years, especially here in Gubbio with its doors of the dead, I've become rather sceptical in this respect...."

"But then ... you did cure her?"

"Not at all. As usually happens in these cases. I spoke to her very seriously, prayed with her a little, and she calmed down. She came to see that the place of the living is with the living."

"Are you sure of that, Ervin?"

"Absolutely sure," he replied with great seriousness. "Unless you choose what I chose. Especially among the living. But why am I preaching this to you? Even you know this."

"She said nothing at all about how Tamás died?"

Ervin did not answer.

"Tell me, would you be able to exorcise the memory of Tamás, and Éva, and all of you, out of me?"

Ervin thought deeply.

"Very difficult. Very difficult. And I don't know if it would be a good thing, because what would you be left with then? Really, it's very hard to counsel you, Mihály. Pilgrims as desperate for help and so hard to help don't often come to Sant' Ubaldo. What I could advise, what my duty should advise, you wouldn't accept. The store of mercy opens only for those who want to share in it."

"But what will become of me? What shall I do tomorrow, and the day after? I expected a miraculous answer from you. I superstitiously believed that you would give me advice. Should I go back to Budapest, like the Prodigal Son, or start a new life, as a worker? Because I have done an apprenticeship. I've got a trade. It would be possible. Don't leave me to myself. I'm so alone already. What shall I do?"

Ervin fished out a large peasant's watch from the depths of his cowl.

"Right now, go and sleep. It's almost midnight. I have to go to chapel. Go and sleep. I'll take you to the room. And during my matutine I'll think about you. Perhaps it'll become clear ... it's happened before. Perhaps I'll be able to tell you something tomorrow morning. Now go and sleep. Come."

He led Mihály to the hospice. Given the deep state of distress that gripped him there seemed a fitness in the semi-darkened hall in which pilgrims down the centuries had dreamed of miraculous cures for their sufferings, yearnings and dearest hopes. Almost all the bunks were empty, though two or three pilgrims were asleep at the farther end.

"Lie down, Mihály, and sleep well. Have a good, peaceful night," said Ervin.

He made the sign of the cross over him, and hurried away.

For a long time Mihály sat on the side of the hard bed, his hands crossed on his lap. He was not in the least bit drowsy, and he was very depressed. Would anyone be able to help him? Would his road ever lead anywhere?

He knelt and prayed, for the first time in years.

Then he lay down. It was difficult to sleep on the hard bed, in unfamiliar surroundings. The pilgrims stirred restlessly on their bunks, sighed, moaned in their sleep. One of them kept calling for aid on Saints Joseph and Catharine and Agatha. When Mihály finally drifted off day was already breaking.

He woke in the morning with the exquisite feeling that he had dreamed of Éva. He did not remember the dream, but his whole body registered the silky euphoria that only that dream could give, or waking passion on very rare occasions. In the context of this bleak, ascetic sleeping-place, this mellow feeling took on a strange, paradoxical, sickly-sweet quality.

He rose, washed himself, an act of no little self-mortification in the antiquated washing-place, and went out into the courtyard. It was a bright, cool, breezy morning. The bell was just tolling for Mass, and brothers, lay people, monastery servants and pilgrims were hurrying from all directions into the chapel. Mihály joined them, and attended devoutly to the timeless Latin of the service. He was filled with a festive, happy feeling. Ervin would surely tell him what to do. Perhaps he would have to do penance. Yes, he would become a simple workman, earning his bread with the labour of his hands.... He had the feeling that something new was beginning in him. It was for him that voices rose in song, for him rang out the crisp and mellow tones of the spring bells. For his special soul.

When Mass was over he went out into the courtyard. Ervin came up to him, smiling:

"How did you sleep?"

"Well, very well. I feel quite different from last night, I have no idea why."

He looked at Ervin, full of expectation; then, when he said nothing, asked:

"Have you thought about what I should do?"

"Yes, Mihály," Ervin said quietly. "I think you should go to Rome."

"To Rome?" he blurted out in astonishment. "Why? How did you arrive at that?"

"Last night in the choir.... I can't really explain this to you, you're not familiar with this type of meditation.... I do know that you must go to Rome."

"But why, Ervin, why?"

"So many pilgrims, exiles, refugees have gone to Rome, over the course of centuries, and so much has happened there ... really, everything has always happened in Rome. That's why they say, 'All roads lead to Rome.' Go to Rome, Mihály, and you'll see. I can't say anything more at present."

"But what shall I do in Rome?"

"What you do doesn't matter. Perhaps visit the four great basilicas of Christendom. Go to the catacombs. Whatever you feel like. It's impossible to be bored in Rome. And above all, do nothing. Trust yourself to chance. Surrender yourself completely, don't plan things.... Can you do that?"

"Yes, Ervin, if you say so."

"Then go immediately. Today you don't have that hunted look on your face that you had yesterday. Use this auspicious day for your setting forth. Go. God be with you."

Without waiting for a reply he embraced Mihály, offered the priestly left cheek and right cheek, and hurried away. Mihály stood for a while in astonishment, then gathered up his pilgrim's bundle and set off down the mountain.

# XII

WHEN ERZSI received the telegram Mihály had sent via the little *fascista* she did not linger in Rome. She had no wish to return home, not knowing how to explain the story of her marriage to people in Budapest. Following a certain geographical pull, she travelled to Paris, as people often do when they have no hopes or plans but wish to start a new life.

In Paris she looked up her childhood friend Sári Tolnai. Even as a young girl Sári had been notorious for her somewhat unfeminine character and practical capability. She had never married, not having the time for it. It always happened that there was some burning need for her services in the company, the business or the newspaper where she was working. Her love life was conducted on the move, as it were, like a commercial traveller's. In due course, having become bored with everything, she emigrated to Paris to begin a new life, and continued in just the same way, but in French companies, businesses and newspapers. At the time when Erzsi arrived in Paris, she was working as the secretary of a large commercial film studio. She was the statuary sole unattractive woman in the house, the pillar of stone who remained untouched by the general erotic ambience of the profession, whose common-sense and impartiality could always be relied upon, who worked so much harder, and expected so much less, than everyone else. Meanwhile, her hair had turned grey. Cut very short, it gave the head on her delicate girlish body the distinction of a military bishop. People would turn to stare at her, of which she was very proud.

"What will you live on?" she asked, after Erzsi had briefly outlined the history of her marriage, softening the tale with a few Budapest witticisms. "How will you live? You've always had so much money."

"Well you know, this business of my money is all rather tricky. When we broke up Zoltán gave back my dowry, and my father's legacy, which by the way was a great deal less than people think. I put most of it into Mihály's family firm, and the rest into the bank in case I should ever need it. That's what I should be living on, only it's very hard to get at. The bank money can't be sent here through legal channels. So I have to depend on what my ex-father-in-law sends me. And that's not a simple matter either. When it comes to paying out money from his own pocket my father-in-law is usually a very difficult person. And we have no proper arrangement about it."

"Hm. You're going to have to get your money out of their business, that's the first thing."

"Yes, but to do that I should have to divorce Mihály."

"Well of course you must divorce Mihály."

"It's not quite so 'of course'."

"What, after all he's done?"

"Yes. But Mihály isn't like other people. That's why I chose him."

"And that was a fine move. I really dislike the sort of people who aren't like other people. It's true other people are so boring. But so are the ones who aren't like them."

"Very good, Sári. Can we just leave this? Really I can't do Mihály the favour of divorcing him just for this."

"But why the devil don't you go back to Budapest, where your money is?"

"I don't want to go back until all this is cleared up. What would people say at home? Can you imagine what my cousin Julie would say?"

"They'll talk anyway, you can be sure of that."

"But at least here I don't have to listen. And then ... no, no, I can't go back, because of Zoltán."

"Because of your ex-husband?"

"Because of him. He'd be waiting at the station with bunches of flowers."

"You don't say. He isn't angry with you, after the callous way you walked out on him?"

"He's not the least bit angry. I believe what he says. He's waiting in all humility for me to go back to him some day. And as a penance he's definitely broken off with the entire typing pool and living a celibate life. If I went back he'd be round my neck all the time. I couldn't bear that. I can put up with anything, but not goodness and forgivingness. Especially not from Zoltán."

"You know what, for once you're dead right. I hate it when men are all good and forgiving."

Erzsi took a room in the same hotel as Sári: a modern hotel, free from smells and aromas, behind the Jardin des Plantes. From it you could see the great cedar of Lebanon, with foreign, oriental dignity stretching out its many-handed branches to the unruly Parisian spring. The cedar was not very good for Erzsi. Its foreignness always made her think of some exotic and wonderful life whose advent she longed for in vain.

Initially she had her own room, then they moved in together because it was cheaper. In defiance of hotel regulations they took things up to their room and made supper together. It became apparent that Sári was as skilled at preparing dinners as she was at everything else. They had to lunch separately because Sári ate in town, coffee and sandwiches, taken standing up before hurrying straight back to the office. Erzsi at first tried various of the better restaurants, but became aware that these places mercilessly overcharged foreigners, so she took instead to visiting little *crémeries*, where "you can buy the identical thing, but so much cheaper." Likewise, at first she would always drink black coffee after lunch because she adored the fine Parisian *café noir*, but then she came to realise that it was not absolutely essential for survival and gave it up, except that once a week, every Monday, she went to the Maison de Café on the Grand Boulevard to regale herself with a cup of the famous beverage.

The day after her arrival she had bought herself a splendid reticule in a very genteel shop near the Madeleine, but this was her sole luxury purchase. She discovered that goods identical to those retailed to foreigners at such high prices in the more fashionable areas could be found in simple shops and flea-markets in the side streets, the rue de Rivoli or the rue de Rennes, and very much cheaper. But her final insight was that not to buy was in fact cheapest of all, and from then on she took a special pleasure in objects she thought she would have liked to purchase, but did not. Following this, she discovered a hotel two streets further along which, while not quite so modern as the one they were living in, did have hot and cold running water in the rooms, and after all they might just as well live there as where they were, only it was so much less expensive, nearly a third. She persuaded Sári, and they moved.

By degrees the saving of money became her chief preoccupation. She realised she had always had a strong inclination to save. As a child, chocolate bonbons given to her as presents would usually be stored away until they went mouldy. She hid her best clothes, any length of silk, pair of fine stockings or expensive gloves, and the maids would find them in the most surprising places, grubby and ruined. Her later life did not permit any expression of this economising passion. As a young girl she had to be on show beside her father, and conspicuous extravagance was required if she was to do him credit. And as Zoltán's wife she could not possibly have dreamed of saving money. If she declined an expensive pair of shoes, Zoltán would surprise her the following day with three even more expensive pairs. Zoltán was a "generous" man. He patronised art and artists (female), and made an absolute point of showering largesse on their husbands, partly to ease his sense of guilt. And in all this Erzsi's ruling passion, the saving of money, remained unexpressed.

Now, in Paris, this repressed yearning erupted in her with overwhelming force. It was helped by the French ambience, the French way of life, which promotes the urge for economy in the most feckless breasts. It was reinforced by subtler factors. Her neglected love, her failed

marriage, the aimlessness of her life, all these somehow
sought compensation in the saving of money. Then, when
Erzsi gave up her daily bath because she had realised the
hotel was grossly overcharging for it, Sári could not let it
go on without saying something:

"Tell me, why the devil are you so worried about
spending money? I can let you have some, on an I.O.U.
of course, as a formality...."

"Thank you, you're very kind, but I do have enough. I
had three thousand *francs* from Mihály's father yesterday."

"Three thousand *francs*! My God, that is a lot of money.
I hate it when a woman skimps and saves the way you
are. There's something not right about it. It's like when a
woman spends the whole day cleaning and then goes
hunting for leftover dust, or spends the whole day washing her hands and carries a special cloth around with her
so that when guests arrive they can wipe their hands on
that. Women can be stupid in so many ways. And while
I'm on the subject, just tell me: what do you do all day
while I'm at the office?"

It became clear that Erzsi had little idea how she spent
her time. All she knew was that she saved money. She
hadn't gone here, and she hadn't gone there, and she
hadn't done this, and she hadn't done that, so that she
wouldn't have to spend money. But what she had actually done apart from that was mysterious, dreamlike....

"Madness!" cried Sári. "I always thought you had
some man and spent all your time with him, and it turns
out that you stare in front of you the whole day, in a

daydream, like these half-mad women (they at least are on the right road). And meanwhile of course you put on weight however little you eat, so of course you're getting fat. You should be ashamed of yourself. Well, it can't go on like this. You must get out among people, and you must take an interest in something. Damn, damn, damn! If only I had enough time for things in this god-awful life...."

"Hey, tonight we're going out," she announced radiantly a few days later. "There's a Hungarian gent who wants to put some shady outfit in touch with the studio. He's buttering me up because he knows I've got the boss's ear. Now he's asked me out to dinner. He says he wants to introduce me to his rich friend, the one he's representing. I told him I'm not interested in the ugly rich, I meet quite enough dowdy characters at the office. He said, 'He really isn't dowdy, he's a very handsome chap, a Persian.' 'Well, alright,' I said, 'then I'll come, but I'm bringing my girlfriend with me.' He said that was splendid. He was just about to suggest it himself, so I wouldn't be the only woman in the party."

"My dear Sári, you know I can't go. What an idea! I really don't want to, and I haven't got a thing to wear, just my rubbishy Budapest things."

"Don't worry about a thing. You look wonderful in them. Listen, compared to these scrawny Paris women, you're the real thing ... and the Hungarian will certainly like you because you're from home."

"There's no question of my going. What's this Hungarian's name?"

"János Szepetneki. At least that's what he said."

"János Szepetneki ... my God, I know him! Do you know, he's a pickpocket!"

"A pickpocket? Could be. I see him more as a burglar, myself. Would you believe it, that's how everyone starts off in the film business. But apart from that, he's very good-looking. Well, are you coming or not?"

"Yes, I'm coming."

The little *auberge* where they went to dine was of the type classified as Old French: check curtains and table-cloths, very few tables, excellent and hugely expensive food. During her earlier visit with Zoltán, Erzsi had often eaten in such places, or better. Now, coming to it from the depths of her penny-pinching, she was strongly affected as she caught the first whiff of the familiar atmosphere of wealth. But this emotion lasted only a moment before the arrival of the greater sensation, János Szepetneki. Not recognising Erzsi, he kissed her hand with elaborate courtesy and formality, complimented Sári on her excellent choice of friends, and led the ladies to the table where his friend was waiting for them.

"Monsieur Suratgar Lutphali," he announced. From behind an aquiline nose two fiercely intense eyes met Erzsi's, causing her to shudder. Sári too was shocked by the penetrating stare. Their first feeling was that they had sat down at table with a somewhat imperfectly tamed tiger.

Erzsi did not know whom to fear the more: Szepetneki the pickpocket, with his rather too good Parisian accent and the studied nonchalance with which he selected their perfectly judged menu, as only a dangerous swindler

could (she remembered Zoltán's timidity before the waiters of these elite Parisian restaurants and how stupid this
fear made him in their eyes), or on the other hand the
Persian, who sat there in silence, a benign European
smile on his face, as quick and inappropriate as a pre-
knotted tie. But the *hors d'oeuvre* and first glass of wine loos-
ened his tongue, and from then on he directed the
conversation, in a strange staccato French sounding from
deep within his chest.

He knew how to captivate an audience with his speech.
A kind of romantic eagerness flowed out from him, something medieval, a more instinctive and authentic humanity, pre-industrial. This man lived not by *francs* and *forints*,
but by the values of the rose, the mountain crag and the
eagle. And yet the feeling remained that they were sitting
at table with an imperfectly tamed tiger—the impression
created by those burning eyes.

It emerged that back home in Persia he owned
rose-gardens and mines and, most important, poppy-
plantations, and his main business was the manufacture
of opium. He had a very low opinion of the League of
Nations, which had banned international traffic in opium
and was causing him severe financial difficulties. He was
obliged to maintain a gang of bandits up on the Turke-
stan border to smuggle his opium through to China.

"But that, sir, makes you a public enemy," declared
Sári. "You're peddling white poison. You're destroying
the lives of hundreds of thousands of destitute Chinese.
And then you're surprised that all thinking people are
united against you."

"*Ma chère*," said the Persian with unexpected anger, "you shouldn't talk of things you know nothing about. You've been taken in by the stupid humanitarian platitudes of the European newspapers. How could this opium harm the 'destitute' Chinese? Do you think those people have money for opium? They're glad of a bellyful of rice. In China only the very rich smoke opium, because it is expensive and the prerogative of the wealthy, like all the other good things of this world. It's as if I were to start worrying about the excessive amounts of champagne consumed by the working classes of Paris. And if they don't stop the Parisian rich drinking champagne when they want to, by what right do they meddle with the Chinese?"

"The comparison doesn't hold. Opium is much more harmful than champagne."

"That's such a European idea. It's true that when a European takes up opium smoking he doesn't know when to stop. Because Europeans take everything to excess—gluttony, house-building, violence, all equally. But we know how to preserve the golden mean. Do you think opium has done me any harm? I smoke it regularly, and I eat it."

He puffed out his powerful chest, then displayed his biceps, somewhat in the circus manner, and was about to raise a leg when Sári intervened: "Slow down. You'd better leave something for next time."

"Excuse me.... Alcohol is another thing Europeans take to excess. What a horrible feeling it is when you've too much wine in your stomach and know that sooner or later you're going to be sick. The effect of the wine gets steadily stronger until you suddenly collapse. It doesn't produce the steady, controlled ecstasy that opium does. There is no greater pleasure on earth.... Really, what do people in Europe know about it? You should consider the circumstances before you meddle in the affairs of other countries."

"This is why we want to make this educational propaganda film with you," said Szepetneki, turning to Sári.

"What? A propaganda film about opium smoking?" said Erzsi. Up to this point she had found the Persian's point of view somewhat attractive. Now she was horrified.

"Not to promote opium smoking, but the free movement of the product and human rights in general. The film is dedicated as a great individualist statement against every form of oppression."

"What's the story-line?" asked Erzsi.

"The opening shots," replied Szepetneki, "take you into a family living peacefully on a simple, kind-hearted, traditional opium farm in Persia. For reasons of social rank they can only marry their daughter (the heroine) to the young man she loves if they can find a buyer for the year's harvest. Whereupon the bad guy, who is also in love with the girl, but is a wicked communist prepared to do anything, betrays the father to the authorities and, in a night ambush, seizes the entire stock. This bit will be very exciting, with car chases and sirens blowing. But later the girl's innocence and nobility of soul so impresses the hard-nosed general that he returns the seized opium, which sets off merrily for China, in tinkling wagons. That would be the outline of the story...."

Erzsi had no idea whether Szepetneki was joking or not. The Persian listened solemnly, with an air of naïve pride. Doubtless the story was his idea.

After the meal they went to a fashionable dancing-place. Here they were joined by some other acquaintances. They sat round a large table and made conversation, in so far as the general din allowed. Erzsi kept her distance from the Persian. János Szepetneki asked her to join him, and they began to dance.

"How do you like him?" he asked as they stepped out. "A very interesting character, don't you agree? A complete romantic."

"Do you know, every time I look at him I think of the words of an old English nonsense poem," said Erzsi, visited suddenly by a flash of her former intellectuality: *"Tiger, Tiger, burning bright /In the forests of the night. . . ."*

Szepetneki looked at her amazed, and Erzsi felt embarrassed.

"A tiger perhaps," said Szepetneki, "but he's come a terribly hard road. And yet he's so naïve, so unsure and cautious in business matters. Even the film people can't take him in. But it isn't for commercial reasons that he wants to make the film. It's for the message. And the other main reason, as I see it, is so that he can make a harem out of the female extras. Now, when did you leave Italy?"

"So you recognised me?"

"Of course. Not just now, a few days ago, in the street, when you were with Sári. I've a pretty sharp eye. I actually arranged this evening so that I could talk to you. . . . Tell me, where did you leave my good friend Mihály?"

"Your good friend is probably still in Italy. We don't write."

"Sensational. You separated on your honeymoon?"

Erzsi nodded.

"Great. That's really great. That's Mihály's style. The old boy hasn't changed one little bit. All his life he's always given up. No stamina for anything. For example, he was the best centre-half, not just in the school but, I dare say, of any school in the whole country. And then one fine day...."

"How do you know that he left me and not the other way around?"

"Forgive me. I shouldn't have asked. But of course. You left him. I get it. You couldn't put up with someone like him. I can imagine how difficult it must have been living with such a cold fish ... someone who never gets angry, who...."

"Yes. He left me."

"I see. My very first thought, by the way. In Ravenna, you remember. You know, I say this in all seriousness, Mihály isn't cut out for a husband. He's ... how do I put this?... a seeker.... All his life he's been looking for something, something different. The sort of thing this Persian no doubt knows a lot more about than we do. Perhaps Mihály should be taking opium. Yes, that's absolutely right—that's what he should do. I must tell you quite frankly, I never understood that man."

And he made a gesture of hopelessness.

But Erzsi sensed that this casual dismissal was simply a pose, and that Szepetneki was dying to know exactly what had passed between her and Mihály. He stuck very closely by her side.

They sat down together. Szepetneki was letting no one near her. Sári was now receiving the attentions of a distinguished elderly Frenchman, and the Persian with the burning eyes was seated between two actress-types.

Erzsi was thinking: "It's interesting how different, and contradictory, things appear from close up." On her first visit to Paris she had been full of the superstitious prejudices acquired in her schooldays. She had thought of Paris as an evil metropolis full of perverts, and the Dôme and the Rotonde in Montparnasse, two harmless coffee-houses for painters and *émigrés*, had been for her the two gleaming fangs in the devil's gullet. And now here she sat, among people who no doubt actually were evil and perverted, and it all seemed perfectly natural.

But she had little time for these reflections because she was listening intently to Szepetneki. He clearly hoped to learn something important about Mihály from her. He chatted happily away about their years together, though of course everything was slanted to fit his point of view, and he painted rather a different picture from Mihály's. Only Tamás remained wonderful: princely, death-marked, a young man who was too good for this world. He had left it young before he had to compromise with it. According to Szepetneki, Tamás was so sensitive he couldn't sleep if someone was moving about three rooms away and a strong smell would have completely finished him off. The only problem was, he was in love with his sister. They had become lovers, and, when Éva fell pregnant,

Tamás killed himself from remorse. In fact, everyone was in love with Éva. Ervin had become a monk because of his hopeless passion for her. Mihály too was hopelessly in love with her. He followed her around like a puppy. It was comical. And how she treated him! She took all his money. And she stole his gold watch. Because of course it was Éva, not himself, who stole it, but he didn't want to say that to Mihály out of delicacy. But she was in love with neither of them. Only with him, János Szepetneki.

"And what has happened to Éva since? Have you seen her?"

"Me? Of course! We still get on very well. She's made a splendid career; not entirely without my help. She's a very great lady."

"How do you mean?"

"Well now, she always has the most aristocratic patrons possible—cheese barons, petroleum kings, actual heirs to thrones, not to mention the great writers and painters she takes on for the publicity."

"And what of her at present?"

"Right now she's in Italy. If she can, she always goes to Italy. It's her passion. And she collects antiques, as her father did."

"Why didn't you tell Mihály that she was in Italy? And while we're on the subject, how did you get to Ravenna that time?"

"Me? I was passing through Budapest and I heard there that Mihály was married and on his honeymoon in Venice. I couldn't resist taking the opportunity to see the old boy and his wife, so I made a detour through Venice

175

on my way back to Paris. I went to Ravenna when I heard that you had gone there."

"And why didn't you mention Éva?"

"I had it in mind. So that he could go looking for her?"

"He wouldn't have gone looking for her—he was with his wife, on honeymoon."

"Forgive me, but I don't believe that would have restrained him."

"Come on. For twenty years he hadn't thought of looking for her."

"Because he never knew where she was. And besides Mihály is so passive. But if he actually knew...."

"And what harm would it do you if Mihály did meet Éva Ulpius? Are you jealous? Are you still in love with her?"

"Me? Not at all. I never was. She was in love with me. But I didn't want to cause any trouble in Mihály's marriage."

"Are you such an angelic little boy, or what?"

"No. Just that I instantly found you so attractive."

"Wonderful. In Ravenna you said exactly the opposite. I was pretty offended."

"Yes, I only said that to see if Mihály would slap my face. But Mihály doesn't slap anyone's face. That's what's wrong with him. He always turns the other cheek. But to get back to the point: from the first moment you had an enormous effect on me."

"Amazing. So now I should feel myself honoured? Tell me, can't you seduce me with a little more wit?"

"I don't know how to seduce wittily. That's for weaklings.

If a woman attracts me, all I think is that I want her to know it. Then she responds or she doesn't. But women usually respond."

"I'm not 'women'."

But she was fully aware that she really did attract János Szepetneki: that he desired her body, in a hungry, adolescent way, devoid of adult restraint, single-mindedly, obscenely. And this so delighted her that through her whole being the blood moved faster under the skin, as if she had been drinking. She wasn't used to this raw instinctuality. Men generally approached her with love and fine words. Their addresses were always to the well-born, well-educated daughter of a good family. And then Szepetneki had come along, that time in Ravenna, and deeply offended her female vanity. Perhaps that had been the start of the collapse of her marriage, and she had ever since carried inside her the sting of Szepetneki's words. Now here was her remedy, her satisfaction. She behaved so coquettishly towards him that she actually ceased to believe what she really knew: that she was at last taking revenge for the insult at Ravenna, a revenge all the colder for the delay.

But above all she responded to Szepetneki's advances because she felt with her woman's instinct that he was treating her essentially as Mihály's wife. She knew what a strange relationship Szepetneki had with Mihály, how he always, by whatever means, wanted to prove that he was the better of the two; and this was why he now wished to seduce Mihály's wife. Erzsi bathed in Szepetneki's desire with a sickly, widow-like need for consolation, and she felt that now, with this desire, this awakening, she was becoming Mihály's authentic wife, she was entering the magic circle, the old Ulpius circle, Mihály's true reality.

"Let's talk about something else," she said, but under their table their knees caressed sensuously. "What are you actually doing in Paris?"

"I make links between large companies. Only very large companies," he said, and began to stroke her thigh. "My finest connections are with the Third Empire. You might say that in some respects I am their local commercial representative. And besides I'm trying to bring together this Lutphali business and the Martini-Alvaert film studio, because I need pocket money. But tell me, why are we talking so much? Come and dance."

They went on till three in the morning. Then the Persian piled the two film studio girls he had been entertaining into a car, invited the others for Sunday afternoon at his villa in Auteuil, and took his leave. The others made their way home. Sári was escorted by the French gentleman, Erzsi by Szepetneki.

"I'm coming up with you," Szepetneki announced when they reached the door.

"How charming. Especially as I share with Sári."

"Damnation. Then come to my place."

"It's clear, Szepetneki, you've been a long time away from Budapest. Otherwise there's no other way to explain how you could so little understand the sort of woman I am. You've ruined everything."

And without a word of parting, she went off in great triumph.

"Hey, what was all that flirting with this Szepetneki?" asked Sári when they had settled into their beds. "Just be careful, that's all."

"It's already over. Can you imagine: he wanted to come up with me."

"Did he now? You're behaving as if you had never left Pest. 'My child, never forget that Budapest is the most moral city in Europe.' That's not how they take these things here."

"But Sári, the first evening.... So all it needs for a woman's dignity is...."

"Of course. But then you should never even talk to men.... Here that's the only way a woman can 'defend her dignity'. Just as I do. But tell me, why should a woman defend her dignity? Just tell me why. Do you think I wouldn't have happily gone with that Persian if he had asked me? But did he ask me? It was in his mind. What a wonderful man! Otherwise, you did well not to get involved with this Szepetneki. He's very good-looking, I won't deny, and very much the man, but I have the feeling ... look, what I'm trying to say, but you know this already, he's a crook. He'll end up taking your money. 'Take very great care, my child.' He once stole five hundred *francs* from me on a similar occasion. So, night night."

"A crook," Erzsi thought to herself, as she lay without sleeping. "That's just what he is." All her life she had been the model of a good girl, adored by her nannies and *fräuleins*, her father's pride and joy, the best pupil in the form, sent abroad to academic competitions. Her whole life had been sheltered and ordered, the good bourgeois life consecrated to a sternly supervised moral order. In due course she married a wealthy man, dressed elegantly, took on a grand house and presided over it as a model housewife. She always wore the identical hat sported by every other woman of the same rank in society. She took her summer holidays where fashion dictated, held the same opinions about theatrical productions, uttered the turns of phrase currently *de rigueur*. In everything she was a conformist, as Mihály would say. Then she began to get bored. The boredom developed into a full neurosis, and then she chose Mihály for herself, because she felt that he was not entirely conformist, that in him there was something utterly alien to the conventions of bourgeois existence. She believed that through him she too could get beyond the walls, into the badlands, the wide flood-plain and what lay there in the unknown distances. But Mihály was simply trying, through her, to become a conformist himself, using her as a means to become a regular bourgeois, only stealing out into the badlands, into the bushes, furtively and alone, until conformity no longer bored him and he was used to it. Now if János Szepetneki, who had no wish to conform, who lived more or less as a professional bandit beyond the walls, who was so much more untamed and vigorous than Mihály ... if he ... "*Tiger, Tiger, burning bright / In the forests of the night....*"

The Sunday afternoon at Auteuil was elegant and dull. The actress-types were not there this time, and the company entirely *mondain* and well-heeled, typical of the French *grande bourgeoisie*. But this world did not interest

180

Erzsi, being even more conformist and devoid of tigers than its Budapest equivalent. She began to breathe freely only when, on the way home, they called to take János Szepetneki out to dinner, and then went on to dance. János was demonic. He drank, showed off, recited poetry, wept and was at times extremely manly. But all this was really quite superfluous. He was thoroughly overdoing his part because, not to put too fine a point on it, Erzsi was without doubt already disposed to spend the night with him, following the inner logic of events, and in quest of the burning tiger.

# PART THREE

# ROME

# XIII

MIHÁLY had now been in Rome for several days, and still nothing had happened to him. No romantic leaflet had fallen out of the sky to direct him, as he had secretly expected after what Ervin had said. All that had happened was Rome itself, so to speak.

Compared with Rome, every other Italian city was simply dwarfed. Venice, where he had been with Erzsi, officially, and Siena, where he went unofficially with Millicent, paled in comparison. For here he was, in Rome alone, and, as he felt, on higher instructions. Everything he saw in Rome seemed to symbolise fatality. The feeling that, in the course of a morning stroll, or late one special summer afternoon, everything would suddenly be filled with a rare and inexpressible significance, was one that he had known before. Now it never left him. He had known streets and houses to stir in him far-reaching pre-sentiments but never with the force of these Roman streets, palaces, ruins, gardens. Wandering among the vast walls of the Teatro Marcello, gazing into the Forum with wonder at the way little baroque churches had sprung up between the ancient columns, looking down from some hill at the star-shape of the Regina Coeli prison, loitering in the alleyways of the ghetto, passing through the different courtyards from Santa Maria sopra Minerva to the Pantheon, with its great millwheel of a roof open to the dark blue summer sky: these filled his days. And in the evening weary, weary to death, he would fall into bed in the ugly little stone-floored hotel room near the station, where he had scuttled in terror on the first evening, and then lacked the energy to change it for something more suitable.

From this general trance he was awakened by a letter from Tivadar, which Ellesley had forwarded from Foligno.

*Dear Misi,*

*We were all very concerned to read that you've been ill. With your usual vagueness you forgot to mention what precisely is wrong with you, and you can imagine how anxious we are to know. Please remedy this in due course. Are you now fully recovered? Your mother is extremely worried. Don't take it amiss that I've not sent you any money before this, but you well know the difficulties with foreign exchange. I hope the delay hasn't caused you any problems. Now, you wrote, send a lot of money. This was a bit vague—'a lot of money' is always relative. You may find what I have sent rather little, since it's not much more than the amount you say you owe. But for us it is a lot of money, considering the state the business is in just now, about which the less said the better, and the major investments we made recently, which will take years to amortise. But at least it will be enough for you to pay off your hotel bills and come home. Luckily you had a return ticket. Because it hardly needs saying, you really have no alternative. You can understand that in the current circumstances the firm really won't stand the strain of continuing to finance one of its partners residing expensively abroad, quite without rhyme or reason.*

*Even less so, since, as you would expect, as a result of the situation she finds herself in, your wife has herself approached us with*

186

*certain demands, quite properly in our view, and these demands we naturally must satisfy as a highest priority. Your wife is at present in Paris, and for the time being has stipulated that we should meet her living expenses there. The final settlement can only be drawn up when she comes home. I really can't overstate what an exceptionally difficult position that final settlement could put us in. As you well know, all the ready money she brought into the firm was invested in machinery, the prestige building, and other current developments, so that liquidating all these sums will not only cause us difficulties, but will practically shake the firm to its foundations. I really do think anybody else would have taken all this into account before abandoning his wife on their honeymoon. I need hardly add that, quite apart from all the financial considerations, your conduct was in itself absolutely and utterly ungentlemanly, particularly towards such a correct and blameless lady as your wife.*

*Well, that's the situation. Your father was not entirely persuaded that I should write to you at all. You can imagine how nervous and distressed these events have made him, and how alarming he finds the prospect that sooner or later we shall have to pay everything back to your wife. He's taken it all so much to heart that we want to send him on a holiday for a break (we're thinking mainly of Gastein), but he won't hear of it because of the extra expense of travelling during the summer holiday season.*

*So, dear Misi, on receipt of this letter be so good as to pack up and come straight home, the sooner the better.*

*Love from everyone,*

*Tivadar*

Tivadar had certainly enjoyed writing that letter, revelling in the fact that he, the feckless playboy of the family, was now in a position to preach morality to the sober and serious Mihály. This in itself, and the superior tone of voice from a totally unsympathetic younger brother, made him very angry. Now, returning home could be seen as nothing more than an imposition, a horrid and hateful command.

But, it seemed, there really was no alternative. If he paid back the loan from Millicent there would be nothing left for him to live on in Rome. What also disturbed him deeply was what Tivadar had said about his father. He knew that Tivadar was not exaggerating. His father had a tendency to depression, and the whole disaster, in which material, social and emotional problems were linked together in such a complicated way, was just the sort of thing to destroy his peace of mind. If the other elements failed to achieve this, it was enough in itself that his favourite son had behaved so impossibly. He really would have to go home, if only to make amends for this, to explain to his father that he simply could not have done other than he did, not even for Erzsi's good. He needed to show that he was not a runaway, that he took full responsibility for his action, as a gentleman should.

And once home he would have to knuckle down to work. Now everything would be work. Work was the promised reward for a young man setting out, for completing his studies, and work was the penitential act and punishment for those who met with failure. If he went home and worked steadily, sooner or later his father would forgive him.

But when he thought in detail about this "work"—his desk, the people he had to deal with, and above all the things that filled his time after work, the bridge parties, the Danube outings, the well-to-do ladies, he felt exasperated to the point of tears.

"What did the shade of Achilles say?" he pondered. "'I would rather be a cotter in my father's house than a prince among the dead.' For me it's the reverse. I'd rather be a cotter here, among the dead, than a prince at home, in my father's house. Only, I'd need to know what exactly a cotter is. . . ."

Here, among the dead . . . for at that moment he was walking in the little Protestant cemetery behind the pyramid of Cestius, beside the city wall. Here lay his fellows, dead men from the North, drawn here by nameless nostalgias, and here overtaken by death. This fine cemetery, with its shady wall, had always lured souls from the North with the illusion that here oblivion would be sweeter. At the end of one of Goethe's Roman elegies there stands, as a memento: *Cestius' Denkmal vorbei, leise zum Orcus herab.* "From the tomb of Cestius, the way leads gently down to Hell." Shelley, in a wonderful letter, wrote that he would like to lie here in death, and so he does, or at least his heart is there, beneath the inscription: *Cor cordium.*

Mihály was on the point of leaving when he noticed a small cluster of tombs standing apart in one corner of the cemetery. He went over and perused the inscriptions on the plain Empire-stones. One of them read simply, in English: "Here lies one whose name is writ in water". On the second a longer text declared that there lay Severn, the painter, the best friend and faithful nurse on his death-bed of John Keats, the great English poet, who had insisted that his name should not be inscribed on the neighbouring stone, under which he lay.

Mihály's eyes filled with tears. So here lay Keats, the greatest poet since the world began ... though such emotion was somewhat irrational, given that the body had been lying there for a very long time, and the spirit was preserved by his verses more faithfully than by any grave-pit. But so wonderful, so truly English, was the manner of this gentle compromise, this innocent sophistry, that perfectly respected his last wishes but nonetheless announced without ambiguity that it was indeed Keats who lay beneath the stone.

When he raised his eyes some rather unusual people were standing beside him. They were an enchantingly beautiful and undoubtedly English woman, a second woman dressed as a nurse, and two lovely English children, a little boy and girl. They simply stood motionless, looking rather awkwardly at the grave, at each other, and at Mihály. He stood and waited for them to say something, but they did not speak. After a while an elegant gentleman arrived, with the same expressionless face as the others. He bore a strong resemblance to his wife: they might have been twins, or at least brother and sister. He stood before the grave, and the wife pointed out the inscription. The Englishman nodded, and with great solemnity and some embarrassment gazed in turn at the grave, at his family, and at Mihály. And he too said nothing. Mihály moved a step further away, thinking that perhaps they were discomposed by his presence, but they simply remained standing, nodding from time to time, and looking self-consciously at one another. The two children's faces were every bit as embarrassed and blankly beautiful as the adults'.

As he was turning away, Mihály suddenly stared at them with undisguised astonishment. He felt that they were not human but ghostly dolls, mindless automata standing here over the poet's grave: inexplicable beings. Had they not been so very beautiful perhaps they would have been less astonishing, but they had the inhuman beauty of people in advertisements, and he was filled with an unspeakable horror.

Then the English family moved away, slowly and still nodding, and Mihály recovered himself. In sober consciousness he reviewed the past few minutes, and became truly anxious.

"What's wrong with me? What sort of mental state have I fallen into again? It was like a dark, shameful reminder of my adolescence. These people were quite clearly nothing other than self-conscious, thoroughly stupid English, confronted by the fact that this was Keats's grave and not knowing where to begin, perhaps because they had no idea who Keats was. Or perhaps they knew, but couldn't think how to behave appropriately at the grave of Keats the famous Englishman, and because of this they were embarrassed in front of each other and of me. A more insignificant or banal scene you really couldn't imagine, and yet I immediately thought of the most unspeakable horror in the world. Yes. Horror isn't at its most intense in things of night and fear. It's when you are staring in full sunlight at some mundane thing, a shop window, an unknown face, between the branches of a tree. . . ."

He thrust his hands in his pockets and quickly made his way back.

He decided that he would travel home the next day. It was too late to leave that day, because Tivadar's letter had not arrived much before noon. He would have to wait until morning to change the cheque he had been sent, and to despatch the money he owed to Millicent. He was spending his last night in Rome. He wandered around the streets with an even greater sense of surrender than before, and found everything even more charged with significance.

He was bidding farewell to Rome. It was not particular buildings that had found their way into his heart. The overwhelming experience was of the life of the city itself. He wandered aimless and uncertain, with the feeling that tucked away in the city were still thousands upon thousands of districts he would now never see. And again he had the feeling that the really important things were happening elsewhere, where he was not; that he had missed the secret signal. His road led absolutely nowhere and his nostalgia now would gnaw him eternally, remain eternally unquenched, until he too departed, *Cestius' Denkmal vorbei, leise zum Orcus herab.* . . .

The light was fading and Mihály walked with lowered head, hardly noticing even the streets, until, in a dark alley-way, he bumped into someone, who muttered, "sorry".

Hearing the English word, he looked up and saw before him the young Englishman who had so struck him at Keats's grave. There must have been something in Mihály's face as he looked at the Englishman, for he raised his hat, murmured something, and hurried off. Mihály turned and stared after him.

But only for a moment. Then, with determined footsteps, he hurried after him, without thinking why he did. As a boy, under the influence of detective novels, one of his favourite pastimes had been to fall in suddenly behind some unknown person and to track him, taking great care not to be noticed, sometimes for long hours. He would not follow just anyone. The chosen person had to have been revealed to him by some means, some cabalistic sign, as had this young Englishman. It could not have been by empty chance that in all this vast city he had met him twice on the same day, and that day such a significant one, and that in both of them the meeting had produced such unprovoked astonishment. Some secret lay hidden in this, and he would have to follow it to its end.

With the excitement of a detective he tracked the Englishman through the narrow streets to the Corso Umberto. He had not lost his boyhood skill. He could still follow unobserved, like a shadow. His quarry walked up and down the Corso for a while, then took a chair on a café terrace. Mihály also sat down, drank a vermouth, and watched him in a fever of anticipation. He knew that something must happen. He had the impression that the Englishman was no longer as calm and expressionless as he had been at the graveside. Under the regular lines of his face and the alarming clarity of his skin some strange life seemed to be throbbing. Of course the restlessness showed on his impeccable English surface no more than the wing of a bird brushing the surface of a lake. But restless he certainly was. Mihály knew that the man was waiting for someone, and he too was infected with the apprehension of waiting, which was amplified in him like a voice through a megaphone.

The Englishman began to glance repeatedly at his watch, and Mihály could hardly bear to remain in his seat. He fidgeted, ordered yet another vermouth, then a maraschino. This was no time for economising. Anyway, he was going home the next day.

At last an elegant limousine drew up outside the café, the door opened and a woman glanced out. Instantly the Englishman sprang up and disappeared into the car, which moved off smoothly and silently.

It took but an instant. The woman had appeared in the open car door for no more than a moment, but Mihály had recognised her, as much by intuition as by sight. It was Éva Ulpius. He too had leapt to his feet, had seen her glance fall on him for just a moment, and caught the very faint smile that appeared on her face. But it was over in a flash, and Éva had disappeared inside the car and vanished into the night.

He paid for his drinks and staggered out of the café. The omens had not lied. It was for this that he had been summoned to Rome: because Éva was here. Now he understood that she was the source and object of his nostalgia. Éva, Éva. . . .

And he knew he would not be travelling home. If he had to wear a donkey jacket and wait for fifty years, then he would wait. At last there was a place in the world where he had reason to be, a place that had meaning. For days, without realising it, he had sensed this meaning everywhere, in the streets, houses, ruins and temples of Rome. It could not be said of the feeling that it was "filled with pleasurable expectation". Rome and its millennia were not by nature associated with happiness, and what Mihály anticipated from the future was not what is usually conjured up by "pleasurable expectation". He was awaiting his fate, the logical, appropriately Roman, ending.

He wrote at once to Tivadar to say that his state of health would not permit an extended journey. He did not send the money to Millicent. Millicent was so rich she could manage without it. If she had waited all this time she could wait a bit longer. The delay was Tivadar's fault for not sending more money.

That evening, in his elation, his nervous excitement after the feverish waiting, he got drunk on his own, and when he woke later in the night with a violently palpitating heart he again knew the terrible feeling of mortality which in his younger days had been the strongest symptom of his passion for Éva. He well knew, now even more clearly than he had the day before, that for a thousand and one reasons he really had to go home; and that if despite that knowledge he remained in Rome because of Éva—and how uncertain it was that he actually had seen her—he was putting everything at risk, perhaps doing irreparable offence against his family and his own status as a bourgeois, and that very uncertain days lay ahead. But not for one minute did it occur to him that there was anything else he could do. All this, the great gamble and the death-haunted feeling, was so much part of those adolescent games. Not tomorrow, and not the day after, but one day he and Éva would meet, and, until then he would live. His life would begin anew, not as it had been during all the wasted years. *Incipit vita nova.*

# XIV

Every day he read the newspapers, but with rather mixed feelings. He enjoyed the paradox that they were written in Italian, that potent and voluminous language, but (in their case) with the effect of a mighty river driving a sewing-machine. But the contents deeply depressed him. The Italian papers were always ecstatically happy, as if they were written not by humans but by saints in triumph, just stepped down from a Fra Angelico in order to celebrate the perfect social system. There was always some cause for happiness: some institution was eleven years old, a road had just turned twelve. So someone would make a monumental speech, and the people would enthusiastically applaud, at least according to accounts in the press.

Like all foreigners, Mihály was exercised by the question of whether the people did actually welcome everything as fervently, and were as steadily, indefatigably, tirelessly happy, as the papers insisted. Naturally he was aware that it was difficult for a foreigner to take an exact measure of Italian contentment and sincerity, especially when he never spoke to anyone, and had no real connection with any aspect of Italian life. But as far as he could judge, from such a distance, and given his general detachment, it seemed to him that the Italian people were indeed indefatigably enthusiastic and happy, ever since these had come into fashion. But he also knew what trifling and stupid things could suffice to make man happy, whether individually or in the mass.

However he did not occupy himself at great length with this question. His instincts told him that in Italy it was all very much the same whoever happened to be in power and whatever the ideas in whose name they ruled. Politics touched only the surface. The people, the vegetative sea of the Italian masses, bore the changing times on their back with astonishing passivity, and lived quite unconnected with their own remarkable history. He suspected that even Republican and Imperial Rome, with its huge gestures, its heroics and bestial stupidities, had been nothing more than a virile drama on the surface, the whole Roman Empire the mere private affair of a few brilliant actors, while down below the Italians placidly ate their pasta, sang songs of love, and begat their countless offspring.

One day a familiar name met his eye in the *Popolo d'Italia*: "The Waldheim Lecture". He studied the article, from which it emerged that Rodolfo Waldheim, the world-famous Hungarian classical philologist and religious historian, had given a lecture at the Accademia Reale, entitled *Aspetti della morte nelle religioni antiche*. The fiery Italian journalist fêted the lecture as shedding entirely new light not just on death-practices in ancient religions but on the nature of death in general. The text was moreover an important document of Hungaro-Italian friendship. The audience had enthusiastically received the famous professor, whose very youthfulness had surprised and delighted them.

This Waldheim, Mihály decided, could be no other than Rudi Waldheim, and he was filled with a kind of pleasure, for this man had at one time been a good friend. They had been at university together. Although neither was very congenial by nature—Mihály because he rather looked down upon anyone who was not of the Ulpius set, Waldheim because he felt that compared with himself everyone else was ignorant, dull and cheap—nonetheless a kind of friendship had grown between them out of their interest in religious history. The relationship had not been a very lasting one. Waldheim's knowledge was already formidable: he had read everything that mattered, in every language, and he willingly and brilliantly expounded to Mihály, whom he found an eager listener, until he realised that his interest in the subject was not very deep. He decided his friend was a dilettante and withdrew into suspicion. Mihály for his part was dismayed and astonished by the vastness of his friend's knowledge. If a mere beginner knew so much, he wondered, how much more would a bearded practitioner know, and he entirely lost heart, particularly as not long afterwards he abandoned his university studies. Waldheim however went on to Germany to perfect himself at the feet of the great masters and the two lost touch completely. Years later Mihály would read in the newspapers of another step in Waldheim's rapid rise up the academic ladder, and when he became a lecturer at the university Mihály had been on the point of writing to congratulate him, but then hadn't. They had never again met in person.

Now, reading his name, he remembered Waldheim's peculiar charm, which he had quite forgotten in the intervening years: the fox-terrier liveliness of his bright, round, shaven head; his miraculous loquacity (for Waldheim held forth unstoppably, at full volume, in long perfectly constructed sentences almost always full of interest, even in his sleep it was generally supposed); his indomitable vitality; his perpetual appetite for women (which keeps this type of man always busily active around his more attractive female colleagues); above all his distinctive quality, which, following Goethe, though with modest reluctance, he himself termed "charisma"; and the fact that the study of the concept of Spirit, in all its detailed workings as well as the abstract whole, held him in a white heat of passion. He was never indifferent, always feverishly busy with something, in raptures over some great and possibly ancient manifestation of the Spirit, or detesting some "dull" or "cheap" or "second-rate" piece of stupidity, and invariably sent into a trance by the very word "Spirit", which for him actually seemed to mean something.

Thoughts of Waldheim's vitality had an unexpectedly invigorating effect on Mihály. Ambushed by a sudden urge to see him again, even if briefly, he suddenly realised how utterly lonely his life had been in recent weeks. Loneliness was an inescapable part of awaiting one's fate, which was his sole occupation in Rome and impossible to share with anyone. It was now brought home to him for the first time how deep he had sunk into this passive, dreamy waiting, this immersion in the sense of mortality. It was like a tangle of seaweed sucking him down towards the wonders of the deep: then suddenly his head had burst out of the water, and he breathed again.

He must meet Waldheim. One possible way of effecting this now seemed to offer itself. In the article reporting the lecture, mention was made of a reception to be given in the Palazzo Falconieri, the headquarters of the *Collegium Hungaricum*. He remembered that there was a branch of that organisation in Rome, a hostel for young aspiring artists and scholars. Here they would at least be able to give him Waldheim's address, if he were not actually living there.

The address of the Palazzo Falconieri was not hard to find. It stood in the Via Giulia, not far from the Teatro Marcello, in the district where Mihály most loved to loiter. Now he cut through the alleyways of the ghetto and soon arrived at the fine old Palazzo.

The porter received Mihály's inquiry sympathetically, and told him that the professor was indeed in the College, but it was his sleeping time. Mihály looked in amazement at his watch. It was ten thirty.

"Yes," said the porter. "The professor always sleeps until twelve, and must not be roused. Not that it's easy to wake him. He sleeps very deeply."

"Then perhaps I can call back after lunch?"

"Sorry, after lunch the professor goes back to sleep, and cannot be disturbed then either."

"And when is he awake?"

"The whole night," said the porter, with a hint of awe in his voice.

"Then it would be better if I left my card and address, and the professor can let me know if he would like to see me."

When he arrived home late that afternoon a telegram

was waiting for him. Waldheim had invited him to dinner. Mihály immediately boarded a tram and set off for the Palazzo Falconieri. He loved the "C" line, that wonderful route which would take him there from the main railway station skirting half the city, passing through various areas of woodland, stopping at the Coliseum, brushing past the Palatine ruins and racing alongside the Tiber, the cavalcade of the millennia passing in procession on either side of the rails, and the whole journey taking just a quarter of an hour.

"Come," shouted Waldheim in answer to Mihály's knocking. But when he tried the door it appeared to be stuck.

"Hang on, I'm coming...." came the shout from within. After some time the door opened.

"It's a bit choked up," said Waldheim, gesturing towards the books and papers piled on the floor. "Don't worry, just come in."

Negotiating entry was not a simple matter, for the entire floor was strewn with objects of every description: not just books and papers, but Waldheim's underwear, some extremely loud summer gear, a surprising quantity of shoes, swimming and other sportswear, newspapers, tins of food, chocolate boxes, letters, art reproductions, and pictures of women.

Mihály looked around him in embarrassment.

"You see, I don't like having the cleaners in while I'm here," his host explained. "They leave everything in such a mess I can never find anything. Please, take a seat. Hang on, just a second...."

He swept a few books from the top of a tall pile, now revealed as a chair, and Mihály sat down nervously. Chaos always disconcerted him, and in addition this particular chaos somehow exuded an aura that demanded respect for the sanctity of learning.

Waldheim also sat down, and immediately began to hold forth. He was explaining the state of disorder. His untidiness was essentially abstract, a manifestation of the spirit, but heredity also played a part in it.

"My father (I must have told you about him) was a painter. Perhaps you've heard of him? He would never allow anyone to lay a finger on the things piled up in his studio. After a while he was the only one who could go in. He was the only person who knew where there were these islands you could safely step on without falling into something. But then even the islands became buried under the flood of litter. So my father would close up that studio, take another, and begin a new life. When he died we discovered that he had five, every one filled to overflowing.

Then he described what had happened to himself since he had last seen Mihály, his academic career and his world fame as a philologist, about which he boasted with the naïve charm of a little boy. He "just happened to have with him" newspaper clippings, in a variety of languages, which deferentially reported his various lectures, among them the one Mihály had seen in the *Popolo d'Italia*. Then he turned up some letters from a string of eminent foreign scholars and writers, all very friendly, and an invitation card to Doorn, to the annual summer convention of the Former Emperor's Society of Post-Imperial German

203

Archaeologists. From somewhere or other he produced a silver goblet inscribed with the ex-Emperor's monogram.

"See this. He presented it to me after the whole society had drunk to my honour in good Hungarian Tokay."

Next he proudly displayed his photographs, flicking through a great pile at high speed. In some he appeared with highly academic-looking gentlemen, in others with various ladies of less scholarly aspect.

"My distinguished self in pyjamas," he expounded. "My distinguished self in the buff ... the lady is covering her face in embarrassment...."

Then, as a final inclusion, Waldheim was pictured with an extremely plain woman and a small boy.

"Who are these? This hideous woman with her brat?" Mihály asked, tactfully.

"Oh dear, that's my family," he replied, and roared with laughter. "My wife and my son."

"You have a family?" Mihály asked in amazement. "Where do you keep them?"

For Waldheim's room, his manners, his whole being were so much that of the perpetual and incurable university student, with the stamp of the "I never want to grow up" *stud. phil.* so clearly upon him, that Mihály simply couldn't imagine him with a wife and child.

"Oh, I've been married for centuries," he said. "It's a very old photo. Since then my son has got a lot bigger, and my wife even uglier. She fell for me at Heidelberg, when I was in my third year. Her name was Katzchen, (isn't that wonderful?) and she was forty-six. But we don't trouble each other very much. She lives in Germany, with my dear father-in-law and his family, and they look down their noses at me. More recently this is not just because of my morals, but because I'm not German."

"But surely you are German, at least by descent?"

"Yes, yes, but an Auslanddeutsche, from Bratislava, my God, such an outpost in the Danube basin! That doesn't count as real German. At least that's what my son says, and he's intensely ashamed of me in front of his friends. But what can I do? Nothing. But please, eat up. Oh dear, haven't I had you to dine here before? Just hang on a second ... the tea's already brewed. But you don't have to drink tea. There's also red wine."

From somewhere among the arcana of the floor he produced a large package, removed several objects and papers from the desk and placed them under it, put the package down and opened it. A mass of raw Italian ham, salami and bread spilled out into view.

"You see I eat only cold meat, nothing else," said Waldheim. "But to make it less boring for you I've arranged for a bit of variety. Just wait a moment...."

After a long search he produced a banana. The smile with which he presented it to Mihály seemed to say, "Did you ever see such thoughtful housekeeping?"

This student-like casualness and incompetence Mihály found enchanting.

"Here's a man who's achieved the impossible," he thought with a touch of envy, as Waldheim stuffed the raw ham into his mouth and continued to hold forth. "There's a man who's managed to stay fixed at the age that suits him. Everyone has one age that's just right for him, that's certain. There are people who remain children all their lives, and there are others who never cease to be awkward and absurd, who never find their place until suddenly they become splendidly wise old men and women: they have come to their real age. The amazing thing about Waldheim is that he's managed to remain a university student at heart without having to give up the world, or success, or the life of the mind. He's gone down a path where his emotional immaturity doesn't seem to be noticed, or is even an advantage, and he pays only as much heed to reality as is consistent with the limitations of his own being. That's wonderful. Now if only I could manage something like that...."

The meal was barely over when Waldheim looked at his watch and muttered excitedly:

"Holy heavens, I've got some really urgent business with a woman, just nearby. Please, if you've nothing better to do, it would be very kind if you would come along and wait for me. It really won't take long. Then we can find a little hostelry and continue our really interesting dialogue...." ("He obviously hasn't noticed that I've not said a single word yet," thought Mihály.)

"I'd be delighted to go with you," he said.

"I'm extremely fond of women," Waldheim announced as they walked along. "Perhaps excessively. You know, when I was young I didn't get my share of women as I wanted to, and as I should have, partly because when you're young you're so stupid, and partly because my strict upbringing forbade it. I was brought up by my mother, who was the daughter of a *pfarrer*, a real Imperial

German parish priest. As a child I was once with them and for some reason I asked the old man who Mozart was. '*Der war ein Scheunepurzler,*' he said, which means, more or less, someone who does somersaults in a barn to amuse the yokels. For the old man all artists fell into that category. So nowadays I feel that I can never do enough to make up for what I missed in the way of women when I was twenty-five. But here we are. Hang on a moment, won't you. I shan't be long."

He disappeared through a dark doorway. Mihály walked up and down, thoughtfully but in good spirits. After a while he heard an odd, amused coughing. He looked up. Waldheim had thrust his bright round head out of a window.

"Ahem. I'm on my way."

"A very nice lady," he said as he emerged. "Breasts hang down a bit, but it's not a problem. You have to get used to that here. I met her in the Forum and made a conquest of her by telling her that the Black Stone was probably a phallic symbol. You really can't imagine how useful religious history can be for getting around women. They eat it out of my hand. Mind you, I fear you could probably do the same with differential calculus or double-entry bookkeeping, so long as you talk about it with the proper intensity. They never listen to what you actually say. Or if they do listen, they never understand. All the same they can sometimes have you on. Sometimes they really are almost human. Never mind. I love them. And they love me, that's the main thing. So, let's go in here."

Mihály made an involuntary grimace when he saw the place Waldheim proposed entering.

"I'm not saying it's pretty, but it's very cheap. But I see, you're still the fussy little boy you were as a student. Never mind. For once we'll go somewhere better, for your sake."

Again came the smile that spoke consciousness of great generosity, as he added that, also as a favour to Mihály, he would be quite happy to pay for his own drinks in the more expensive place.

They went into an establishment that was possibly a shade or two better. Waldheim again held forth for a while, then seemed to become rather tired. For a few moments he seemed lost in thought, then turned with alarming suddenness towards Mihály:

"But what have you been doing all these years?"

Mihály smiled.

"I learned the trade, and worked in my father's firm."

"You worked? In the past tense? And now?"

"At the moment, nothing. I ran away from home. I loaf around here and try to think about what I should be doing with myself."

"What you should be doing? How can there be a question? Take up religious history. Believe me, it's the most topical subject today."

"But why do you think I should become a student? What have I to do with the academic life?"

"Because anyone who isn't actually stupid ought to study, in the interests of his soul's salvation. It's the only thing worth doing. I don't know, perhaps also art and music ... but to spend your time doing anything else, like working in a commercial company, for a man who isn't totally stupid ... I'll tell you what that is: affectation."

"Affectation? How do you mean?"

"Look. I remember you started off as a pretty decent religious historian. I'm not saying ... well, you were a bit slow on the uptake but hard work can make up for a lot of things and people with far less talent than you have gone on to become excellent scholars, in fact.... And then, I don't know the facts but I can imagine what went on in your middle-class soul. You found that the academic path doesn't guarantee a living, that you didn't want the boring routine of schoolteaching, and this and that, so really you had to go for something practical, considering all the supposed necessities of a wealthy person. This is what I call affectation. Because even you realise that these supposed necessities aren't real. The practical career is a myth, a humbug, invented to cheer themselves up by people who aren't capable of doing anything intellectual. But you've got too much sense to be taken in by them. With you it's just an affectation. And it's high time you gave up this pose, and got back where you belong, in the academic life."

"And what do I live on?"

"My God, it's not a problem. You see, even I manage."

"Yes, on your salary as a university teacher."

"True. But I could equally live without it. People shouldn't throw money about. I'll teach you how to live on tea and salami. Very healthy. You people don't know how to economise, that's the trouble."

"But Rudi, there's another problem. I'm not very sure that a life of scholarship would be as satisfying for me as it is for you ... I don't have the enthusiasm ... I can't really believe in the importance of these things...."

"What sort of things are you talking about?"

"Well, for example, the factual basis of religious history. What I'm saying ... sometimes I think ... does it really matter exactly why the wolf reared Romulus and Remus?..."

"How the hell could it not matter?' You're utterly crazy. No, it's just affectation. But that's enough talk for now. It's time to go back and work."

"Now? But it's past midnight!"

"Yes, that's when I'm able to work: no interruptions, and for some reason I don't even think about women then. I'll work now until four, and then run for an hour."

"You'll do what?"

"Run. Otherwise I can't sleep. I go to the river bank and run up and down beside the Tiber. The police know me and they leave me alone. It's just like at home. Come. On the way I'll tell you what I'm working on at present. It's really sensational. You remember that Sophron fragment that came to light a little while ago...."

By the time he had finished his exposition they were standing outside the Falconieri building.

"But going back to the question of what you should do," he said unexpectedly. "The only difficulty is starting. You know what? Tomorrow I'll get up a bit earlier for your sake. Come for me, let's say, at eleven-thirty. No, twelve. I'll take you to the Villa Giulia. I bet you haven't been to the Etruscan Museum, right? Well, if that doesn't give you the urge to take up the old threads, then you really are a lost man. Then you better had go back to your father's factory. So, God be with you."

And he hurried into the darkened building.

# XV

THE NEXT DAY they did indeed visit the Villa Giulia. They looked at the graves and the sarcophagi, with their lids supporting terracotta statues of the old Etruscan dead enjoying their lives—eating, drinking, embracing their spouses, and proclaiming the Etruscan philosophy. This, being wise enough not to have developed literature in the evolution of their cultural life, they never committed to writing, though of course it can be read unmistakably on the faces of their statues: only the present matters, and moments of beauty are eternal.

Waldheim pointed out some broad drinking bowls. These were for wine, as the inscription proclaimed: *Foied vinom pipafo, cra carefo.*

"Enjoy the wine today, tomorrow there will be none," Waldheim translated. "Tell me, could it be expressed more succinctly or truly? That statement, in its archaic splendour, is as definitive and unshakeable as any polygonic city-walls or cyclopean buildings. *Foied vinom pipafo, cra carefo.*"

Whole sets of figurines were displayed in a glass case: dreamy-eyed men, being led onwards by women, and dreamy-eyed women led, or clutched at, by satyrs.

"What are these?" Mihály asked in amazement.

"That's death," said Waldheim, and his voice took on an edge, as it always did when some serious academic issue arose. "That's death. Or rather, dying. They're not the same thing. Those women luring the men on, and those

212

satyrs clutching at the women, are death-demons. Are you with me? The male demons take the women, and the female demons the men. Those Etruscans were perfectly aware that dying is an erotic act."

A strange frisson shot through Mihály. Could it be that others had known this, and not just himself and Tamás Ulpius? Was it possible that this most basic element in his own sense of life was once something that, for the Etruscans, could be expressed in art, a self-evident spiritual truth, and that Waldheim's brilliant scholarly intuition had been able to understand that truth, just as he had so many of the mysteries and horrors of ancient belief?

The question so troubled him that he said not a word, neither in the museum nor on the tram going back afterwards. But that evening, when he again called on Waldheim, and had been lent courage by the red wine, he managed to ask, taking care not to let his voice tremble: "But tell me, how did you mean 'dying is an erotic act'?"

"I meant it just as I stated it. I'm not a symbolist poet. Dying is an erotic process, or if you like, a form of sexual pleasure. At least in the perception of ancient cultures like the Etruscans, the Homeric Greeks, the Celts."

"I don't understand," said Mihály disingenuously. "I always thought that the Greeks had a horror of death. Surely the afterlife had no consolations for the Homeric Greeks, if I remember my Rodhe correctly. And the Etruscans, who lived for the fleeting moment, would have feared it even more."

"That's all true. These peoples probably feared death even more than we do. Our civilisation presents us with a marvellous mental machinery designed to help us forget, for most of our lives, that one day we too will die. In time we manage to push death out of our consciousness, just as we have done with the existence of God. That's what civilisation does. But for these archaic peoples nothing was more immediately apparent than death and the dead, I mean actual dead people, whose mysterious para-existence, fate, and vengeful fury constantly preoccupied them. They had a tremendous horror of death and the dead. But then of course in their minds everything was more ambiguous than it is for us. Opposites sat much closer. The fear of death and the desire for death were intimately juxtaposed in their minds, and the fear was often a form of desire, the desire a form of fear."

"My God, the death-wish isn't some archaic thing, but eternally human," said Mihály, fending off his real inner-most thoughts. "There always were and always will be people worn out and weary of life, who long for the release of death."

"Don't talk rubbish, and don't pretend you don't under-stand me. I'm not talking about the death-wish of the weary and the sick, or potential suicides, but about peo-ple in the fullness of their life, people who in fact because their lives are so fulfilled yearn for death as for the great-est ecstasy, as in the common phrase, mortal passion. Either you understand this or you don't. I can't explain it. But for those ancient people it was self-evident. That's why I say that dying is an erotic act. Because they yearned after it, and in the final analysis every desire is sexual at base, or rather what we call erotic, in which the god Eros, that is to say, yearning or desire, exists. A man always yearns after woman, according to our friends the Etruscans, so death, dying, must be a woman. For a man it was a woman, but for a woman an importunate male satyr. That's what those figures tell us, the ones we saw this afternoon. But I could show you other things too: portraits of the death-hetaira on various ancient reliefs. Death is a harlot tempting young men, and she is depicted with a hideously vast vagina. And this vagina probably means something more again. We come from it and we return to it, that's what they are telling us. We are born as the result of an erotic act and through a woman, and we have to die through an erotic act involving a woman, the death-hetaira, the great inseparable and contrary aspect of the Earth Mother.... So when we die we are born again ... do you follow? Actually this is what I was saying the other day, in my lecture at the Accademia Reale entitled *Aspetti della morte*. It was a great success with the Italian newspapers. It just so happens I have a copy with me. Hang on a moment...."

Mihály looked around with a shiver at the cheerful chaos of Waldheims's room. It reminded him subtly of that other room, in the Ulpius house. He was looking for a sign, something specific to focus ... perhaps the near-presence of Tamás, Tamás whose inner thoughts Waldheim, with his brilliant scholarly objectivity and clarity, had expressed here, this summer night. Waldheim's voice was again edged with that sharp, inspired quality it always took on when he talked about the "divine essence". Mihály rapidly downed a glass of wine and went over to the window for a breath of air. Something oppressed him deeply.

"The death-yearning was one of the strongest sources of myth," Waldheim continued, talking now rather to himself than to Mihály in his excitement. "If we read the Odyssey aright, it speaks of nothing else. There are the death-hetaira, Circe, Calypso, who from their caves lured men on to the journey towards the happy islands and never let them go; the whole empire of death, the Lotus-Eaters, the land of the Phaia. And who knows, perhaps the land of the dead was Ithaca itself? Far to the west ... the dead are always sailing by day into the west ... and Ulysses's nostalgia for and his journey back to Ithaca perhaps represents the nostalgia for non-being, signifying rebirth.... Perhaps the name Penelope actually carries its latent meaning of 'duck', and originally was the spirit-bird, but for the time being I can't be sure of that. You see this is the sort of idea that really should be looked into without delay. And you.... You could do the groundwork for a section, so that you can get into the professional way of doing things. For example, it would be really interesting if you wrote something about Penelope as the spirit-duck."

Mihály politely declined this commission. For the moment it did not much interest him.

"But why was it only the ancient Greeks who were so aware of this death symbolism?" he asked.

"Because the nature of civilisation everywhere was such that, even with the Greeks, it diverted people's minds away from the reality of death, and compensated

216

for the yearning for death just when the basic appetite for life was declining. It was Christian civilisation that did this. But perhaps those peoples Christianity had to subdue brought with them an even greater death-cult than existed among the Greeks. The Greeks were not in fact a particularly death-centred race. It was just that they were able to express everything so much better than other people. The real death-cultists were the races of the north, the Germans, woodsmen of the long nights, and the Celts. Especially the Celts. The Celtic legends are full of the islands of the dead. These islands later Christian observers, in their usual fashion, transformed to islands of the blessed, or happy isles, and simple-minded folklore-collectors generally followed them in this error. But tell me, was that an island of the 'blessed' that sent its fairy envoy to Prince Bran with such overwhelming constraint? Or was it, I ask, from 'happiness' that a man was turned to dust and ashes the moment he left the island? And why do you think they laughed, those people on the island, the 'other island'? Because they were happy? Like hell they were. They were laughing because they were dead, and their grins were nothing more than the hideous leer of a corpse, like those you see on the faces of Indian masks and Peruvian mummies. Sadly it isn't my field, the Celts. But you should take them up. You would have to learn, quickly and without fail, Irish and Welsh, there's no other way. And you would have to go to Dublin."

"Fine," said Mihály. "But say a bit more, if you would. You've no idea how much this interests me. Why did it come to an end, this human yearning for the islands of the dead? Or perhaps the feeling is still with us? In a word, where does the story end?"

"I can only answer with a bit of home-made Spengler-ism. When the people of the north came into the community of Christendom, in other words European civilisation, one of the first consequences was, if you remember, that for two hundred years everything revolved around death. I'm referring to the tenth and eleventh centuries, the centuries of the monastic reforms begun at Cluny. In early Roman times Christianity lived under constant physical threat, so that it became the darkest of death-cults, rather like the religion of the Mexican Indians. Later of course it took on its truly Mediterranean and humane character. What happened? The Mediterraneans succeeded in sublimating and rationalising the yearning for death, or, in plain language, they watered down the desire for death into desire for the next world, they translated the terrifying sex-appeal of the death-sirens into the heavenly choirs and rows of angels singing praises. Nowadays you can yearn comfortably after the glorious death that awaits the believer: not the dying pagan's yearning for erotic pleasure, but the civilised and respectable longing for heaven. The raw, ancestral pagan death-desire has gone into exile, into the dark understrata of religion. Superstition, witchcraft, Satanism, are among its manifestations. The stronger civilisation becomes, the more our yearning for death thrives in the subconscious.

"Think about it. In civilised society death is the most absolute of all taboo-subjects. It isn't done to mention it. We use circumlocutions to name it in writing, as if it were some sort of ridiculous solecism, so that the dead person, the corpse, becomes the 'deceased', the 'dear departed', the 'late', in the same way as we euphemise the acts of digestion. And what you don't talk about, it isn't done to think about either. This is civilisation's defence against the potential danger of a contrary instinct working in man against the instinct for life, an instinct which is really cunning, calling man towards annihilation with a sweet and strong enticement. To the civilised mind this instinct is all the more dangerous because in civilised man the raw appetite for life is so much weaker. Which is why it has to suppress the other instinct with every weapon available. But this suppression isn't always successful. The counter-instinct breaks surface in times of decadence, and manages to overrun the territory of the mind to a surprising degree. Sometimes whole classes of society almost consciously dig their own graves, like the French aristocracy before the Revolution. And, I'm afraid, the most current example today are the Hungarians of Transdanubia. . . .

"I don't know if you're still following me? People usually get me spectacularly wrong whenever I talk on this subject. But I can do a little test. Do you recognise this feeling? A man is walking on a wet pavement and slips. His one leg collapses under him, and he starts to fall backwards. At the precise moment when I lose my balance, I am filled with a sudden ecstasy. Of course it lasts only a second, then I automatically jerk back my leg, recover my balance, and rejoice in the fact that I didn't fall. But that one moment! For just one moment I was

suddenly released from the oppressive laws of equilibrium. I was free. I began to fly off into annihilating freedom.... Do you recognise this feeling?"

"I know rather more about this whole business than
you think," Mihály said quietly.

Waldheim suddenly looked at him in surprise.

"Eh, you say that in a strange voice, old chap! And
you've gone so pale! What's wrong with you? Come out
on to the balcony."

Out on the balcony Mihály recovered himself in an
instant.

"What is this, damn you?" said Waldheim. "Are you
hot? Or hysterical? You should consider that if you were
to commit suicide under the influence of what I've said I
shall deny that I ever knew you. What I am saying is of a
completely theoretical significance. I really detest those
people who like to draw practical conclusions from scholarly truths, who 'apply learning to real life', like engineers
who turn the propositions of chemistry into insecticides
for bedbugs. It translates, in Goethe's words, as: 'life is
always grey, and the golden tree of theory is always
green'. Especially when the theory itself is still as green as
this is. Now I hope I've restored your equilibrium. Here's
a general rule ... don't try to live the life of the soul. I
think that's your problem. An intelligent person doesn't
have a spiritual life. And tomorrow you must come with
me to the garden party at the American Institute of
Archaeology. You'll have a bit of fun. Now go to hell, I've
still got work to do."

# XVI

THE AMERICAN ARCHAEOLOGICAL INSTITUTE occu-
pied a resplendent building set in a large garden on
the Gianicolo hill. Its annual garden party was a major
event in the social calendar of Rome's Anglo-Saxon community. Its organisers were not just the American Archaeologists, but more importantly the American painters
and sculptors living in Rome, and the guests all those
closely or loosely connected with them. It was always a
particularly varied and particularly interesting group of
people who assembled on the night.

But Mihály experienced little of the variety and interest of the company. He was again in that state of mind in
which everything seemed to reach him through a veil of
fog—the scented enchantment of the summer night, blend-
ing with the dance-music, the drinks and the women he
chatted to, he had no idea about what. His Pierrot costume
and his domino mask and cape completely distanced
him. It wasn't himself there, but someone else, a dream-
locked domino mask.

The hours passed in a pleasant daze. The night was
now much advanced, and he stood once more on top of
the grassy hillock under the umbrella pine, listening to
those strange inexplicable voices which had troubled him
again and again in the course of the evening.

The voices came from behind a wall, a truly massive
wall, which as the night went on seemed to grow steadily
higher, soaring into the sky. The voices swelled out from

behind the wall, sometimes stronger, sometimes fainter, sometimes with ear-splitting intensity, and sometimes no louder than the far-off lamentation of mourners on the distant shore of some lake or sea, under an ashen sky ... then they fell silent, were totally silent for long stretches of time. Mihály would start to forget about them and feel again like a man at a garden-party, and allowed Waldheim, brilliantly in his element, to introduce him to one woman after another, until once again the distant voices rose.

They did so just at a time when the general mood had begun to develop agreeably, as everyone slipped towards the subtler, deeper stages of drunkenness, the effect of the night rather than the alcohol. They had passed beyond the threshold of dreams, the habitual hour of sleep. Now distinctions were becoming blurred, rational morality was in retreat as they surrendered themselves to the night. Waldheim was singing extracts from *The Fair Helen*, Mihály was busy with a Polish lady and everything was quite delightful, when he again heard the voices. He excused himself, went back to the top of the mound, and stood there alone, his heart palpitating in the tenseness of his concentration, as if everything depended on resolving this enigma.

Now he could hear quite distinctly that the voices beyond the wall were singing, and there were several of them, probably men, intoning a dirge unlike anything ever heard, in which certain distinct but unintelligible words rhythmically recurred. There was a profound, tragic desolation in the song, something not quite human, from a different order of experience, something reminiscent of the howling of animals on long dark nights, some ancient grief from the great age of trees, from the era of the umbrella pines. Mihály sat back under the pine and closed his eyes. No, the singers beyond the wall were not men but women, and he could already see them in his mind's eye, a strange company, something out of *Naconxipan*, the mad Gulácsy painting of the denizens of wonderland in their oppressive lilac-coloured attire, and he thought that this was how one would mourn for the death of a god, Attis, Adonis, Tamás ... Tamás, who had died unmourned at the beginning of time, and now lay in state out there beyond the wall, with the sunrise of tomorrow dawning on his face.

When he opened his eyes a woman stood before him, leaning with her shoulder against the umbrella pine, in classical costume, exactly as Goethe imagined the Greeks, and masked. Mihály politely straightened his posture, and asked her in English: "You don't know who those men or women are, singing through the wall?"

"But of course," she replied. "There's a Syrian monastery next door. The monks chant their psalms every second hour. Spooky, isn't it?"

"It certainly is," said Mihály.

They were silent for a while. At last she spoke:

"I've a message for you. From a very old acquaintance."

Mihály promptly stood up.

"Éva Ulpius?"

"Yes, a message from Éva Ulpius. That you are not to look for her. You won't find her anyway. It's too late. You

223

should have, she says, in that house in London, when she was hiding behind the curtain. But you shouted out Tamás's name, she says. And now it's too late."

"Even to speak to her?"

"Much too late."

The cry of pain swelling up through the wall as if in grief for the rising dawn, in lamentation for the passing of night, now lost its strength, became a faltering, broken wail, tearing at itself, murderously. The woman shuddered.

"Look," she said. "The dome of St Peter's."

Above the grey city the cupola hovered, white and very cold, like unconquerable eternity itself. The woman ran off down the hill.

Mihály felt an immeasurable fatigue. It was as if he had all the while been anxiously clutching his life in his hands, and had just let it slip away.

Then he suddenly pulled himself together and rushed after the woman, who had now vanished.

Down below there was a tight crush of people. Most were taking their leave, but Waldheim was still reading aloud from the Symposium and holding forth. Mihály scurried here and there in the seething crowd, then raced to the main gate hoping to find the girl in the press of people boarding coaches.

He arrived just in time. She was climbing into a splendidly old-world open carriage, where the shape of a second woman was already seated, and the coach moved off briskly. The other woman he recognised instantly. It was Éva.

# XVII

THE BANKERS' DISCUSSION was becoming intermin-
able. The matter could in fact have been resolved
quite simply if all those round the table had been equally
intelligent. But in this life that is rarely given. The lawyers
dazzled one another with their skill in sliding down the
very steepest sentences without falling off, while the powerful financiers said little, listened suspiciously, their
silence saying more eloquently than any words: "Count
me out."

"No deal will come of this," thought Zoltán Pataki,
Erzsi's first husband, with resignation.

He grew steadily more restless and impatient. He had
noted several times of late that his mind would wander
during discussions, and ever since he had noticed that
fact he had become even more restless and impatient.

The protracted blast of a car-horn sounded beneath
the window. Previously, Erzsi would often wait in the car
down below if the discussion went on at length.

"Erzsi ... try not to think of her. It's still painful, but
time will cure that. Just keep going. Just keep going.
Emptily, like an abandoned car. But just keep going."

His hand made a gesture of resignation, he pursed his
lips oddly, and he felt very very tired. In recent days these
four connected acts kept recurring in automatic sequence,
like a sort of nervous tic. Thirty times a day he thought of
Erzsi, made the resigned gesture, pulled the wry face, and
felt a wave of exhaustion. "Perhaps I should see the

doctor about this tiredness after all? Oh, come off it. We're getting on, old chap, getting on in years."

His concentration returned. They were saying that someone should go to Paris to negotiate with a certain finance group. Someone else was arguing that this was quite unnecessary, it could all be settled by letter.

"Erzsi's in Paris now ... Mihály in Italy ... Erzsi doesn't write a single line, but she must be horribly lonely. Does she have enough money? Perhaps the poor thing has to travel by Metro. If she leaves before nine and goes back after two she can get a return ticket. It's so much cheaper—poor thing, that's surely what she's doing. But perhaps she isn't alone. In Paris it's difficult for a woman to remain on her own, and Erzsi is so attractive...."

This time what followed was not the gesture of resignation, but a rush of blood to the head and: "Death, death, there's nothing else for it...."

Meanwhile the meeting was moving towards the consensus that they really would have to send someone. Pataki asked to speak. He threw all his energy behind the view that it was absolutely essential to pursue the matter with the French interest on a personal basis. When he began to speak he was not entirely clear what the issue was, but as he spoke it came back to him, and he produced unassailable arguments. He carried the meeting with him. Then the exhaustion once again overwhelmed him.

"Of course someone's got to go to Paris. But I can't go. I can't leave the bank just now. And anyway, what would I be going for? Erzsi hasn't invited me. For me to run after her, to run the risk of a highly probable rejection, that's quite impossible.... After all, a man has his pride."

He brought his words to an abrupt close. Persuaded, the meeting agreed to send a young director, the son-in-law of one of the big financiers, who spoke exceptionally good French. "It'll be an education for him," the older men thought to themselves with fatherly benevolence.

After the meeting came the most difficult part of the day, the evening. Pataki had once read that the most important difference between a married man and a bachelor was that the married man always knew who he would dine with that evening. And indeed, since Erzsi had left him, this had been the greatest problem in Pataki's life: who would he dine with? He had never got on with men, had never known the institution of male friendship. Women? This was the oddest thing. While he was married to Erzsi he had needed endless women, one after the other. Every one seemed to please him, one because she was so thin, another because so plump, a third because she was so exactly in between. All his free time, and much that was not free, was filled with women. There had been a *maîtresse de titre* obscurely connected with the theatre, who had cost him a great deal of money (though she had brought with her a degree of publicity for the bank), then various gentlemanly diversions, the wives of one or two colleagues, but chiefly the typists, with the occasional maid-servant for the sake of variety: an inglorious collection. Erzsi had a real grievance in law, and Pataki in his more optimistic moments reckoned that this was why she had left him. In his more pessimistic mode he had to acknowledge that there was another reason, certain needs which he had been unable to meet, and that consciousness was particularly humiliating. When Erzsi left he had discharged the *maîtresse de titre* with a handsome redundancy payment, that is to say, made her directly over to an older colleague who had long aspired to the honour, he had "reorganised" his secretarial staff, surrounded himself with one of the ugliest workforces in the bank, and lived a life of self-denial.

"There should have been a child," he thought, and was filled with the sudden sense of how much he would have loved his child had there been one, Erzsi's child. With rapid decisiveness he telephoned a cousin who had two positively golden children, and went there to dinner. En route he purchased a horrifying quantity of sweets. The two golden children probably never knew what they had to thank for three days of stomach-ache.

After dinner he sat on in a coffee-house, read the newspapers, vacillated over the question of whether to go yet again and play cards for a bit in the club, could not finally make up his mind, and went home.

Without Erzsi, the flat was now unspeakably oppressive. He really would have to do something with her furniture. Her room couldn't just stand there as if she might return at any moment, although.... "I'll have to get them to take it all up to the attic, or have it stored. I'll have it fitted out like a club-room, with huge armchairs."

Again the gesture of resignation, the grimace, the wave of exhaustion. Decidedly he couldn't bear it in the flat. He would have to move. To live in a hotel, like an artist.

And change the hotel constantly. Or perhaps move into a sanatorium. Pataki adored sanatoria, with their bleached tranquillity and doctorly reassurance. "Yes, I'll move out to Svábhegy. My nerves could really do with it. Any more of this runaway wife business and I'll go mad."

He lay down, then got up again because he felt he couldn't possibly sleep. He dressed, but had absolutely no idea where to go. Instead, although he knew perfectly well it would be of no use, he took a Szevenal, and once again undressed.

As soon as he was in bed the alternative again stood before him in all its misery. Erzsi in Paris: either she was alone, horribly alone, perhaps not eating properly (who knows what ghastly little *prix-fixe* places she was going to); or indeed she was not alone. That thought was not to be borne. Mihály he had somehow got used to. For some odd reason he was unable to take Mihály seriously, even though he had actually run off with her. Mihály didn't count. Mihály wasn't human. Deep in his consciousness lurked the conviction that one day, somehow, it would transpire that no such person existed ... his affair with Erzsi had been a chance thing, they had lived in a marriage but had never had a real relationship, man and woman. That was something he could not imagine of Mihály. But now, in Paris ... the unknown man ... the unknown man was a hundred times more disturbing than any familiar seducer. No, the thought could not be endured.

He must go to Paris. He must see for himself what Erzsi was doing. Perhaps she was hungry. But what of his pride? Erzsi didn't care a hoot for him. He didn't need Erzsi. Erzsi had no wish to see him....

"And then? Isn't it enough that I want to see her? The rest will sort itself out.

"Pride! Since when did you have all this pride, Mr Pataki? If you'd always been so proud in your business life, where would you be now, pray? In a flourishing greengrocer's in Szabadka, like your dear old dad's. And why exactly all this pride with regard to Erzsi? A man's pride should come out where there is some risk involved: in dealing with presidents, or, say, secretaries of state, with the Krychlovaces of this world. (Well, no, that's going a bit far.) But proud towards women? That's not chivalrous, not gentlemanly. Just daft."

The next day he produced a storm of activity. He persuaded the bank and all others concerned that the son-in-law was not the ideal person: someone with more experience was needed after all, to negotiate with the French.

The interested parties came gradually to understand that this person of more experience would be Pataki himself.

"But, Mr Director, do you speak French?"

"Not a great deal, but for that very reason they won't sell me anything. And in any case the people we're dealing with will surely speak German, just like you or me. Did you ever meet a businessman who didn't speak German? *Deutsch ist eine Weltsprache.*"

The next morning he was already on his way.

The business side of his trip he despatched in half an

hour. His French counterpart, whose name was Loew, did in fact speak German, and also happened to be intelligent. The matter was soon settled because Pataki, in contrast to less skilled or experienced men, did not take business and financial matters too seriously. He regarded them the way a doctor regards his patients. He knew that here too it is just like anywhere else: the talentless often do much better than the able, the inexpert come good more often than the expert. A bunch of pseudo-financiers sit in the highest places directing the world economy, while the real ones meditate in the Schwartzer or the Markó. The quest is for a myth, a groundless fiction, just as it is in the world of learning, where men pursue a non-existent and seductive Truth. In business it is Wealth on a scale that defies comprehension, in pursuit of which they sacrifice the wealth that can be understood. And in the last analysis the whole rat-race is as frivolous as everything else in this world.

He was very proud of the fact that he knew this and that Mihály, for example, did not. Mihály was an intellectual, and for precisely that reason believed in money while at the same time calling everything else into doubt. He would say such things as, for instance: "Psychology in its present state is a thoroughly primitive, unscientific discipline ... " or, "Modern lyric poetry is utterly meaningless," or "Humanism? there's no point in making speeches against war: it comes upon us wordlessly...." But, on the other hand: "The Váraljai Hemp and Flax Company, that's real. You can't say a word against that. That's about money. Money's no joking matter." Pataki chuckled to himself. "Váraljai Hemp and Flax, my God.... If Mihály and his friends only knew.... Even lyric poetry is more serious."

"And now we must proceed calmly to the second item on our little agenda." Pataki had obtained Erzsi's Paris address from Mihály's family. For Pataki, as he did with everyone, had maintained good relations with them (after all they could hardly be held responsible) and he had even brought a present for Erzsi from Mihály's married sister. He was very pleased to establish that she no longer lodged on the left bank, the dubious Parisian Buda, full of bohemians and immigrants, but on the respectable right bank, close to the Étoile.

It was twelve o'clock. With a café waiter he telephoned Erzsi's hotel, not sufficiently trusting his own command of French to negotiate the complexities of the Paris exchange. Madame was not in. Pataki went on reconnaissance.

He entered the little hotel and asked for a room. His French was so bad it was not difficult to play the stupid foreigner. He indicated through gestures that the room he had seen was too expensive, and left. He had however established that it was a regular, genteel sort of place, probably full of English, though a hint of seediness was just perceptible, especially in the faces of the room-girls. No doubt there were certain rooms which elderly Frenchmen would hire as a *pied-à-terre*, paying for a whole month but actually using for only a couple of hours a week. Why had Erzsi moved here from the other side of the river? Did she wish to live more elegantly, or had she found a more elegant lover?

At four that afternoon he telephoned again. This time Madame was in.

"Hello, Erzsi? Zoltán here."

"Oh, Zoltán...."

Pataki thought he could hear suppressed agitation in her voice. Was this a good sign?

"How are you, Erzsi? Is everything all right?"

"Yes, Zoltán."

"I'm here in Paris. You know, the Váraljai Hemp and Flax contract was a real tangle, I had to come. Endless running around. I'll be on my feet for three days. I'm getting really bored with this town...."

"Yes, Zoltán."

"And I thought, well, here I am, and today I've got a little spare time to catch a breath or two, I might inquire how you are."

"Yes.... Very kind of you."

"Are you well?"

"Very well."

"Tell me.... Hello.... Could I possibly see you?"

"What for?" asked Erzsi, from an immense distance. Pataki experienced a brief dizziness, and leaned against the wall. To conceal this he continued jovially:

"What's this 'what for'? Of course I should see you, since I'm here in Paris, don't you think?"

"True."

"Can I come over?"

"All right, Zoltán. No, don't come here. We'll meet somewhere."

"Splendid. I know a very nice teashop. Do you know

where Smith's is, the English bookshop in the rue de Rivoli?"

"I think so."

"Well I never! On the first floor there's an English teashop. You go up from inside the bookshop. Do come. I'll wait for you there."

"Fine."

He had in fact selected this venue because, where Erzsi was concerned, he had a morbid suspicion of everything French. In his imagination Paris and the French symbolised for Erzsi everything lacking in him, everything he could not give her. In the French cafés (which he particularly loathed, because the waiters were insufficiently respectful, and never brought water with his coffee) the entire French nation would aid Erzsi in her resistance to him, and she would have the advantage. In the interests of fair play he had chosen the cool, neutral extra-territoriality of the English teashop.

Erzsi appeared. They ordered, and Pataki strove to behave as if nothing had happened between them: no marriage, no divorce. Two clever Budapesti, a man and a woman, happening to meet in Paris. He treated her to the latest gossip from home, full and fully spiced, concerning their close acquaintances. Erzsi listened attentively.

Meanwhile he was thinking:

"Here's Erzsi. Essentially she hasn't changed, not even after all that's happened and all the time that's passed since she was my wife. She's wearing one or two bits and pieces of Paris clothing, chic enough, but, I fear, not of the best quality. She's a bit down. In her voice there's a certain, very slight, veiled quality that breaks my heart. Poor little thing! That bastard Mihály! What did she need him for? It seems she hasn't yet got over him ... or perhaps she's suffered new disappointments in Paris? The unknown man.... Oh my God, my God, here am I chattering on about Peter Bodrogi when I'd rather die.

"Here is Erzsi. As large as life. Here is the one woman I cannot live without. Why, why, why? Why should she be the only woman I find desirable, at a time when my general desire for women is non-existent? So many of the others were so much 'better women', Gizi for example, not to mention Maria.... Just to look at them made my blood well up. And above all, they were so much younger. Erzsi's no longer exactly.... Why, despite all this, here and now, in sober mind and free from the heat of passion, would I give up half my fortune to lie with her?"

Erzsi rarely looked at Zoltán, but listened to his gossip with a smile, and thought:

"How much he knows about everyone! People are so much at home with him. (Mihály never knew anything about anyone. He was incapable of noticing who was whose brother-in-law or girlfriend.) I don't understand what I was afraid of, why I got so anxious. That old cliché of the 'deserted husband', how much truth is there in it? I really might have known that Zoltán could never get into the way of being the tiniest bit tragic. He finds a smile in everything. He abhors everything that's on a grand scale. If his fate led him to a martyr's death he'd no doubt make a joke and a bit of gossip even at the stake, to take the edge off the tragic situation. And yet he surely has suffered a lot. He's older than he was. But at the same time he's played down the suffering. And occasionally he's felt wonderful. You can't feel too sorry for him."

"Well, what's the matter?" Zoltán asked suddenly.

"With me? What should there be? I'm sure you know all about why I came to Paris...."

"Yes, I'm aware of the broad outline, but I don't know why everything turned out as it did. You wouldn't care to tell me?"

"No, Zoltán. Don't be offended. I really can't think why I should discuss with you what happened between me and Mihály. I never talked to him about you. It's only natural."

"That's Erzsi," thought Zoltán. "A fine lady, real breeding. Nothing, however catastrophic, could make her indiscreet. Self-control on two legs. And how she looks at me, with such cool, withering politeness! She's still got the knack—she's only to look at me to make me feel like a grocer's assistant. But I can't let myself be so easily intimidated."

"All the same, you can perhaps at least tell me what your plans are," he said.

"For the time being I really don't have any. I'm staying on in Paris."

"Are you happy here?"

"Happy enough."

"Have you filed for divorce yet?"

"No."

"Why not?"

"Zoltán, you ask so many questions! I haven't, because it isn't yet time for that."

"But do you really think he'll still ... do excuse me ... that he'll still come back to you?"

"I don't know. Perhaps. I don't know whether I would want him if he did. Perhaps I'd have nothing to say to him. We aren't really suited. But ... Mihály isn't like other people. First I would have to know what his intentions were. For all I know he could wake up one fine morning and look around for me. And remember in a panic that he left me on the train. And look for me high and low all over Italy."

"Do you really think so?"

Erzsi lowered her head.

"You're right. I don't really think so."

"Why was I so frank?" The question gnawed at her. "Why did I give myself away, as I have to no one else? It seems there's still something between me and Zoltán. Some sort of intimacy, that can't be wished away. You can't undo four years of marriage. There's no other person in the world I would have discussed Mihály with."

"My time hasn't yet come," thought Zoltán. "She's still in love with that oaf. With a bit of luck Mihály will mess it up in the fullness of time."

"What news have you had of him?" he asked.

"Nothing. I only guess he's in Italy. One of his friends is here, someone I also know, by the name of János Szepetneki. He tells me he's tracking him closely and will soon know where he is, and what he's doing."

"How will he find out?"

"I don't know. Szepetneki is a very unusual man."

"Truly?" Zoltán raised his head and gazed at her steadily. Erzsi withstood the gaze defiantly.

"Truly. A very unusual man. The most unusual man I ever met. And then there's a Persian here too...."

Pataki dropped his head, and took a large mouthful of tea. "Which of the two was it? Or was it both? My God, my God, better to be dead...."

The *tête-à-tête* did not last very much longer. Erzsi had some business, she didn't say what.

"Where are you staying?" she asked absent-mindedly.

"At the Edward VII."

"Well, goodbye, Zoltán. Really, it was very nice seeing you again. And ... don't worry, and don't think about me," she said quietly, with a sad smile.

That night Pataki took a little Parisienne back to the hotel. "After all, when you're in Paris," he thought, and was filled with unspeakable revulsion against the smelly little stranger snoring in the bed beside him.

In the morning, after she had gone and Pataki was up and beginning to shave, there was a knock at the door.

"*Entrez!*"

A tall, too-elegantly dressed, sharp-featured man made his entrance.

"I'm looking for Mr Pataki, the Director. It's important. A matter of great importance to him."

"That's me. With whom do I have the pleasure?"

"My name is János Szepetneki."

# PART FOUR

# AT HELL'S GATE

*V. A porta inferi R. erue, Domine,
animam eius.*
OFFICIUM DEFUNCTORUM

# XVIII

NIGHT WAS FALLING. Slowly, with a slight dragging of the feet, Mihály trudged over the Tiber.

For some time now he had been living on the Gianicolo Hill, in a shabby little room Waldheim had discovered, where a scruffy crone cooked most of his meals, simple *pasta asciutta*, which Mihály supplemented with a bit of cheese and sometimes an orange. Despite its creaking antiquity it was much more the real thing than any hotel room. The furniture was ancient—real furniture, large and nobly proportioned, not the pseudo-furniture one finds in large hotels. Mihály would have been very fond of his room had its state of cleanliness and hygiene not constantly provoked the painful sense of having come down in the world. He even complained to Waldheim, who simply laughed and delivered lengthy and not very appetising lectures on his experiences in Greece and Albania.

Thus he came face to face with poverty. Now he really did have to ponder every *centesimo* before parting with it. He gave up drinking black coffee, and smoked cigarettes so foul he could take only a few at a time. His throat was permanently inflamed. And the thought was seldom from his mind that what money he had would soon run out. Waldheim was always assuring him that he would find a job. There were so many stupid old American women running about in Rome that one of them was sure to hire him as a secretary or tutor for her grandchildren, or perhaps as a caretaker, a really cosy position that. But at present these American women existed entirely in Waldheim's imagination, and besides, Mihály had a dread of any occupation he might equally find in Budapest.

Anyway, he already had two occupations, and between them they were quite enough for him. The first was, on Waldheim's instructions, to "read up" on everything Etruscan, to frequent libraries and museums, and listen every evening to the conversation of Waldheim and his current academic friends. Mihály did not for a moment feel anything of Waldheim's immense, genuine enthusiasm for the subject, but he clung desperately to the routine of study for the slight relief it gave from the suffocating middle-class guilt which he still felt, so pointlessly, about his life of idleness. Mihály had never really liked work, but in his bourgeois years had applied himself obsessively because he loved the feeling at night of having done a good day's worth. Moreover, study momentarily diverted his attention away from his second and more important occupation: waiting for a meeting with Éva.

He simply could not accept the possibility that he would never see her again. The day after that memorable night he had wandered round the city in a stupor, with no idea of what he wanted, though he later saw clearly that there was only one thing he could want, so far as the word "want" had any meaning in the case. The academics had taught him that there are degrees of Being, and that only the Perfect was wholly, truly alive. The time he spent in quest of Éva had been more alive, far more truly caught up in reality, than all the months and years without her.

However good or bad, however bound up with hideous anxiety and trouble, he knew that this was the life, and that without Éva there was no reality other than in thinking of her and waiting for her.

He was tired, oppressed with the sense of his own mortality, and he dragged his feet as if lame. Reaching the river bank he became aware of a feeling that he was being followed. But he dismissed it, persuading himself that it was just his nervous imagination.

However as he trudged through the alleyways of the Trastevere quarter the feeling became ever more insistent. A strong wind began to blow. There were far fewer people than usual about in the streets. "If someone is following me," he thought, "I must get a glimpse of him," and he turned round periodically to look. But people kept coming. "Perhaps someone is following me, and perhaps not."

As he made his way up the narrow streets the feeling gradually became so insistent again that he decided not to turn left, up towards the hill, but to continue on through the Trastevere alleyways with the idea of waiting for the pursuer in some suitable place. He stopped outside a little tavern.

"If he wants to attack me," he thought (in the Trastevere district this was not difficult to imagine) "here at least I can count on help. Someone's bound to come out of the bar if I shout. But in any case I'll wait and see."

He stood outside the little inn and waited. More people came along, having followed him out of the alleys, but none took the slightest notice of him. They simply

continued on their way. He was just about to move on
when a man approached in the semi-darkness, and Mihály
instantly knew that this was he. With beating heart he
realised that the man was making straight for him.

As the shape loomed closer he recognised János Szepetneki. In the whole episode the strangest thing, perhaps
the only strange thing, was that he was not particularly
surprised.

"Hello," he said quietly.

"Hello, Mihály," said Szepetneki, loudly and jovially.
"I'm glad you decided to wait for me. This is just the
place I wanted to take you. Well, come on in."

They entered the little tavern, whose strongest feature,
apart from the smell, was the darkness. The smell Mihály
could tolerate. For some reason the smells of Italy did not
bother his normally sensitive nostrils. In this particular
smell there was something romantic, a hint of fatality.
But the darkness he did not like. Szepetneki immediately
shouted for a lamp. It was brought by a ravishing, distinctly slovenly Italian girl, shockingly thin, with flashing
eyes and huge earrings. It appeared Szepetneki was an
old acquaintance. He slapped her on the back, at which
she smiled with her great white teeth and launched into
a story in the Trastevere dialect, of which Mihály understood not a single word, though János, who, like all con-
men, had a flair for languages, interjected skilfully. The
girl brought wine, sat down at the table, and talked. János
listened with delight, ignoring Mihály completely, or, at
most, offering the occasional comment in Hungarian,
such as:

"Fantastic girl, hey? They know a thing or two, these Italians!" or:

"How's that for a pair of eyes, eh! You don't see them like that in Pest" or:

"She says, all the men who were going to marry her got locked up, and I'm sure to be the next ... what a wit, eh?"

Mihály nervously downed one glass of wine after another. He knew János Szepetneki, knew that he would take ages to get round to what he really wanted to say. For everything he had to establish an appropriately romantic context. So Mihály would have to wait for this little farce with the Italian girl to run its course. Perhaps Szepetneki ran a gang of burglars in the Trastevere and this girl and this tavern were part of it, at least as a setting. But he also knew that Szepetneki hadn't come to sort out his gang but because he wanted something from him; and he was profoundly troubled about what it might be.

"Just leave the girl alone and tell me why you followed me, and what you want from me. I haven't got the time or inclination to witness this little comedy."

"But why?" asked Szepetneki with a face of innocence. "Perhaps you don't fancy the lady? Or the hostelry? I just thought we could have a bit of fun. It's such a long time since we were together...."

And he resumed his chat with the woman.

Mihály stood up and made to leave.

"No, Mihály, for God's sake, don't go yet. The only reason I came to Rome was to talk to you. Just stick around for one minute." And with that he turned to the girl: "Just be quiet a moment."

"How did you know I was in Rome?" asked Mihály.

"Oh, I always know everything about you, my Mihály. Have done for years. But until now none of it's been worth knowing. Now you begin to be interesting. That's why we'll be meeting more often."

"Fine. And now be so kind as to tell me what you want from me."

"I've something to discuss with you."

"You've got something else to discuss? And what's that about?"

"You're going to laugh. Business matters."

Mihály's face darkened.

"Have you been talking to my father? Or my brother?"

"No. Not at present. For the time being I've no business with them, only you. But tell me truly, isn't this girl fantastic? See what a fine hand she's got. Pity it's so dirty."

And once again he turned to the girl and began to rattle away in Italian.

Mihály leaped to his feet and rushed out. He struggled up towards the hill. Szepetneki ran after him and soon caught up with him. Mihály did not turn round, but simply left Szepetneki to address him from behind his back, over his left shoulder, like a familiar.

János spoke quickly and low, panting slightly from the uphill walk.

"Mihály, listen here. I happened to meet a man, a man by the name of Zoltán Pataki, who, it turns out, was your wife's first husband. But that's nothing. It also turns out, that this Pataki, believe it or not, still loves her ladyship to death. He wants to take her back. He hopes that now you've chucked her over, she'll perhaps come to her senses, and go back to him. Which would undoubtedly be, for all three of you, the best solution. Well, have you nothing to say? Great. You still don't understand where the business lies in this, and what business it is of mine. But you know me, I gave up tact a long time ago. In my profession.... So, listen to this. Your lady wife not only doesn't want to divorce you, she still secretly believes that one day you'll make a happy and contented couple, and perhaps heaven will bless the marriage with children. She knows that you're not like other people, though she really has no idea what that actually means. She thinks about you a very great deal, to the point of nuisance, and at times when she really shouldn't. But you needn't feel bad about her. She's getting along very nicely, though I don't want to spread gossip. She's doing very nicely without you."

"What do you want?" shouted Mihály, stopping in his tracks.

"Nothing at all. It's a question of a little business arrangement. Mr Pataki believes that, if you were to take a decisive step, your wife would see that she can no longer expect anything from you, and that it's all over."

"What kind of decisive step are you talking about?"

"Well, for example, you might sue for divorce."

"How the devil would I do that? Since I was the one that left her. And besides, even if she had left me I wouldn't do it. That's the woman's part."

"Well, yes, naturally. But if the woman doesn't want to

do it, then it's up to you. At least, that's Mr Pataki's point of view."

"Pataki's point of view is none of my business, and the whole affair is none of my business. You talk to Erzsi. I'll fall in with whatever she wants."

"Look Mihály, this is precisely what our business is about. Use your common sense. Mr Pataki isn't asking you to give this divorce for nothing. He's prepared to make substantial material sacrifices. He's horribly rich, and he can't live without Erzsi. So he's authorised me to make you the immediate down payment of a small sum, quite a tidy little sum."

"Rubbish. On what grounds could I sue for divorce? Against Erzsi? When I was the one who left her? If the court decides that we have to live together again and she comes back to me, what would I do then?"

"But, Mihály, have no fear of that. You sue for the divorce, we'll see to the rest."

"On what grounds?"

"Adultery."

"You're crazy!"

"Not in the least. Just trust me. I'll guarantee a wonderful adultery, pure as the driven snow. I'm an expert in these things."

By this time they had reached Mihály's door. He could hardly wait to get inside.

"God preserve you, János Szepetneki. This time I don't offer you my hand. What you have said is a lot of disgraceful drivel. I hope I don't see you for a very long time."

And he rushed up to his room.

# XIX

"I DON'T KNOW what all this is about but I'm quite sure your anxieties are ridiculous," said Waldheim with great energy. "You're still the pious son of your respected grey-haired father, still a petty-bourgeois. If someone wants to give you money, whatever the source, you should take it. Every religious-historical authority agrees about that. But you still haven't learned that money ... quite simply, is unimportant. Where essential things are concerned it doesn't count. Money is always there of necessity, and it's there even when you don't bother about it. How much and for how long and where it came from, that's completely immaterial. Because everything that depends on money is immaterial. You can acquire nothing of importance with money. What you can buy might happen to be life's necessities, but really isn't important.

"The things really worth living for can never be had for money. Scholarship, the fact that your mind can take in the thousand-fold splendour of things, doesn't cost a penny. The fact that you are in Italy, that the Italian sky stretches above you, that you can walk down Italian streets and sit in the shade of Italian trees, and in the evening the sun sets in the Italian manner, none of this is a question of money. If a woman likes you and gives herself to you, it doesn't cost a penny. Feeling happy from time to time, that doesn't cost you a penny. The only things that do cost money are peripheral, the external trimmings of happiness, the stupid and boring accessories. Being in Italy costs nothing, but what does cost money is travelling here, and having got here, sleeping with a roof over your head. Having a woman who loves you doesn't cost money, only that meanwhile she has to eat and drink, and dress herself up so that she can then get undressed. But the petty-bourgeoisie have lived so long by supplying one another with unimportant things with a cash value they've forgotten the things that aren't to be had for money, and they attach importance only to things that are expensive. That is the greatest madness. No, Mihály, you should pay no attention to money. You should take it in like the air you breathe and not ask where it came from, unless it actually smells.

"And now, go to hell. I've still got to write my Oxford lecture. Have I shown you the letter, the one inviting me to Oxford? Just wait, it won't take a second.... Isn't it wonderful what he says about me? Of course if you read it as it stands it doesn't say very much, but if you take into account that the English love to *understate* their real meaning, then you can see what it means when they describe my work as *meritorious*...."

Mihály left, deep in thought. He set off south alongside the Tiber, walking away from the city centre towards the great dead Maremma. On the city boundary there is a strange hill, the Monte Testaccio, and this he climbed. Its name, "shard hill", reflects the fact that it is made up entirely of pieces of broken pottery. In Roman times the wine-market stood here. Here the wines of Spain were brought in sealed amphoras which were then broken and the wine decanted into goatskins. The shards were then swept up into a heap, which eventually formed the present hill.

Mihály dreamily picked up a few reddish bits of pottery and put them in his pocket.

"Relics," he thought. "Real shards, from the age of the Caesars. And no doubt of their genuineness, which can't be said of every souvenir."

On the hill young Roman boys, late descendants of the *quirites*, were playing at soldiers, hurling shards at one another, fragments of pottery two thousand years old, without a trace of emotion.

"That's Italy," thought Mihály. "They pelt one another with history. Two thousand years are as natural to them as the smell of manure in a village."

Night was already falling when he reached the little tavern in the Trastevere quarter where he had met János Szepetneki the evening before. Following the local custom, he pressed his shabby old hat down on his head and stepped into the smoky interior. His eyes could distinguish nothing, but Szepetneki's voice was immediately audible. As before, Szepetneki was busy with the girl.

"I hope I'm not disturbing you?" Mihály asked with a laugh.

"Disturbing us, what the hell. Sit yourself down. I've been waiting for you with mounting impatience."

Indignation rose in Mihály, then he was overcome with embarrassment.

"Sorry.... I just dropped in for a glass of wine. I was passing by and I had the feeling you might be here."

251

"My dear Mihály, don't say anything. Let's consider the matter settled. I'm very glad you're here, speaking for myself and for all the interested parties. And now, listen here. This little witch Vannina is wonderful at reading palms. She told me who I am, what I am. Not over-flattering, but she painted a very accurate picture of me. This is the first woman who hasn't been taken in by me, and she doesn't believe I'm a crook. All the same she predicts a bad end for me: a long and difficult old age.... Now, let her do you. I'm curious what she'll say about you."

A lamp was brought and the girl immersed herself in the examination of Mihály's palm.

"Oh, the *signore* is a lucky man," she said. "He will find money in an unexpected quarter."

"What are you saying?"

"Somewhere abroad a woman thinks often about the *signore*. A bald man also thinks often about the *signore*, but this is not altogether good. This line signifies much conflict. The *signore* can go with women without worrying, because there will be no children."

"How do you mean?"

"It's not as if you cannot make children, but all the same there will be none. The line of fatherhood is missing. In summer you should not eat oysters. Soon you will take part in a christening. An older man will arrive from beyond the mountains. The dead visit you often...."

Mihály abruptly pulled his hand away, and asked for wine. He looked more closely at the girl. Her large-breasted thinness he now found much more beautiful than he had the night before. And she was much more frightening, much more like a witch. Her eyes had an Italian glitter, and the whites seem to enlarge as he looked into them. That northern idea again flitted through his head: the whole race was mad, that was their greatness.

The girl seized his hand and continued to prophesy, now in real earnest.

"Soon you will receive very bad news. Beware of women. All your trouble is because of women. Oh.... the *signore* has a very good soul, but not one for this world. Oh, *dio mio*, poor *signore*...."

With that she pulled Mihály to her and kissed him fiercely, with tears in her eyes. János laughed out loud and cried "*Bravo!*" Mihály was overcome with embarrassment.

"You must come here again, *signore*," said Vannina. "Yes, come again, and often. You'll be happy here. You will come again, won't you? You will come?"

"Yes, of course. Since you ask so kindly...."

"You really will come? Do you know what? My cousin is having a baby soon. She's always longed for a foreign godfather for the infant. It's such a fine thing to have. Wouldn't you like to be godfather to the little *bambino*?"

"But of course, with great pleasure."

"Promise."

"I promise."

János was a tactful villain. Through all this he had not once mentioned "business matters". Only when it was late, and Mihály was slowly preparing to leave, did he send the girl away and say:

"Please, Mihály. It is Mr Pataki's wish that you should

write to him about this matter, in your own handwriting, in detail, making it absolutely clear that you authorise him to file a divorce in your name against your wife, and that you acknowledge that he will pay you the twenty thousand dollars in two instalments. You see, Pataki somehow doesn't trust me one hundred percent, and I'm not surprised. He wants to negotiate with you directly. Meanwhile I am to hand over to you, now, five thousand *lire* as a down payment."

He counted the money out on to the table and Mihály crammed it, with some embarrassment, into his pocket. "There," he thought, "that's how the die is cast. That's how you cross the Rubicon. So easily no one would even notice."

"Would you please write to Pataki as follows," said Szepetneki: "you have received, from me, the money he sent. But you mustn't specify the exact sum. After all, it shouldn't really be like a receipt or a business letter. That would be rather indelicate, as I'm sure you'll understand."

Mihály understood. In his head he instantly calculated how much Szepetneki had pocketed of the money sent to him. Perhaps fifty percent, certainly not more. Never mind, let him have it.

"Well then, God be with you," said János. "I've done my part in this, and tomorrow I'm leaving. But the rest of the evening I'll spend with Vannina. A splendid girl, I can tell you. Call on her often when I'm not here."

# XX

It BECAME STEADILY HOTTER. Mihály lay naked on his bed, but could not sleep. Since he had accepted Pataki's money and written that letter, he had not been able to settle.

He got up, washed, and set off for a stroll in the summer night. Soon he reached the Acqua Paola and stood delighting in the classical waterfall as, with timeless calm and proud dignity, it exercised its mystery in the moonlight. He remembered the little Hungarian sculptor in the *Collegium Hungaricum* whom he had got to know through Waldheim. The sculptor had walked from Drezda to Rome along the Via Flaminia, which, as Mihály knew from school, was the route always taken by victorious invaders from the north. Then on his first evening he had come up here, on to the Gianicolo. He had waited for them to clear everyone from the park and lock the gate, then he climbed over the wall and lay down in a bush, high above Rome, with the city at his feet. When morning came he rose, undressed and bathed in the pool of the Acqua Paolo, the classical waterfall.

That was how a conqueror marches into Rome. Perhaps nothing would ever come of the little sculptor. Perhaps his fate would be permanent hunger and who knows what else. Nonetheless a conqueror he was, needing only an army and "simple luck, nothing more". The road of his life led upwards, even if he perished in the ascent. Mihály's road led downwards, even if he survived,

survived everything and came to tranquil tedious old age. We carry within ourselves the direction our lives will take. Within ourselves burn the timeless, fateful stars.

He wandered for hours on the Gianicolo, along the bank of the Tiber and down the alleyways of the Trastevere. The night was late, but this was an Italian summer night, with people therefore awake on every side, hammering away or singing without embarrassment. This nation is quite innocent of northern notions of sleep as a time of consecrated stupor. At any moment you might stumble without rhyme or reason upon small children playing marbles in the street between three and four in the morning, or a barber will suddenly open his shop at three-thirty to shave a few merry bridegrooms.

On the Tiber tow-boats glided downstream with a calm, classical dignity: not tow-boats, but pictures from a school Latin book illustrating the word *Navis, navis.* On one a man played a guitar, a woman washed her stockings, a little dog barked. And behind it sailed another ship, the spectre-vessel, the Isola Tiberina, which even in ancient times had been built boat-shaped by men who doubted its fixedness, convinced that it slipped away on occasional night expeditions to the sea, carrying the hospital and all its death agonies on its back.

Across the water the moon rode at anchor over the huge oppressive ruins of the Teatro Marcello. From the nearby synagogue, Mihály seemed to remember, a crowd of long-bearded old Jews, with veils of the dead on their necks, would process to the Tiber bank and scatter their sins on the water with a murmuring lamentation. In the sky three aeroplanes circled, their headlights occasionally stroking one another's sides. Then they flew off towards the Castelli Romani, like large birds winging to rest on the craggy peaks.

Then with a tremendous rumbling a huge lorry drove up. "Daybreak," thought Mihály. Shapes clad in dark grey leapt from the lorry with alarming speed and poured through an archway door which opened before them. Then a bell tinkled, and a herd-boy appeared, singing out commands to a miraculous Vergilian heifer.

Now the door of a tavern opened and two workmen came up to him. They asked him to order some red wine for them and to tell them his life history. Mihály ordered the wine, indeed helped them finish the bottle, and even sent for some cheese to accompany it, though his difficulties with the language prevented the telling of his tale. Yet he felt an immense friendliness towards these people, who really seemed to sense his abandonment and grappled him to their hearts, and said such kind things it was a pity he could not understand what they were. But then, quite suddenly, he became afraid of them, paid, and made his escape.

He was in the Trastevere quarter. In the narrow alleyways with their myriad places of ambush, his mind filled again with images of violent death, as it had so often in his adolescence when he "played games" at the Ulpius house. What absurd rashness to get into conversation with those workmen! They could have murdered him and thrown him in the Danube, the Tiber, for his thirty *forints*. And to be wandering around in the satanic

Trastevere at such an hour, where under any of the gap-ing archways he might be struck dead three times over before he could open his mouth. What madness ... and what madness to harbour in his mind the very thing that lured him on, tempting him towards sin and death.

Then he found himself standing outside the house where Vannina lived. The house was dark, a small Italian house with a flat, tiled roof and window-arches faced with brick. Who might be living there? What deeds might lurk in the darkness of such a house? What horrors might befall him if he went in? Would Vannina ... yes, Vannina had surely had a purpose in inviting him there so often and so insistently in recent days. She could well have known he had had a lot of money from János. All her prospective husbands had been locked up ... yes, Vannina would be quite capable.... And when he knew that for certain, he would go in.

He stood for a long time outside the house, plunged in sick imaginings. Then suddenly a leaden weariness seized him, and again he felt the nostalgia that had haunted him at every stage of his journey through Italy. But his weari-ness told him that now he was near the last resting place of all.

# XXI

THE NEXT DAY he received a letter. The handwriting was familiar, very familiar, though he found, with some sense of shame, that he couldn't quite place it. It was from Erzsi. She informed him that she had come to Rome because she wished absolutely to talk to him, on a matter of great importance, great importance concerning him. He would be able to appreciate that this was not a question of some womanly caprice. Her self-respect would not permit her to seek a connection with him if she did not wish to defend his interests with respect to an extremely painful matter; but she considered she owed him that much. Therefore she strongly desired him to call on her, at her hotel, that afternoon.

Mihály was at a loss what to do. The thought of a meeting with Erzsi filled him with dread. His sense of guilt was particularly bad at that moment, and besides he could not imagine what she might want from him. But this soon gave way to the feeling that he had hurt Erzsi so much in the past he could not hurt her yet again by not meeting with her. He took his new hat, bought out of the money received from Pataki, and hurried off to the hotel where she was staying.

Word was sent up to her, and she soon came down to greet Mihály unsmilingly. His first impression was that he could expect little good from this meeting. Her brows were knitted into the frown she wore when she was angry, and she did not relax it. She was beautiful, tall, in every matter of taste elegant, but an angel with a flaming sword.... After a few terse inquiries about the journey and one another's health, they walked together in silence.

"Where are we going?" he asked.

"It's all the same to me. It's so hot. Let's sit in a pâtisserie."

The ice-cream and *aranciata* brought momentary relief. But they soon got to the point.

"Mihály," she said with suppressed anger, "I always knew you were pretty useless, and had no idea about anything going on around you, but I had thought there was a limit to your stupidity."

"That's a good start," said Mihály. But he was secretly rather pleased that she considered him a fool and not a villain.

She was surely right.

"How could you have written this?" she asked, and placed on the table the letter he had written to Pataki at Szepetneki's behest.

Mihály reddened, and in his shame felt such weariness he could not speak.

"Say something!" shouted Erzsi, the angel with the flaming sword.

"What should I say, Erzsi?" he said in a desultory tone. "You're an intelligent person, you know why I wrote it. I needed the money. I don't want to go back to Pest, for a thousand reasons. ... And this was the only way I could raise money."

"You're crazy."

"Maybe. But that doesn't explain such incredible

immorality. What an incredible pimp I am. Anyway, I know it. If the only reason you came to Rome, in this heat, was to tell me that...."

"The devil you're a pimp," she said in extreme exasperation. " If only you were! But you're just an idiot."

She fell silent. "Really," she thought, "I shouldn't take that tone with him, seeing I'm no longer his wife...."

After a while he asked: "Tell me, Erzsi, how did that letter come your way?"

"What do you mean? So, you still haven't worked the whole thing out? They conned you, János Szepetneki and that disgusting Zoltán. All he wanted was to show me your total lack of principle, in writing. He sent the letter on to me immediately, but first he made a photo-copy, duly notarised, which he kept."

"Zoltán? Zoltán does that sort of thing? Duly notarised? Such incredibly dark doings as that, something that would never even enter my mind, such fantastic shabbiness?... I don't understand it."

"Well of course you don't understand," she said, more gently. "You're not a pimp, just a fool. And Zoltán, unfortunately, is well aware of the fact."

"But he wrote me such a kind letter...."

"Oh yes, Zoltán is kind, but he's clever. You're not kind, but you are a fool."

"But then why is he doing all this?"

"Why? Because he wants me to go back to him. He wants to show me just what sort of lad you are. He doesn't take into account that I know it anyway, have known it a lot longer than he has, and that I also know what baseness lies behind his goodness and his gentle devotedness. Now if it were simply a question of getting me back, then the whole business has had the opposite result to what he wanted, and that wouldn't have been so clever. But it's not just about that."

"Go on."

"Listen to this." Erzsi's facial expression changed from exasperation to horror. "Zoltán wants to destroy you, Mihály. He wants to wipe you off the face of the earth."

"Really. But he isn't big enough for that yet. How do you think he'd try?"

"Look Mihály, I don't know exactly, because I'm not as cunning as Zoltán. I'm only guessing. First of all, I'd do everything I could to make your position in your family impossible. Which, at least for the time being, won't be difficult, because you can imagine what sort of face your father will make, or has already made, seeing this letter."

"My father? But you don't think he'd show it to him?"

"I'm quite sure of it."

Now he was horrified. A shivering, adolescent dread filled him, dread of his father, the old, old terror of losing his father's goodwill. He put down the glass of *aranciata* and buried his head in his hands. Erzsi understood his motives, he knew that. But he could never explain them to his father. He had lost credit with his father, once and for all.

"And after that he'll get to work in Pest," Erzsi continued. "He'll make up such a story about you, you won't be able to walk down the street. Because, my God, I know that the crime you wanted to commit is not so very unusual. There are hordes of people running around Pest who in one way or another have sold their wives and continue to enjoy general respect, especially if they're in the money and God's blessing goes with their businesses—but Zoltán will make quite sure that the weekly press, and other leaders of public opinion, will see it in a way that will mean you won't be able to walk down the street. You'll have to live abroad, which won't worry you very much, except that your family will barely be able to support you, or in fact not at all, since Zoltán will certainly do his utmost to destroy your father's business."

"Erzsi!"

"Oh yes. For example he'll find a way of forcing me to take my money out of the firm. When news of that gets out—and I will have to do it, your father himself will insist—that in itself will be a terrible blow to your people."

For a long time they sat in silence.

"I'd just like to know," Mihály said at last, "why he hates me so much. Because he used to be so understanding and forgiving it really wasn't natural."

"That's exactly why he hates you so much now. You really can't imagine how much resentment was stored up behind his goodness even then, what frantic loathing there was precisely in that forgivingness. No doubt he himself believed he had forgiven you, until the opportunity for revenge presented itself. And then like some wild animal reared on milk, suddenly given its first taste of meat...."

"I always thought of him as such a soft, slimy creature."

"Me too. And, I have to confess, now that he's assumed

such Shylockian proportions, he impresses me much more favourably. A decent chap, after all. . . ."

There was another long silence.

"Tell me," began Mihály, "presumably you've some plan, something I, or we, must do, that brought you to Rome."

"In the first place, I want to warn you. Zoltán believes that you'll walk as unsuspecting into his other traps as you have into this. For example, he wants to offer you a wonderful job, so that you'll go back to Pest. So that you'll be right on the spot when the scandal breaks. But you mustn't go back, at any price. And then I want to warn you about a . . . friend of yours. You know who."

"János Szepetneki?"

"Yes."

"How did you meet him in Paris?"

"In company."

"Were you with him often?"

"Yes, often enough. Zoltán also got to know him through me."

"And how did you find János? He's really unusual, don't you think?"

"Yes, really unusual."

But she said this with so much apparent deliberation that suspicion flashed through Mihály's mind. Was it really? . . . How strange it would be. . . . But his considerable discretion instantly rebelled and he suppressed his curiosity. If it were at all like that, then he should say nothing more about János Szepetneki.

"Thank you, Erzsi, for the warning. You're very good

to me, and I know how little I deserve it. And I can't believe that in time you too will come to hate me as bitterly as Zoltán Pataki does."

"I would think not," said Erzsi, very solemnly. "I don't feel any desire for revenge against you. There's no reason why I should, really."

"I see there's still something you want to say. Is there something else I should do?"

"There is something else I must warn you about, but it's rather painful because you might perhaps misunderstand my reason for saying it. Would you still think I'm speaking out of jealousy?"

"Jealousy? I'm not so conceited. I know I've thrown away every legal claim on your jealousy."

Deep down, he was well aware that Erzsi was not disinterested. Otherwise she would not have come to Rome. But he felt, and chivalry dictated, that he ought to ignore the fact (which his male ego would normally have insisted on) that she might still be attracted to him.

"Perhaps we should leave this—this question of my feelings," Erzsi said with some exasperation. "They really have nothing to do with it. So . . . as I say . . . look, Mihály, I know perfectly well on whose account you're in Rome. János told me. The person concerned wrote to him that you'd seen each other."

Mihály lowered his head. He sensed how very much it hurt Erzsi that he loved Éva. But what could he say to alter what was true and unchangeable?

"Yes, Erzsi. If you know about it, good. You know the background to all this. In Ravenna I told you everything there was to know about me. Everything is as it had to be. Only it shouldn't have to be so hard on you...."

"Please, drop it. I haven't said a thing about it being hard on me. That really isn't the point. But tell me ... do you know what this woman is? What sort of life she leads nowadays?"

"I don't know. I've never inquired about it."

"Mihály, I've always marvelled at your coolness, but you begin to surpass yourself. I never heard of such a thing, someone in love with a woman who has no inter-est in who or what sort of...."

"Because all that interests me is what she was then, in the Ulpius house."

"Perhaps you aren't aware that she won't be here much longer? She's managed to hook a young Englishman who's taking her with him to India. They leave in the next few days."

"That's not true."

"Oh, but it is. Take a look at this."

She drew another letter from her reticule. The hand-writing was Éva's. It was addressed to János. It gave a brief account of her impending trip to India, and the fact that she did not propose returning to Europe.

"You didn't know ?" asked Erzsi.

"You win," said Mihály. He got up, paid, and went out, leaving his hat behind.

Outside he staggered for a while in a blind daze, his hand pressed against his heart. Only after some time did he notice that Erzsi was walking beside him, and had brought him his hat.

Erzsi was now quite changed: meek, timid, her eyes all tears. It was almost moving, the tall dignified woman in this posture of a small girl, as she walked beside him, in silence, with his hat in her hand. Mihály smiled, and took his hat.

"Thank you," he said, and kissed Erzsi's hand. Timidly, she stroked his face.

"Well, if you've no more letters in your reticule, then perhaps we can go and dine," he said with a sigh.

During the meal they exchanged few words, but those were full of intimacy and tender feeling. Erzsi was filled with a loving desire to console, Mihály with his own suffering, and the great quantity of wine he got through in his unhappiness made him gentle. He saw how much Erzsi still loved him, even now. What happiness, if he in turn could love her, and thus free himself of the past and the dead. But he knew it was impossible.

"Erzsi, in the depths of my heart I wasn't to blame for what happened between us," he said. "True, that is easily said. But you see, for so many years I had done everything to make myself conform, and I only married you, as a kind of reward, when I really thought that at last everything was all right, that I had at last made my peace with the world. And then all the demons turned on me—my entire youth and all that nostalgia and rebellion. There's no cure for nostalgia. Perhaps I should never have come to Italy. This country was created out of nostalgia, by kings and poets. Italy is the earthly paradise, but only as Dante saw it: the earthly paradise on the peak of Mount Purgatory, a mere stopping place on a journey, a supernatural airport

267

where spirits take off for the distant circles of heaven, when Beatrice lifts her veil, and the soul 'feels the great power of the old yearning....'"

"Oh, Mihály, the world won't tolerate a man giving himself up to nostalgia."

"It doesn't tolerate it. It doesn't tolerate any deviation from the norm. Any desertion or defiance, and sooner or later it turns the Zoltáns on you."

"And what do you want to do?"

"That I don't know. What are your plans, Erzsi?"

"I'll go back to Paris. We've talked about everything now—I think it's time I went to my room. I'm leaving early tomorrow morning."

Mihály paid, and escorted her back.

"I would love to know that you will be all right," he said as they walked. "Say something to reassure me."

"It's not as bad for me as you think," said Erzsi, and her smile was now genuinely proud and satisfied. "My life is very full now, and who knows what wonderful things lie in store for me? In Paris I've found myself to some extent, and what I want in life. My only regret is that you're not part of it."

They were standing outside Erzsi's hotel. Taking his leave of her, Mihály looked again at Erzsi. Yes, she had changed a great deal. For better or worse, who could say? She was no longer the fine presence she had been: there was something broken in her, some inner coarsening of texture that showed in the way she dressed and spoke, and overpainted her face in the Parisian fashion. Erzsi had become somehow more common, was somehow surrounded by the ambience of some stranger, some mysterious and enviable stranger. Or perhaps of János, his arch-rival.... This element of newness in the woman he had so long known was inexpressibly seductive and disturbing.

"What will you do now, Mihály?"

"I don't know. I don't want to go home, for a thousand and one reasons, and I really don't want to be alone."

For an instant their eyes met, in the conspiratorial glance developed by the year they had spent together, then, without another word, they hurried up to Erzsi's room.

The passion that had driven them so painfully together when Erzsi was still Zoltán's wife now rose again in both of them. During those months they had both tried to fend off their desire, but the desire had been stronger and opposition only made it more savage. Now again they met in the teeth of a major obstacle. All that had happened between them, the seemingly irreparable grievances driving them so violently apart, served only to intensify the passion that threw them into one another's arms. With the miraculous joy of recognition Mihály discovered it all again: Erzsi's body which, physically, he desired more than the body of any other woman, Erzsi's gentleness, Erzsi's wildness, Erzsi's whole night-time being which was utterly unlike the Erzsi who was revealed in the words and deeds of daylight, the passionate, loving Erzsi, so wise in the ways of love. And Erzsi revelled in her capacity to strip Mihály of the lethargic indifference in which he spent so much of his days.

Later, all conflict resolved, they gazed delightedly at one another, exhausted and fulfilled, with eyes of wonder. Only now did it occur to them what had happened. Erzsi began to laugh.

"Well, would you have believed this, this morning?"

"Not me. Would you?"

"Me neither. Or, I don't know. I did come to do you a favour."

"Erzsi! You're the most wonderful woman in the whole world."

He really thought that. He had been stunned by the womanly warmth in which she bathed him, and was gratefully, childishly happy.

"Yes, Mihály, I must always be good to you. That's what I feel. No one should ever hurt you."

"Tell me ... shouldn't we give our marriage one more try?"

Erzsi grew serious. She had of course expected this question, if only because her sexual vanity required it ... but could it be a realistic proposition?... For a long time she gazed at Mihály, hesitant and questioning.

"We should have another try," he said. "Our bodies understand each other so well. And they are usually right. Nature's voice, don't you think?... What we mess up with our minds our bodies can still put right. We must have another go at living together."

"Why did you leave me there if ... if that's the case?"

"Nostalgia, Erzsi. But now it's as if I've been released from a kind of spell. True, I was a most willing slave and victim. But now I feel healthy and strong. I must stay with

270

you, it's quite clear. But of course I'm being selfish. The question is, what would be best for you?"

"I don't know, Mihály. I love you so much more than you love me, and it frightens me how much suffering you cause me. And ... I don't know where you stand with the other woman."

"With Éva? But did you think I had spoken to her? I just yearned after her. A spiritual illness. I'm going to be cured of it."

"First get yourself cured, then we can discuss it."

"Fine. You'll see, we'll talk about it soon enough. Sleep well, my dear, dear one."

But during the night he woke, and reached out for Éva. Grasping the hand that lay on the blanket he remembered it was Erzsi's and, overcome with guilt, released it. Then he thought, wryly, sadly, wearily, how very different Éva was after all. From time to time he might feel an intense desire for Erzsi, but even this desire played itself out, and after it nothing remained but the sober and boring acknowledgement of facts. Erzsi was desirable and good and clever and everything, but she lacked mystery.

*Consummatum est.* Erzsi was the last connection with the world of humanity. Now there was only the one who wasn't: Éva, Éva.... And when Éva went, only death would remain.

And towards dawn Erzsi woke and thought:

"Mihály hasn't changed, but I have. Once he stood for the great adventure, rebellion, the stranger, the man of mystery. I now know he just passively lets outside forces carry him along. He's no tiger. Or at least, there are people far more remarkable than he is. János Szepetneki. And the ones I haven't yet met. Mihály returns my love at the moment simply because he's looking to me for bourgeois order and security, and everything I actually ran to him to escape from. No, it doesn't make sense. I'm cured of him."

She rose, washed, and began to dress. Mihály also woke. Somehow he immediately took in the situation and also got dressed, and they breakfasted with barely a word. He escorted Erzsi to the train and waved her goodbye. Both knew it was now finally over between them.

# XXII

THE DAYS that followed Erzsi's departure were dreadful. Shortly afterwards Waldheim left too, for Oxford, and Mihály was completely on his own. He had no interest in anything. He did not move out of the house, but lay all day long on his bed, fully dressed.

The reality-content of Erzsi's news had run through his whole system like a poison. He thought endlessly, and with ever-increasing anxiety, about his father, whom his own behaviour and the impending financial crisis had surely reduced to a dreadful state of mind. He could see the old man before him: presiding disconsolately over the family dinner, twirling his moustache or rubbing his knee in his distress, struggling to act as if nothing was wrong, his forced jollity making the others even more depressed, and everyone ignoring his sallies, becoming gradually more silent, eating at double speed to get away as fast as possible from the miseries of the family gathering.

And if Mihály did occasionally manage to forget his father, his thoughts turned to Éva. That Éva would leave for an impossibly distant country, perhaps for ever, was worse than anything. Because, dreadful as it was that she had no desire to know about him, life was nonetheless bearable so long as one knew she was living in the same city, and that they might chance to meet, or at least she might be glimpsed from afar.... But if she went away to India, there was nothing left for him. Nothing.

One afternoon a letter arrived from Foligno, from Ellesley.

*Dear Mike,*

*I have some very sad news for you. Father Severinus, the Gubbio monk, recently fell seriously ill. More precisely, he had a long-standing tubercular condition which got to the stage where he could no longer remain in the monastery and they brought him to the hospital here. During those hours when neither his illness nor his devotions claimed him, I had the opportunity to talk with him, and gained some small insight into his remarkable state of mind. I have no doubt that in earlier centuries this man would have been venerated as a saint. He spoke of you often and in terms of the greatest affection, and I learned from him—how mysterious are the ways of Providence—that in your youth you and he had been close friends and always very attached to one another. He asked me to let you know when the inevitable happened. This request I now fulfil, for Father Severinus died in the night, towards dawn this morning. He was alert to the last, praying with his fellow Franciscans seated by his bed, when the moment of departure came.*

*Dear Mike, if you had the absolute faith in eternal life that I have you would take some comfort in this news, because you would trust that your friend was now where his fragmentary mortal existence received its deserved complement, the Life Eternal.*

*Don't forget me completely. Write sometimes to your devoted*

*Ellesley*

*P.S. Millicent Ingram duly received the money. She finds your apologies absurd between friends, sends you many greetings and thinks of you with affection. I can now also mention that she is my fiancée.*

The day was appallingly hot. In the afternoon Mihály walked in a daze round the Borghese gardens, went to bed early, fell asleep in his exhaustion, and later woke again.

In a half-dream he saw before him a wild, precipitous landscape. The prospect seemed somehow familiar and, still in his dream, he wondered where he could possibly have known that narrow valley, those storm-tossed trees, those seemingly stylised ruins. Perhaps he had seen them from the train, in that wonderful stretch of country between Bologna and Florence, perhaps in his wanderings above Spoleto, or in a painting by Salvator Rosa in some museum. The mood of the landscape was ominous and heavy with mortality. Mortality hung over the tiny figure, the traveller, who, leaning on his stick, made his way across the landscape under a brilliant moon. He knew that the traveller had been journeying through that increasingly abandoned landscape, between tumultuous trees and stylised ruins, terrified by tempests and wolves, for an immense period of time, and that he, and no one else in all the world, would roam abroad on such a night, so utterly alone.

The bell rang. Mihály switched on the light and looked at his watch. It was past midnight. Who could it be? Surely no one could have rung. He turned on his other side.

The bell sounded again. Troubled, he got up, put something on, and went out. At the door stood Éva.

In his embarrassment he forgot even to greet her.

That's how it is. You yearn for someone, maniacally, mortally, to the verges of hell and death. You look for them

275

everywhere, pursue them, to no avail, and your life wastes away in nostalgia. Since coming to Rome Mihály had never stopped waiting for this moment, had prepared for it, and had only just come to believe that never again would he speak with Éva. And then suddenly she appears, just at the moment when you've pulled on a pair of cheap pyjamas, are ashamed to be so unkempt and unshaven, ashamed to death of your lodgings, and you'd actually rather this person, for whom you've yearned so inexpressibly, were simply not there.

But Éva paid no attention to any of that. Without greeting or invitation she stepped quickly into his room, sat down in an armchair, and stared stiffly in front of her.

Mihály shuffled in after her.

She had not changed in the slightest. Love preserves one moment for ever, the moment of its birth. The beloved never ages. In love's eye she is always seventeen, her dishevelled hair and light summer frock tousled for the rest of time by the same friendly breeze that blew in the first fatal moment.

Mihály was so discomposed all he could ask was:

"How did you find my address?"

Éva motioned restlessly with her hand.

"I telephoned your brother, in Pest. Mihály, Ervin's dead."

"I know," he said.

"How did you know?"

"Ellesley, the doctor, wrote to me. I know you also met him once, in Gubbio, in the house where the door of the dead was open."

"Yes, I remember."

"He nursed Ervin in his last hours, in the Foligno hospital. Here's his letter."

Éva read the letter and fell into a reverie.

"Do you remember his enormous grey coat," she said, after a while, "and how he always turned the collar up as he walked along, with his head bowed?..."

"And somehow his head always went in front of him, and he came after it, like those big snakes that throw their head forward and their bodies slither along behind.... And how much he smoked! No matter how many cigarettes I put in front of him, they all went."

"And how sweet he was, when he was in good humour, or tipsy...."

Father Severinus vanished. In the dead man of Foligno only Ervin had died, the remarkable boy and dear friend and the finest memory of their youth.

"I knew he was very ill," said Mihály. "I tried to persuade him to get himself seen to. Do you think I should perhaps have tried a bit harder? Perhaps I should have stayed in Gubbio and not left until something was done about getting him well?"

"I think our concern, our tenderness, our anxiety would never have got through to him—to Father Severinus. For him the illness wasn't as it would be for other people— not a misfortune but rather a gift. What do we know about that? And how easy it would have been for him to die."

"He was so used to the ways of death. In the last few years I think he dealt with nothing else."

277

"All the same, it might well have been horrible for him to die. There are very few people who die their own, proper death, like ... like Tamás."

The warm orange glow from the lampshade fell on Éva's face and it became much more like the face she had shown in those years in the Ulpius house when ... when they played their games and Tamás and Mihály died for her, or at her hands. What kind of fantasy, or memory, might now be stirring in her? He clutched his hand to his aching, pounding heart, and a thousand things flitted through his head: memories of the sick pleasure of the old games, the Etruscan statues in the Villa Giulia, Waldheims's explanations, the Other Wish and the death-hetaira.

"Éva, you killed Tamás," he said.

Éva gave a start, her facial expression changed totally, and she clapped her hand to her forehead.

"It's not true! Not true! How could you think it?"

"Éva, you killed Tamás."

"No, Mihály, I swear I didn't. It wasn't me that killed him ... you can't see it like that. Tamás committed suicide. I told Ervin, and Ervin gave me absolution, as a priest."

"Then tell me too."

"Yes, I'll tell you. Listen. I'll tell you how Tamás died."

Éva's hand in Mihály's was cold as ice. He too felt shivers of horror running through him, and his heart grew unspeakably heavy. Relentlessly they descended into the mines, the passageways, the pits, through brackish underground lakes until they reached the cave where, amid the blackness at the very centre of things, lurked the secret, and the spectre.

"You remember, don't you, how it was. That suitor of mine, and how violent my father was, and how I asked him if I could travel with Tamás for a few days before I got married."

"I remember."

"We went to Hallstatt. The place was Tamás's idea. The moment I arrived there I understood. I really can't describe it ... an ancient, black town, beside a dead, black lake. You see these hill towns in Italy too, but this was much darker, much more chilling, the sort of place where all you can do is die. Tamás had already told me on the way there that he was going to die soon. You remember, don't you, the office ... and how he couldn't bear being torn away from me ... and in particular, you remember, how he always longed for death, and you know, too, how he didn't want to die in some random way, but prepared for, carefully....

"I know that anyone else would have reasoned with him, or sent off telegrams right and left, called for help from his friends and the police and the emergency services and whatever else one does. That was my first feeling too, that I ought to do something, I ought to call for help. I didn't, and I watched his preparations with despair. But then suddenly it dawned on me that Tamás was right. How I knew this I can't say ... but you remember how close we always were, how I always knew what was going on inside him—and now I knew that he was beyond help. If it didn't happen now, then some other time, soon; and if I wasn't there then he would die alone, and that would be terrible, for both of us.

"Tamás realised I had become resigned to the idea and he told me the day when it would happen. That day we went boating on the dead lake, but in the afternoon the rain came down and we went into our room. There was never such an autumn since the world began, Mihály.

"Tamás wrote a farewell note, in meaningless phrases, giving no reasons. Then he asked me to prepare the poison, and to give it to him....

"Why did I have to do it? ... and why did I do it? ... you see, this is something perhaps only you can understand, Mihály. You played and acted with us, in those years.

"I've never felt any pangs of remorse. Tamás wanted to die, and there was no way I could have prevented it. And I didn't even want to, because I knew it was better for him this way. I carried out his last wishes. I did the right thing. I've never regretted it. Perhaps if I hadn't been there, if I hadn't given him the poison, he wouldn't have had the strength of mind, he would have struggled with himself for hours and then taken it after all, and gone to his death ashamed of his lack of courage, shamefaced. But this way he killed himself bravely, without hesitation, because it was play-acting, he played at being killed by me, he was performing a scene we had rehearsed so many times at home.

"Afterwards he lay down calmly and I sat on the edge of the bed. When the drowsiness of death drew near, I pulled him to me and kissed him. And I carried on kissing him until his arm fell away from me. Those weren't the kisses of a brother and sister, Mihály, it's true. We were no longer brother and sister but someone who would live on and someone who was dying ... then at last he was free, as I believe."

For a long time they sat in silence.

"Éva, why did you send me that message not to look for you?" Mihály finally asked. "Why don't you want to see me?"

"Oh, but don't you see, Mihály, don't you see, it's impossible?.... When we're together it's not just the two of us.... At any moment Tamás might appear. And now Ervin too.... I can't be with you, Mihály, I can't."

She rose.

"Just sit down for one more minute," he said, as softly as a man speaking in extreme anger. "Is it true you're going to India?" he asked. "For a very long time?"

Éva nodded.

He wrung his hands.

"You really are going, and I shan't see you any more?"

"That's true. What will become of you?"

"There's only one thing for me: to die my own, proper death. Like ... like Tamás."

They were silent.

"Do you seriously think so?" Éva asked eventually.

"Absolutely seriously. There's no point in my staying in Rome. And there's even less point in my going home. There's no point in my doing anything."

"Could I possibly be of help?" she asked, without enthusiasm.

"No. Or rather, there is a way, after all. Could you do something for me, Éva?"

"Well?"

"I'm afraid to ask, it's so difficult."

"Ask away."

"Éva ... be at my side, when I die ... like you were with Tamás, Éva."

Éva considered.

"Would you do it? Would you do it? Éva, this is all I ask of you, and after it, nothing ever again, till the end of the world."

"All right."

"Do you promise?"

"I promise."

# XXIII

Erzsi arrived back in Paris. She telephoned János, who came for her in the evening to take her out to dinner. But she found him rather distracted, and not especially pleased to see her. This suspicion grew stronger when he announced:

"Tonight we're dining with the Persian."

"Why? On our first night!"

"True, but I can't do anything about it. He insisted on it, and you know how I have to butter him up."

During the dinner János was mostly silent, and the conversation flowed between Erzsi and the Persian.

The Persian was talking about his homeland. There, love was a difficult and romantic business. Even today it was still the case that the young man in love had to climb a ten-foot wall and hide in the garden of his beloved's father, to watch for the moment when the lady might walk by with her companion and they might exchange a few words in secret. But the young man was playing with his life.

"And this is a good thing?" asked Erzsi.

"Yes, a very good thing," he replied. "Very good. People tend to value things much more highly when they have had to wait for them, to struggle and suffer. I often think Europeans don't know what passion is. And really they don't, technically speaking."

His eyes glowed, his gestures were exaggerated but noble—untamed, genuine gestures.

"I am delighted you have returned, Madame," he suddenly announced. "I was just beginning to be afraid you would stay in Italy. But that would have been a shame.... I should have been very sorry."

Erzsi, in a gesture of thanks, placed her hand for a moment on the Persian's. Beneath it he closed his, making it like a claw. She was alarmed, and withdrew hers.

"I would very much like to ask you something," continued the Persian. "Would you accept a small gift from me? On the happy occasion of your return."

He produced a beautifully wrought gold *tabatière*.

"Strictly speaking it's for opium," he said. "But you can also use it for cigarettes."

"I'm not sure on what basis I can accept this," Erzsi said, in some confusion.

"On no basis whatever. On the basis that I am happy to be alive. On the basis that I am not a European, but come from a country where people make gifts lightly and with the best of intentions, and are grateful when they are accepted. Accept it because I am Suratgar Lutphali, and who knows when you will ever meet such a bird again."

Erzsi looked inquiringly at János. She greatly admired the *tabatière*, and would have loved to accept it. János gave her a look of approval.

"Then I accept," she said, "and thank you very much. I would accept it from no one else, only you. Because who knows when I shall ever meet such a bird again in my life."

The Persian met the bill for all three of them. Erzsi was a little irritated by this. It was almost as if János had found her for the Persian, as if, not to put too fine a point on it, he were his impresario, now withdrawing modestly into the background ... but she dismissed this thought. Most likely János was again out of funds and that was why he allowed the Persian to pay. Or the Persian, with his oriental magnificence, had insisted on it. Besides, in Paris one person always paid.

That night János fell asleep early, and Erzsi had time to reflect:

"It's coming to an end with János, that's for certain, and I'm not sorry. What is interesting in him I already know by heart. I was always so afraid of him—that he might stab me, or steal my money. But it seems this fear was misplaced, and I'm a bit disappointed in him. What comes next? Perhaps the Persian? It rather seems he fancies me."

She thought for a long time about what the Persian would be like at close quarters. Oh yes, he certainly was the real *Tiger, Tiger, burning bright/ In the forests of the night.* How his eye glowed.... It could be quite terrifying. Yes, quite terrifying. She really should give him a try. Love has so many unexplored landscapes, so many secret, wonderful, paradisal places....

Two days later the Persian invited them on an outing by car to Paris-Plage. They bathed in the sea, had dinner, and set out for home in the dark.

The journey was a long one and the Persian, who was driving, began to be more and more uncertain.

"Tell me, did we see that lake when we came?" he asked János.

János looked thoughtfully into the dark.

"Perhaps you did. I didn't."

They stopped and studied the map.

"The devil knows where we might be. I don't see any kind of lake here."

"I said at the time the driver shouldn't drink so much," said János in exasperation.

They drove further on, in some uncertainty. No one, not a vehicle, in the whole countryside.

"This car's not right," said János. "Have you noticed it spluttering from time to time?"

"Yes, it certainly is."

As they drove on the spluttering became quite pronounced.

Do you understand this contraption?" asked the Persian. "Because I don't know the first thing about it. For me, the mechanics of a car are still the work of the devil."

"Pull over. I'll see what the trouble is."

János got out, lifted up the bonnet, and started to investigate.

"The fan belt is completely ruined. How on earth could you drive around with a fan belt like that? You really should look at your car occasionally."

Suddenly he swore, copiously and brutally.

"..., the belt's torn! Now we've done it!"

"Now you've done it."

"I've certainly done it. We can't go on until we find another belt. You might as well get out."

They got out. Meanwhile it had started to rain. Erzsi fastened up her waterproof coat.

286

The Persian was angry and impatient.

"Hell and damnation, what do we do now? Here we are in the middle of the main road, and, I've a strong suspicion, this isn't the main road any more."

"I can see some sort of house over there," said János. "Let's try our luck there."

"What, at this time of night? By now the whole French countryside is asleep, and anyone who is up won't be talking to suspicious-looking foreigners."

"But there's a light on," said Erzsi, pointing to the house.

"Let's try it," said János.

They locked the car, and made off towards the house. A wall enclosed the hill on which it stood, but the gate was open. They went up to the house.

It was a very grand-looking building. In the darkness it seemed like a miniature *château*, bristling with marquesses and the noble families of France.

They knocked. An old peasant-woman thrust her head out of a small opening in the door. János explained what had brought them there.

"I'll just have a word with their lordship and ladyship."

Soon a middle-aged Frenchman in country attire stood before them. He looked them up and down while János repeated his account of what had happened. His face slowly brightened, and he became immensely friendly.

"God has brought you amongst us, Madame and Gentlemen. Come in and tell us all about it."

He led them into an old-fashioned room, reminiscent of a hunting lodge, where a lady sat at a table over her embroidery, evidently his wife. The man briefly explained the situation and made his visitors sit down.

"Your misfortune is our good luck," said the lady. "You can't imagine how dull these evenings are in the country. But of course one can't leave one's estates at this time of year, can one?"

Erzsi felt somehow ill at ease. The whole mansion seemed unreal, or indeed too real, like the set of a naturalistic play. And either these two people had sat there forever under the lamp, wordlessly waiting, or they had sprung into being at the precise moment of their arrival. Deep down she had the feeling that something was not quite right.

It emerged that the nearest village where they might find a garage was three kilometres off, but the hospitable couple had no one they could send, as that night the male staff were sleeping out at the farmhouse.

"Do spend the night here," suggested the wife. "There's sleeping-room for all three of you."

But János and the Persian were insistent that they still had to be in Paris that night.

"I am expected," said the Persian, his discreet smile implying it was a question of a lady.

"There's nothing else for it," said János. "One of us will have to walk to the village. Three kilometres really isn't much. Naturally I shall go, since I broke the fanbelt."

"Not at all," said the Persian. "I'll go. Since you are my guests, I must see to it."

"Well, let's draw lots," suggested János.

The draw determined that János should go.

"I'll be straight back," he said, and hurried off.

The host brought wine, his own vintage. They sat around the table, drinking and talking quietly, listening occasionally to the patter of rain on the window-pane.

Erzsi's sense of unreality grew and grew. She no longer knew what the host and his lady were talking about. Probably they were explaining the tedious round of their country life, in tones as unvaried and soporific as the rain. Or perhaps it was the patter of rain that was so soothing; or the fact that she no longer belonged to anyone, anywhere. Here she sat at the end of the world, in a French *château* whose name she did not even know, and where she had arrived quite without rhyme or reason, for one might equally sit thus at the other end of the world, in another *château*, with no more cause or explanation.

Then she sensed that this was not what was soothing and lulling her, but the glance with which the Persian caressed her from time to time. It was a tender, warm, emotional glance, quite different from the cold blue gaze of a European eye. In the Persian's glance there was animal warmth and reassurance. Soothing and lulling. Yes, this man loved women ... but not merely as ... he loved them not because he was a man, but because they were women, dear creatures, needing love. That was it: he loved them the way a true dog-fancier loves dogs. And perhaps that is the best love a woman can have.

In her half-trance she became aware that, under the table, the Persian was holding her hand in his and stroking it.

He did not betray himself by the slightest movement as

289

he conversed politely with the hosts. Yet Erzsi still felt that everyone was posing, so outrageously that she almost expected them to stick out their tongues at her. And the Persian was just waiting, perhaps without any particular plan in his head, at that late hour of night....

"Does he think I am some unapproachable Persian woman? My God, we ought to go out for a stroll ... but it's raining."

Suddenly there was a knock at the door. The peasant-woman brought in a thoroughly sodden youth, who was obviously known to the host couple. From what the lad had to say it transpired that János had reached the neigh-bouring village but had not found a suitable fan belt there. However he had sprained his leg, and thought it best to spend the night with the local doctor, who was a most kindly man. He asked if they would come and col-lect him, should they somehow manage to repair the car.

This news was received with dismay. Then they decided that if that was the way things stood, it would be better to go to bed, as it was already long past midnight. The lady of the house conducted them upstairs. When it had been tactfully established that Erzsi and the Persian were not together, each was assigned a separate room, and the hostess took her leave. Erzsi took her leave of the Persian and went into her room, where the old peasant-woman made up her bed, and bade her goodnight.

It was as if everything had been prepared in advance. Of this Erzsi no longer had any doubt. The little play being enacted in her honour was no doubt the brainchild of János: the problem with the car, the little *château* by the roadside, his accident, and now the final scene with the happy ending.

She looked round her room. She carefully locked the door, and then had to smile. There was another door in the room, and this had no key. She cautiously opened this second door. It revealed an unlit room. But in the far wall of the darkened room was another door, under which a strip of light appeared. She tip-toed over to it. Someone was walking about in the next room. She thought back to the arrangement of the rooms as they had gone along the corridor, and decided that the one behind the door was the Persian's. He was certainly not going to lock his door. Through it he would make his way comfortably to her room. And this was quite natural, after the intimate way they had sat together down below, under the lamp. She returned to her room.

Her mirror showed her how deeply she was blushing. János had sold her to the Persian and the Persian had bought her, as he might a calf. He had made her a down payment in the form of the *tabatière* (which Sári had established was a great deal more valuable than you might think at first glance)—and János had certainly had his "pocket money". She was filled with deep humiliation and anger. How she could have loved the Persian ... but that he should treat her like a commodity! Oh how stupid men were! By this he had spoiled everything.

"Why do they all try to sell me? Mihály sold me to Zoltán—even his letter made it clear that there had been a deal—and now János sells me to the Persian, and, God knows, in time the Persian will sell me to some Greek or

Armenian; and after that I'll be sold again and again by men who don't even view me as their own property." She racked her brains to discover what there might be in her that made men do this. Or perhaps the fault lay not in her, but in the men she fell in with, Mihály and János, and the fact that both of them had loved Éva, a woman who was for sale, and were therefore unable to see her as any different?

A few minutes more and the Persian would come, and, in the most natural way in the world, would wish to complete the transaction. What nonsense! She must do something. Go to the lady of the house, and make a great scene, call for her protection? It would be ridiculous, since the people of the house were the Persian's hired lackeys (Who could they be? They had played their parts very well. Perhaps they were actors, since he was now a film entrepreneur.) She walked up and down, at her wits' end.

"Perhaps you're quite mistaken. Perhaps the thought never entered his brain."

It struck her that if the Persian didn't come, that would be every bit as insulting as if he did.

If he came.... Perhaps it wouldn't be so insulting and humiliating. He knew perfectly well that Erzsi admired him. She herself had issued the invitation to come. He was not coming as to a slave-girl in his harem, but to a woman who loved him, and whom he loved, after carefully removing every obstacle in the way. Had she been sold? Indeed, she had. But properly speaking, the fact that men laid out vast sums for her need not really be so humiliating. On the contrary, it was very flattering, for people spend money only on the things they value.... She began suddenly to undress.

She stood in front of the mirror, and for a few moments studied her shoulders and arms with satisfaction, as a sample of the whole item "for which men laid out vast sums of money". The thought was now decidedly pleasurable. Well, was she worth it? If she was worth it to them....

Before this, under the lamp downstairs, she had longed for the Persian's embraces. Not perhaps with the most single-minded passion: there was more curiosity in it, a yearning for the exotic. For she had not thought at the time that it might become reality. But now, such a short while later, she was going to feel, with her whole body, the volcanic glow she sensed in the Persian. How strange and fearful was the preparation and the waiting!

She was filled with trembling excitement. This would be the supreme night of her life. The goal, the great fulfilment, towards which her road had always led. Now, now at last she was putting behind her every petty-bourgeois convention, everything that was still Budapest in her, and somewhere in the depths of France, that night, in an ancient *château*, she would give herself to a man who had purchased her, would give herself to an exotic wild animal and lose forever her genteel character, like some Eastern whore in the Bible or the *Thousand and One Nights*. Always this same wish-image had lurked at the base of her fantasies, not least when she was deceiving Zoltán with Mihály.... And her instinct had chosen correctly, for the road taken with Mihály had really led all along to this.

And now here was the man who would perhaps prove final. The real tiger. The exotic one. The man of passion. A few minutes, and she would know. A shiver went through her. Of cold? No, a shiver of fear.

Quickly she pulled her blouse back on. She stood at the door that opened on to the corridor, and pressed her hand against her heart, with the naïve, artless gesture she had so often seen in the cinema.

In her imagination she was confronting the great secret: formless, headless, terrifying, the secret of the East, the secret of men, the secret of love. With what appalling, tormenting, lacerating movements and actions would he approach her, this stranger, this man with the tiger-strangeness. And might he not annihilate her, as the gods once annihilated mortal women in their arms? What unspoken, mysterious horrors?...

Suddenly it all enfolded her once again: her good upbringing, her character as genteel lady, as model pupil, her thrift, everything she had once fled. No, no, she did not dare.... Fear lent her strength and cunning. Within seconds she had piled up every bit of furniture against the unlocked door. She even seized hold of the massive bed and, sobbing, gulping down her tears, dragged that too up to the door. Then she collapsed on to it, exhausted.

Just in time. From the neighbouring room she could hear the soft steps of the Persian. He was standing outside the door. He listened, then turned the handle.

The door, with every piece of furniture in the room

leaning against it, stood firm. The Persian did not try to force it.

"Elizabeth," he said quietly.

She did not answer. Again he tried to open the door, this time, it seemed, with the weight of his shoulder. The pile of furniture gave a little.

"Don't come in!" Erzsi cried.

The Persian stopped, and for a short while there was complete silence.

"Elizabeth, open the door," he said more loudly.

She did not reply.

He hissed something, and applied his full strength to the door.

"Don't come in!" she screamed.

The Persian released the door.

"Elizabeth," he said again, but his voice seemed distant, and dying away.

Then, after another pause, he said "Good night," and went back to his room.

She lay on the bed, fully dressed, her teeth chattering. She was sobbing, and horribly tired. This was the moment of truth, when a person sees the whole pattern of their life. She did not prettify the incident to herself. She knew that she had denied the Persian not because she was bothered by the humiliating circumstances, not even because she was a respectable woman, but because she was a coward. She had come up against the mystery she had sought again and again, and she had fled before it. All her life she had been a petty-bourgeoise, and that was what she would remain.

Oh, if only the Persian were to return, now she would let him in. . . . Of course she wouldn't die, nothing truly horrible could happen. Oh how stupid had been her childish fear! If the Persian came back this terrible exhaustion would fall away from her, as would everything else, everything. . . .

But the Persian did not return. Erzsi undressed, lay down and slept.

She managed to sleep for an hour or two. When she woke it was already becoming light outside. It was half past three. She leapt out of bed, washed her face and hands, dressed, and stole out into the corridor. Without even thinking about it she knew she must get away. She knew she could never see the Persian again. She was ashamed, and rejoiced to have escaped with her skin intact. Her spirits were high, and when she finally managed to prise open the main door of the house, which was bolted but not locked, and made it through the garden to the main road without being observed, she was filled with adolescent bravado and felt that, despite all her cowardice, she was the victor, the one who had triumphed.

She ran blithely down the main road, and soon reached a small village. As luck would have it, there was even a railway station nearby, and indeed a dawn market train leaving for Paris. It was still early morning when she reached the capital.

Back in her hotel room, she lay down and slept deeply, and perhaps contentedly, until the afternoon. When she woke she felt as if she had truly awakened after some enduring, beautiful and terrifying dream. She hurried off to Sári in a taxi, though she could have done it quite comfortably by bus or Métro. Now that she was truly awake her economising days were over.

She told Sári the whole story, with the cynical candour women use when talking amongst themselves about their love lives. Sári spiced the narrative with little exclamations and truisms.

"And what will you do now?" she finally asked, in a gentle, consoling tone.

"What will I do? But don't you see? I'll go back to Zoltán. That's why I came here."

"You'll go back to Zoltán? So, is that why you walked out on him? And you think it'll be any better now? Because it can't be said you've any great love for him. I don't understand you.... But you're quite right. You're absolutely right. I would do the same in your position. After all, certainty is certainty, and you weren't born to live like a student in Paris for the rest of your life, and keep changing your lovers as if you lived off them."

"And I certainly wasn't born for that! And just because.... Excuse me, but I've just realised what was the basis of my fear yesterday. I started thinking where all this would lead. After the Persian there would be a Venezuelan, then a Japanese, and perhaps a Negro ... I reckoned that once a girl starts off down that road there's no going back: what the devil is there to stop you? And that's not all. It could be that I really am like that, yes? That's what I was frightened of—myself, and everything I might be capable of, and everything that could still happen to me. But no, it's not that either. There has to be something to hold a woman back. And in that case, better Zoltán."

"What's this 'better'? He's wonderful. A rich man, a good man, he worships you, I can't understand how you ever left him. Now, this minute, write to him, pack up your things, and go. My Erzsi.... How nice for you. And how I shall miss you."

"No, I shan't write to him. You shall."

"Are you afraid he won't want you after all?"

"No, my dear, truly I'm not afraid of that. But I don't want to write to him, because he must never know that I'm going to him as a refugee. He mustn't know that he's the only answer. Let him think I felt sorry for him. Otherwise, he'd be so full of himself!"

"How right you are!"

"Write and tell him that you've tried hard to reason with me to go back to him, and you think I would be willing, only my pride won't let me admit it; that it would be better if he came to Paris and tried to talk with me. You'll prepare the way. Write a good letter, my Sárika. You can be sure Zoltán will be very gallant towards you."

"Splendid. I'll write straight away, here, right here, right now. Now, Erzsi, when you're in Pest, and Zoltán's wife again, you can send me a really nice pair of shoes. You know, they're so much cheaper and better in Pest, and they last so much longer."

# XXIV

FOIED VINOM PIPAFO, CRA CAREFO. Enjoy the wine today, tomorrow there'll be none. The wine had run out: the mysterious inner spring that wakes a man day after day and sustains him with the illusion that life is worth getting up for, had run dry. And as the spring, like the wine, ran dry, it had been replaced from below by waters rising from the dark sea, the inner lake, connected through its depths to the great ocean, the Other Wish, antagonistic to life and more powerful than it.

The legacy of Tamás that had lain within him like a seed had now grown to reality. This growth—his own, special death—had burgeoned inside him, had fed itself on his sap, had thought with his thoughts and reasoned with his reasons, drunk in all the fine sights for its own purposes, until it reached wholeness, and now the time had come for it to move out into the world as a reality.

He wrote to Éva with the exact time: Saturday night. She replied: "I'll be there".

That was all. Éva's curt, matter-of-fact reply filled him with dismay. Was that all he got? Such a routine attitude towards death! It was terrifying.

He felt a kind of chill beginning to spread through him, a strange sickly chill, like a limb going progressively numb under local anaesthetic, when your own body becomes alien and frightening. And so whatever it was inside him that stood for Éva slowly died. Mihály was well acquainted with love's pauses, its blank intermissions, when, between the more ardent periods of passion, we become suddenly quite indifferent to the beloved, and look into the beautiful unfamiliar face wondering whether this actually is the woman ... this was one of those pauses, but more pronounced than any he had known before. Éva had gone cold.

But then what would become of the Tamás-like sweetness of his final moments?

An odd, untimely humour put strength into him, and he acknowledged that the great act had got off to a decidedly poor start.

This was Saturday afternoon. He submitted himself, in these his last remaining hours, to some searching questions. What does a man do when nothing has meaning any longer? "The last hours of a suicide": the phrase, so applicable to his situation, dismayed him even more than his earlier decision that he was "mad with love" or that "he could live no longer without her". How distressing that the most sublime moments and stages of our lives can be approached only with the most banal expressions; and that, probably, these are indeed our most banal moments. At such times we are no different from anyone else. Mihály was now "preparing himself for death" just as any other man would do who knew he would soon have to die.

Yes, there was nothing else for it. He could not escape the law by which, even in his last moments, he was compelled to conform. He too would write a farewell note, as convention required. It would not be right to leave his father and mother without a farewell. He would write them a letter.

That was the first real moment of pain, when this idea struck him. Until then he had felt nothing more than a weary, dull depression, a fog, through which filtered the mysterious green glitter of the awaited climax of his last moments, and his thoughts of Tamás. But as he began to consider his parents he felt a sharp pang, a sharp, bright pang: the fog cleared, and he began to pity them, and to pity himself, stupidly, sentimentally, absurdly. Feeling ashamed, he took out his pen. With exemplary discipline and detachment, but therefore in words warm with feeling, he would announce his deed, calmly, masterfully, as one experienced in death.

As he sat there with the pen in his hand, waiting for the words of exemplary discipline to enter his head, there was a sudden knocking at the door. Mihály started violently. A week could go by and no one called on him. Who could this be, just now? For a moment nameless suspicions flitted through his head. The lady of the house was not at home. No, he wouldn't open the door. There was truly no reason now why he should. He had no business with anyone now.

But the knocking became increasingly vigorous and impatient. Mihály shrugged his shoulders, as if to say: "What are they doing, making all this commotion?" and he went out. As he did so he experienced a subtle sense of relief.

At the door he found, to his immense surprise, Vannina and another Italian girl. They were dressed very festively, with black silk scarves on their heads, and had apparently washed with more than usual thoroughness.

"Oh," said Mihály, "I am delighted," and began one of his longer stammerings, since he utterly failed to grasp the situation but had insufficient Italian to cover his embarrassment.

"Well then, are you coming, *signore?*" Vannina inquired.

"Me? Where to?"

"To the christening, of course."

"What christening?"

"Why, the christening of my cousin's baby. Perhaps you didn't get my letter?"

"I didn't get it. Did you write to me? How did you know my name and my address?"

"Your friend told me. Here it is, written down."

She took out a crumpled note. He recognised Szepetneki's writing. It read: "The Rotund Cabbage," followed by Mihály's address.

"Did you write to this name?" he asked.

"Yes. Funny name. You didn't get my letter?"

"No, absolutely not, I can't think why. But do come in."

They went into the room. Vannina looked round, and asked:

"Is the *signora* not at home?"

"No, there is no *signora.*"

"Really? It would be so nice to sit here a while.... But we still have to christen the *bambino.* Come along, come quickly. People are already starting to arrive, and we can't keep the priest waiting."

"But my dear ... and ... I never did get your letter. I'm so sorry about that, but really I wasn't prepared, today...."

"Maybe, but it doesn't matter. You aren't doing anything. Foreigners never have anything to do. Get your hat and come. *Avanti*."

"But just at the moment I've a lot to do.... An awful lot, and very important."

And he became quite serious. It all came home to him, and he saw the familiar ghastliness of the situation. In the middle of composing his suicide note they were pestering him to go to a christening. They burst in on him with their precious stupid business, the way people always burst in on him with their precious stupid business when life was sublime and terrible. And sublime and terrible things always happened to him when life was stupid and precious. Life was not an art-form, or rather, it was an extremely mixed genre.

Vannina got up, came over to him and put her hand on his shoulder.

"What is this important business?"

"Er, well ... I have letters to write. Very important letters."

She gazed into his face, and he turned away in embarrassment.

"It would be better for you if you came now," she said. "After the christening there's a big celebration dinner at our place. Have some wine, and after that you can write those letters, if you still want to."

Mihály looked at her in amazement. He remembered her gift of prophecy. He had the distinct feeling that the girl could see into him and had understood the situation. He suddenly felt ashamed, like a schoolboy caught red-handed.

Now he saw nothing sublime in his wish to die. The elevated gave way to the mundane, as always happened. One really couldn't keep the priest waiting.... He put some money in his wallet, took his hat, and they set off.

But as he let the two women go on ahead down the darkened stairwell, and stood there alone, it suddenly struck him what unqualified stupidity it was, going off to a christening with these Italian proles he didn't know from Adam. That sort of thing could happen only to him. He was on the point of running back and locking the door behind him, but the girl, as if sensing this, locked her arm in his and pulled him into the street. She hauled him along towards the Trastevere like a calf. Mihály felt that wonderful feeling of old, from the adolescent games, when he had been the sacrifice.

The relatives and friends, some fifteen or twenty strong, were already gathered in the tavern. They talked a very great deal, to him as well, but he understood nothing as they spoke in the Trastevere dialect, and besides he was not really paying attention.

Only when the young mother appeared with the *bambino* in her arms did he feel the full horror. The skinny, sickly ugliness of the mother and the yellowness of the baby terrified him. He had never liked children, whether new-born or in their later stages. He detested and feared them, and had always felt uncomfortable with their mothers. But this mother and this new-born babe were loathsome in a quite special way. In the ugly mother's tenderness and the ugly babe's defencelessness he sensed some kind of satanic parody of the Madonna, some malicious uglification of European man's greatest symbol. It was such an apocalyptic kind of thing ... as if the last mother had given birth to the last child, and none of those present had any idea that they were the last people alive, the excremental deposit of history, the dying Time-god's final and absolute gesture of self-mockery.

From then on he lived through everything that happened from the grotesque, melancholy perspective of the last day and night on earth. Remembering how they had crowded through the narrow Trastevere streets, shouting out here and there to their teeming friends as they swarmed along to the little church, their every movement so strangely nimble and busily diminutive, he saw with ever greater clarity: "They're rats. These people are rats, living here among the ruins. That's why they're so nimble and ugly, and why they breed so fast."

Meanwhile he mechanically performed his function as godfather, with Vannina standing at his side directing him. At the conclusion of the service he gave the mother two hundred *lire*, and with enormous effort managed to kiss his godson, who now bore the name Michele.

*("Saint Michael Archangel, defend us in our struggles; be our shield against the wickedness of Satan and his snares. As God commands you, so we humbly beseech you; and you who command the Heavenly Armies, with the strength of the Lord deliver unto eternal damnation Satan and all the evil spirits who lead us into danger.")*

The service dragged on for ages. After it they all went back to the little tavern. Dinner had already been laid out in the courtyard. As usual, Mihály was hungry. He knew he had now done his duty sufficiently, and ought to be going home to write those letters. But it was no use. He was seduced by his deep culinary curiosity about the celebratory meal, what it would consist of, what interesting traditional dishes would be served. Would anyone else at such a point in his life, he wondered, feel so hungry and so curious about his pasta?

The meal was good. The unusual green pasta they served, pleasantly aromatic with vegetables, was a real speciality and well repaid his curiosity. The hosts were no less proud of the meat, a rare dish in the Trastevere, but Mihály was not so taken with it, viewing the cheese with much greater favour. It was a type he had never encountered before and a real experience, as is any new cheese. Meanwhile he drank a great deal, all the more because Vannina beside him kept generously topping him up, and since he could follow nothing of what was being said, he hoped by that means at least to participate in the general conviviality.

But the wine did not make him any merrier, merely more uncertain, incalculably less certain. It was now evening, Éva would be arriving soon at his lodgings.... He really should get up and go back. There was now nothing to prevent it, only that the Italian girl would not let him. But by this time it was all extremely distant, Éva and his resolution and the desire itself, it was all very far away, drifting, an island drifting down the Tiber by night, and Mihály felt as impersonal and vegetable as the mulberry tree in the courtyard, and he too dandled his branches in this last night, no longer merely his own last night but the last night of all humanity.

It was now quite dark, and Italian stars loitered above the courtyard. He stood up, and felt utterly drunk. He had no idea how it had happened, because he did not remember—or perhaps he had simply not noticed—what a huge amount he was drinking, and he had at no time felt the crescendo of desire which usually overtakes drunkenness. From one minute to the next he was completely intoxicated.

He took a few steps in the courtyard, then staggered and fell. And that was very pleasant. He stroked the ground, and was happy. "Oh how lovely," he thought, "this is where I'll stay. Now I can't fall down."

He became aware that the Italians were lifting him up, and, with a tremendous chattering, were taking him into the house, while he modestly and apologetically protested he really had no wish to be a burden to anybody: the wonderful celebration that was so full of promise should just carry on, should just carry on....

Then he was lying on a bed, and instantly fell asleep.

When he woke it was pitch-black. His head ached, but otherwise he felt sober enough, only his heart was palpitating violently and he was very restless. Why had he got so drunk? It must surely have had a lot to do with the state of mind he had been in when he had sat down to drink: his resistance was so much reduced. Really, there hadn't been any resistance in him: the Italian girl had done what she wanted with him. Why would she want him to get so very drunk?

His restlessness became intense. He thought of that night when he had wandered the streets of Rome until dawn and then found himself outside this same little house, when his imagination conjured up all the mysterious and criminal things that went on behind its silent walls. This was the house where the murders took place. And here he was, inside the house. The walls were alarmingly silent. Here he lay delivered over to the darkness, as he had wanted.

He remained prostrate for a while, in steadily increasing restlessness, then tried to get up. But his movements ran into difficulty, and the blood throbbed painfully in his head. Better to stay lying down. He listened intently. His eyes became used to the darkness and his ears to the silence. A thousand little noises, strange, nearby, distinctly Italian sounds, could be heard all around. The house was more or less awake. A dim light came in from under the door.

If these people were planning something.... What madness it was to have brought money with him! And where had he put his money? But of course, he had lain down fully dressed. It must be in his wallet. He groped for the wallet. It was not in its place. It was not in any of his pockets.

Well, that much was certain: they had stolen his money. Perhaps two hundred *lire*. Never mind that ... what else might they want? Would they allow him to leave and report them? That would be madness. No, these people were going to kill him, without question.

Then the door opened and Vannina came in, carrying some sort of night-light. She looked furtively towards the bed and, when she saw that Mihály was awake, put on the face of someone surprised and came up to the bed. She even said something he did not understand, but which did not sound very pleasant.

Then she put the night-light down and sat on the edge of the bed. She stroked his hair and face, murmuring encouragements in Italian to sleep peacefully.

"Of course, she's waiting for me to fall sleep, and then ... I shan't sleep!"

Then he remembered with horror what force of suggestion there was in this girl, and realised that he certainly would sleep if she willed it. And indeed, closing his eyes as the girl smoothed down his eyelashes, he fell instantly into a babbling half-dream.

In this half-dream he seemed to hear them talking in the next room. There was a man's voice that seemed to growl roughly, the rapid speech of another man from time to time, and the constant staccato whispering of the girl. Without doubt they were now discussing whether to kill him. The girl was perhaps protecting him, perhaps the opposite. Now, now, he really ought to wake. How often had he had this dream, that some terrible danger was approaching and he couldn't wake however hard he tried: and now it was coming true. Then he dreamed that something was flashing before his eyes, and, with a rattle in his throat, he awoke.

There was light in the room. The night-light was burning on the table. He sat up and looked fearfully around, but saw no one there. The murmur of speech still came through from the next room, but it was now much quieter, and he could not distinguish between the speakers.

The terror of death ran through and through him. He was afraid in his whole body. He could feel them closing in on him, with knives, the rat-people. He wrung his hands in despair. Something was holding him down. He could not get out of the bed.

The only thing that calmed him slightly was the night-light, which flared and cast the sort of shadows on the walls he remembered in his room as a child. The night-light led him to think of Vannina's finely-shaped hand: earlier, when it held the lamp, he had stared at it for some time without really paying attention.

"Why am I afraid?" he suddenly started. For this, this thing that was about to happen right now, was what he had wanted, what he had planned. Yes, he was going to die—but he wanted to die—and there beside him, in the flesh, perhaps even taking part, would be a beautiful girl bearing a special secret, in the role of death-demon, as on the Etruscan tombs.

Now he really longed for it. His teeth chattered and his arms were numb with terror, but he wanted it to happen. They would open the door and the girl would come in to him, come to the bed and kiss and embrace him, while the murder weapon went about its work. . . . Let her come and embrace him . . . only let her come . . . only let them open the door. . . .

But the door did not open. Already outside the early morning cocks were crowing, the next room was completely silent, the night-light itself was flickering low, and he fell into a deep sleep.

Then it was morning, like any other morning. He woke

in a bright room, a bright friendly room, to Vannina coming in and asking how he had slept. It was morning, a normal, friendly Italian summer morning. Soon it would be horribly hot, but now it was still pleasant. Only the aftertaste of last night's drunkenness troubled him, nothing else.

The girl was saying something, about how drunk he had been the night before, but this had endeared him and made him very popular with all the party, and they had kept him there overnight because they were afraid he wouldn't be able to make it home.

Talk of going home reminded him of Éva, who surely must have called on him the evening before to be with him when.... What would she think of him? That he had run away: had run away from her?

Then it occurred to him that in the course of the whole alarming and visionary night he had not once thought of Éva. The love-pause. The longest pause of his life. Strange thing, to die for a woman and never think of her the entire night—and what a night!

He got his clothes more or less in order and took his leave of a few people sitting outside in the bar area who greeted him like their dear old friend. How the sun shone in through the little window! Really there was nothing rat-like about these people. They were the good honest Italian proletariat.

"And these people wanted to kill me?" he wondered. "True, it's not really certain that they did intend to kill me. But it's strange that they didn't after all, in fact they must have really longed to while they were stealing my wallet. No, these Italians are really quite different."

His hand unconsciously groped for his wallet. The wallet was there in its place, next to his heart, where the Middle-European, not entirely without a touch of symbolism, keeps his money. He stopped in surprise, and took the wallet out. The two hundred *lire* and the small change, a few ten-*lira* coins, were unmistakably there.

Perhaps they had put the wallet back while he slept—but there would have been no sense in that. More probably they had never taken it. It had been there in his pocket all the time he had believed it gone. Mihály calmed down. This was not the first time in his life that he had seen black as white, and his impressions and suppositions made themselves entirely independent of objective reality.

Vannina accompanied him out the door, then came with him a short way towards the Gianicolo.

"Do come again. And you must visit the *bambino*. A godfather has his duties. You mustn't neglect them. Come again. Often. Always...."

Mihály presented the girl with the two hundred *lire*, then suddenly kissed her on the mouth and hurried off.

# XXV

HE ARRIVED BACK in his room. "I'll rest for a bit, and think carefully about what I actually want, and whether I really want it; and only then will I write to Éva. Because my position with her is rather ridiculous, and if I were to tell her why I didn't come home last night, perhaps she wouldn't believe me, it's all so stupid."

He automatically undressed and began to wash. Was there any point in still washing? But he hesitated only for a moment, then washed, brewed himself some tea, took out a book, lay down and fell asleep.

He woke to the sound of the doorbell. He hurried out, feeling fresh and rested. It had been raining, and the air was cooler now than in recent days.

He opened the door and let in an elderly gentleman. His father.

"Hello, son," said his father. "I've just arrived on the midday train. I'm so glad to find you at home. And I'm hungry. I'd like you to come out to lunch with me."

Mihály was immensely surprised at his father's unexpected appearance, but surprise was not in fact his predominant feeling. Nor indeed was it the embarrassment and shame when his father looked around the room, struggling painfully to stop his face betraying his horror at the shabby milieu. A quite different feeling filled him, a feeling he had known of old, in lesser degree, in the days when he often went abroad. The same feeling had always affected him when he came home from his longer absences: the terror that his father had in the meantime grown older. But never, never, had his father aged so much. When he had last seen him he was still the self-confident man of the commanding gestures he had known all his life. Or at least that was how Mihály had still thought of him, because he had then been at home for some years, and if any change had occurred in his father during that time he had not noticed its gradual workings. He now registered it all the more sharply because he had not seen his father for a few months. Time had punished his face and his figure. There were, just a few but quite undeniable, signs of anxiety: his mouth had lost its old severity, his eyes were tired and sunken (true, he had been travelling all night, who knows, perhaps third class, he was such a parsimonious man), his hair was even whiter, his speech seemed rather less precise, with a strange, and at first quite alarming hint of a lisp. It was impossible to say exactly what it was, but there was the fact, in all its dreadful reality. His father had grown old.

And compared with this everything else was as nothing—Éva, the planned suicide, even Italy itself.

"Just don't let me burst out crying, not just now. Father would deeply despise that, and he might also guess my tears were for him."

Mihály pulled himself together and put on his most expressionless face, the face he habitually adopted for anything to do with his family.

"It was very kind of you to come, Father. You must have had important reasons for making this long journey, in summer...."

"Yes of course, son, my reasons were important. But

nothing unpleasant. There isn't anything wrong. Although you haven't asked, your mother and the family are well. And I see there's nothing particularly wrong with you. Well then, let's go and have lunch. Take me somewhere where they don't cook in oil."

"Erzsi and Zoltán Pataki were with me the day before yesterday," his father said during the meal.

"What's that? Erzsi's in Pest? And they were together?"

"Oh yes. Pataki went to Paris, they made up, and he brought Erzsi home."

"But why, and how?"

"My son, I truly do not know, and you can imagine, I didn't inquire. We talked only about business matters. You know that your ... how can I put this? ... your odd, but I have to say not entirely surprising, behaviour placed me in an absurd situation with regard to Erzsi. An absurd financial situation. For Erzsi to liquidate her investment, in today's climate ... but you know all this, I think. Tivadar told you all about it in his letter."

"Yes, I do know. Perhaps you won't believe this, but I've been terribly worried about what might happen. Erzsi said that Zoltán ... but do go on."

"Thank God, there's no harm done. That's precisely why they came to see me, to discuss the terms under which I could pay them back the money. But I have to say they were so reasonable I was really very surprised. We agreed on all the details. They really are not too oppressive, and I hope we can resolve the whole matter without further difficulty. All the more so, because your uncle Péter managed to find a wonderful new lawyer."

"But tell me: Zoltán, I mean Pataki, has behaved really decently? I don't understand."

"He has conducted himself like an absolute gentleman. Just between us, I think it's because he's so glad Erzsi went back to him. And he's certainly carrying out her intentions. Erzsi is a really wonderful woman. It's bad enough … but I have made up my mind not to reproach you. You always were a strange boy, and you know what you have done."

"And Zoltán didn't abuse me? He didn't say that…."

"He said nothing. Not a word about you, which was only natural, given the circumstances. On the other hand, Erzsi did mention you."

"Erzsi?"

"Yes. She said you had met in Rome. She gave absolutely no details, and naturally I didn't inquire, but she hinted that you were in a very critical situation, and thought that your family had turned against you. No, don't say anything. As a family we've always respected each other's privacy, and we'll keep it that way. I'm not interested in the details. But Erzsi did advise that, if it were at all possible, I should come to Rome myself and talk to you about your going back to Pest. Her actual words were, that I should 'bring you home'."

Bring him home? Yes, Erzsi knew what she was saying, and how well she knew Mihály! She saw clearly that his father could lead him home like a truanting schoolboy. She well knew it was his nature to submit, as indeed he was submitting, like a child caught running away: but of course always with the mental reservation that, when the next opportunity presented itself, he would run away again.

Erzsi was so right. There was no other course but to go home. There might have been another solution, but ... the external circumstances he had wanted to escape through suicide seemed to have vanished. Zoltán had made his peace; his family were waiting for him with open arms; nobody was after him.

"So, here I am," continued his father, "and I would like you to wind up all your business here immediately and come home. On tonight's train, in fact. You know I haven't much time."

"Please, this is all a bit sudden," said Mihály, emerging from his day-dream. "This morning I was thinking of anything but going home to Pest."

"I'm sure, but what objection is there to your coming home?"

"Nothing. Just let me catch my breath. Look, it would do you no harm to lie down here for a while and take a siesta. While you're resting I'll get my thoughts in order."

"Of course, as you think best."

Mihály placed his father in the comfort of the bed. He himself sat in a large armchair, with the firm resolution of doing some thinking. His meditation took the form of recalling certain feelings in turn, and scrutinising their intensities. That was how he usually decided what he wanted, and whether he really did want what he thought he wanted.

Did he really want to die? Did he still hanker after a death like Tamás's? He focused his mind on that longing and looked for the sweetness associated with it. But now he could discover no sweetness, but, on the contrary, nausea and fatigue, such as a man feels after lovemaking.

Then he realised why he felt this nausea. The desire had already been satisfied. Last night, in the Italian house, in his terror and vision he had already realised the wish that had haunted him since adolescence. He had fulfilled it, if not in external reality, at least in the reality of the mind. And with that the desire had been, if not permanently, at least for the time being, assuaged. He was freed from it, freed from the ghost of Tamás.

And Éva?

He noticed a letter on his desk. It had been put there while he had been out to lunch. It must have arrived the day before, but the lady next door had forgotten to give it to him. He got up, and read Éva's parting words.

> *Mihály,*
>
> *When you read this I will be already on my way to Bombay. I'm not coming to you. You aren't going to die. You're not Tamás. Tamás's death was right for Tamás alone. Everyone has to find his own way to die.*
>
> *God be with you,*
>
> *Éva.*

By evening they were in fact already on the train. They were discussing business matters, his father describing what had been happening in the firm while he had been away, what the prospects were, and what new responsibilities he had in mind for him.

318

Mihály listened in silence. He was going home. He would attempt once more what he had failed to do for fifteen years: to conform. Perhaps this time he would succeed. That was his fate. He was giving in. The facts were stronger than he was. There was no escaping. They were all too strong: the fathers, the Zoltáns, the business world, people.

His father fell asleep, and Mihály stared out of the window, trying to make out the contours of the Tuscan landscape by the light of the moon. He would have to remain with the living. He too would live: like the rats among the ruins, but nonetheless alive. And while there is life there is always the chance that something might happen....

# AFTERWORD

In 1991 a friend placed in my hand a slim novel entitled *Utas és Holdvilág*. "You must read this," he insisted.
"This is the novel we all read as students. Every educated
Hungarian knows and loves this book." I too fell under its
spell. The gently ironical tone, the deceptive casualness
with which the story unfolds, the amused scepticism playing on every variety of pretension, inspired an immediate
trust. That trust deepened as the quality of the writing
became apparent. The opening scene, moving between
the Grand Canal of Venice and its seedy back-alleys with
their melancholy view of the Island of the Dead, typifies
Antal Szerb's gift for loading details with an almost symbolic resonance, Mihály's little escapade neatly prefigures
the larger action that will follow, defines the terms of the
conflict, and establishes the faintly surreal tone with its
constant hint of irony.

This irony, distinctively Middle-European in character, operates on every level. First, as with Jane Austen at
her most sly, Szerb's authorial voice constantly mingles
with that of his hero, repeatedly wrong-footing the reader
to leave him peculiarly vulnerable to events. Then there
are the ironic perspectives imposed by the neatly sym-
metrical plot, with its parallels and contrasts, each a logical consequence of Mihály and Erzsi's deeply paradoxical
marriage. Such irony goes beyond mere technique,
investing everything with a disturbing ambiguity. Mihály
is both anti-hero (as often noted) and hero. His actions

are immoral, absurd, farcical, yet somehow our sympathies are never quite alienated. Some principle at the core of his being calls to us. His progress is both a collapse into adolescent disarray and, in its own way, a genuine spiritual journey, though pursued "by moonlight" and leading to inevitable defeat. However daft his actions, he has an attractive intelligence, a surprising capacity for self-honesty, a certain reckless courage in pursuing his wild quest. Its predictably wry conclusion discredits an entire social structure, that of "the fathers, the Zoltáns, the whole punitive middle-class establishment". Mihály is truly one of those "failures and misfits of a civilisation by which we best understand its weaknesses".

This is novelistic art of a high order. The man who produced it was no less remarkable. Born in Budapest in 1901, he lived through perhaps the most traumatic years of Hungarian, indeed European, history. Just seventeen when the Empire collapsed in military defeat, his student years saw the bloody communist revolution of 1919, foreign occupation, the "white terror" and the Second World War. His technically Jewish ancestry and his life-long stance against fascism attracted mounting official persecution from the age of 37, and he died horribly, at 43, in the forced-labour camp at Balf. Yet little of this is reflected in his major writings, or indeed the man himself: life-loving, playful, a brilliantly ironical but never cynical mind, more in keeping with the eighteenth than the twentieth century. A cradle Catholic (the family were, like most Budapest Jews, entirely assimilated), educated in a Piarist seminary, he became the quintessential Hungarian man of letters, not just admired but widely loved. The narrative of *Journey by Moonlight* coincides with rising fascism at home and abroad, and probes the national obsession with suicide, yet the touch is ever light, the focus personal and psychological. All his literary connections reveal a cast of mind humane rather than ideological, mystical rather than political, scholarly but boldly original in its interests and methods.

Those interests were wide-ranging. Antal Szerb was a lifelong Anglophile, an authority on the German, Italian, French and English traditions, and his enduring monument is, besides the fiction, a ground-breaking *History of World Literature*. As a despairing colleague wrote: "He knew everything". The intelligence that pervades *Journey by Moonlight* is of an exceptional order: an intelligence not just of the head, but of the heart.

LEN RIX, March 2001

HENRY JAMES

# Letters from the Palazzo Barbaro

HENRY JAMES first came to Venice as a tourist but was soon fascinated by the city and particularly by the splendid gothic Palazzo Barbaro, situated on the Grand Canal, home of the expatriate American Curtis family. In the gilded and stucco salon of the palace, Sargent painted family portraits and Browning read his poems. James frequently returned to the palace to write, completing *The Aspern Papers* there. This selection of letters covers the period 1869–1907.

The letters have been selected and edited by Rosella Mamoli Zorzi, Professor of Anglo-American Literature at the University of Venice, Ca' Foscari. The late Leon Edel, the great James biographer and editor, provided an Introduction to this volume which contains previously unpublished manuscript letters. Patricia Curtis, a member of the present generation of the family living in the palace, has contributed an Afterword specially written for the Pushkin Press edition.

ISBN 1-901285-07-3 · 224pp · £8/$14

ARTHUR SCHNITZLER

# Casanova's Return to Venice

ONE OF SCHNITZLER'S most poignant evocations of the passing of time and the ironies of sentiment and love, *Casanova's Return to Venice* tells the story of an ageing Casanova's desperate desire to return to the city he truly loves after a life of exile, a desire which is contrasted with his still libidinous, sensuous yet weary pursuit of women, money and prestige.

Arthur Schnitzler was born in Vienna in 1862, the son of a prominent Jewish doctor, and studied medicine at the University of Vienna. In later years, he devoted his time to writing and was successful as a novelist, dramatist and short story writer. His work shows a remarkable ability to create atmosphere and a profound analysis of human motives.

ISBN 1-901285-16-2 • 192pp • £7/$14

FRANÇOIS AUGIÉRAS

# The Sorcerer's Apprentice

IN THE DEPTHS of the Sarladais, 'a land of ghosts, cool caves and woods', a teenage boy is sent to live with a thirty-five-year-old priest. The man becomes more than just his teacher. Soon the adolescent meets a young boy in the village square; they make love to each other like shadows in a cave. The priest knows of their involvement and guides his pupil to seek out his own soul in strange, almost supernatural rituals. *The Sorcerer's Apprentice* is 'a galant, almost magical book' that is one of modern literature's esoteric, underground texts.

Augiéras was born in 1925 in Rochester, New York State. His first book, *The Old Man and the Child*, written under the pseudonym Abdullah Chaanba, caught the attention of André Gide, who referred to it as a 'bizarre delight'. Among Augiéras's best loved works is *Journey to Mount Athos*, inspired by his retreats to Mount Athos. This elusive, anti-Christian nomad died in 1971, aged forty-five.

ISBN 1-901285-44-8 · 112pp · £9/$14